Just Between Us

MADISON WRIGHT

Copyright © 2022 by Madison Wright

All rights reserved.

Cover Design by Sam at Ink and Laurel

Editing by Beth at V.B. Edits

No portion of this book may be reproduced in any form without written permission from the publisher or author, except as permitted by U.S. copyright law.

This is a work of fiction. Any names or characters, businesses or places, events or incidents, are fictitious. Any resemblance to actual persons, living or dead, or actual events is purely coincidental.

To the Pancakes,
for helping me make this one
golden brown instead of burnt.

One

ELLIE

I feel his eyes on me from across the room.

It's hot and sticky with all the bodies between us, trying and failing to press closer to the stage to hear the band, but it's his gaze that makes me feel flushed all over. I press my sweating drink to my cheek as he pushes through the maze of people, closing the distance between us inch by inch.

My stomach coils into a tight knot the closer he gets; until I'm strung so tight I'm afraid I might snap. I let out a shaky breath when he gets close enough for me to see the dark blue of his eyes, the dusting of hair on his forearms under his rolled-up flannel, the sharp line of his stubbled jaw, the rich brown of his wavy hair.

When he's just a step away from my table, my fingers tap against the side of my glass, itching to release some of the energy suddenly pulsing through me.

And then he keeps going, passing right by my table, not stopping until he reaches the bar. All the air releases from me like a deflating balloon. I watch as he orders a drink, and I slide down in my seat to hide the blush creeping up my neck and into my cheeks.

More than anything, I want to retreat to my car, but I remember why I'm here. I know the people on that stage, strumming out country covers and riling up the entire audience. The band is good, and they worked really hard to secure this gig downtown. Hundreds of tourists will flit in and out of here tonight to hear them play. And I want to be supportive.

So I stay in my chair, although reluctantly.

But I can't help but let my eyes drift back to those broad shoulders and the mop of perfectly tousled chestnut hair that walked right past me.

He's not there, though, and I sigh.

"Mind if I sit?" a deep, warm voice asks from my other side, and I almost jump out of my skin. Turning, I look right back into those deep blue eyes, just as easily mesmerized by them as I was a few minutes ago.

"Oh," I say on a whoosh of air before gathering myself enough to gesture to the seat next to me. "Yes. Yeah, of course."

The chair scrapes against the floor as he pulls it out and lowers himself into it next to me. Suddenly, this table feels a lot smaller.

He reaches out a hand, and I slip my own into it, although the moment he tries to introduce himself, the crowd erupts in applause and I miss his name.

I point to my ear, shaking my head, and he tugs on my hand until I'm leaning forward. His breath is warm on my neck, and his lips brush against the shell of my ear, making goose bumps break out across my skin. "I'm Sam," he says right as a cheer breaks out again.

"Ellie," I yell back. He holds on to my hand for a second longer than necessary before releasing it. Immediately, I find my drink again, letting my fingers tap their steady rhythm against it once more.

"You from around here or just visiting?" I ask once the music has started again and the horde of people begin to quiet.

CHAPTER ONE

"Just visiting," he says, taking a sip of his drink. I'm distracted by the fullness of his lips and the way his throat bobs when he swallows.

I wait for him to elaborate, but he doesn't, instead keeping his eyes fixed on the band. I turn back to the stage too, willing myself to get lost in the music like I was before I felt his stare like a caress. It's useless, though.

"They're really good," I say, projecting my voice over the music.

Sam just nods. From the corner of my eye, I watch his long legs stretch out, foot tapping against the floor. He's all long limbs and clean lines, and it's absolutely distracting. I rack my brain for something else to say, needing to fill this silence between us in a room full of nothing but noise.

"They're local," I try again.

"They do have good vocals," he calls back.

I think about trying to correct him, but I lose my train of thought when his eyes fasten on mine. "You should hear some of their originals."

His eyebrows pull together, creating two half-moons between them that my fingers itch to smooth away. "Do you know them?"

The crowd begins yelling again, so I just nod vigorously, not wanting him to drift back into his head again. I like having his full attention squarely on me. It's thrilling.

He asks another question, but I can't hear him over the noise, so I lean closer. "What?"

I hear his voice this time, but the individual words are drowned out again. I shake my head. Before I know what's happening, his warm fingers have slipped beneath my hair and wrapped around the back of my neck. I am hot and cold all at once as he gently pulls me closer, bringing his mouth to my ear again.

This time his voice is as clear as day, his lips brushing against my ear as he enunciates every word. "I asked if you're with one of them."

I pull back just barely, enough for him to see my wide eyes as I shake my head.

For the first time since I saw him across the room, a smile curves those full lips. It's almost too much, being this close and witnessing the corner of his mouth kick up, feeling his breath fan my face as he says, "Good. Want to dance?"

Absolutely nothing could stop me.

I'm not sure how much time passes while I dance with Sam, but with every song, my inhibitions drop a little more. By the time I'm starting to feel dead on my feet, he's got one hand wrapped around my waist, burning a hole through the fabric of my shirt, the other back under my hair, his fingers drawing little circles on the back of my neck. The band has switched to a ballad, and we're moving so slowly it can't even be considered dancing anymore.

My eyes are fluttering closed against my will, lashes brushing up against his flannel where I've rested my head against his chest. His heart beats out a steady rhythm in my ear, and I'd like to listen to it next time I'm staring at my ceiling, unable to fall asleep. It's positively hypnotic.

"Hey," he whispers, no longer needing to yell when I'm this close, wrapped around his body like English ivy. I don't know how I'll ever be able to untangle myself, and I'm not sure I want to.

I hum against his chest, and it rumbles with laughter beneath me.

"Want to get some fresh air?"

I nod and let him lead me toward the door. When we're almost there, I tug on his hand, pulling him to a stop. "Wait."

Sam turns back around, his free hand finding my waist like he just can't help it.

"Are you taking me outside to murder me?"

A small, devastating smile tips up one corner of his mouth. "You've got me figured out. I really thought that plan was going to work," he says.

"If you're going to put my body parts in canning jars, please don't put them in a fluorescent liquid. I don't look good in neon."

His dark eyes trail from my face all the way down to my toes. He leans forward, so close he doesn't even have to yell above the music. "I doubt there's anything you don't look good in."

My entire body flushes at his words, and I am fully aware of how stifling the heat in here has become. My skin is practically boiling under my striped sweater and mustard tights, damp with perspiration that is sure to cool and leave me chilled in the October air.

"Come on," he says, leading me through the door.

I don't have to worry about the cold because Sam's arms come back around me as soon as we step onto the quiet sidewalk. Country music drifts from inside and from bars down the street, but we're alone out here. Suddenly, I'm not so sleepy anymore.

Sam's fingers reach up to trace a line from my cheekbone to the corner of my mouth. My breath hitches at his gaze, warm as cocoa and just as dark.

My eyes catch on a flash of light in the night sky behind him. "Shooting star," I whisper.

"Make a wish," he says before brushing his lips against mine in the gentlest of kisses. I sigh into him, everything inside me melting until I see, taste, and feel nothing but him.

His warm body pressing me against the cool, scratchy building at my back. His thumbs brushing maddeningly over my jaw before sweeping down my neck. His mouth tasting of cinnamon and spice.

Sam pulls back just far enough to trail a line of kisses to the shell of my ear. "What did you wish for?"

My heart beats erratically in my chest, and my breath comes out uneven. "This."

Two

CAMDEN

I WAKE UP IN an unfamiliar bed. Blinking, I slowly try to make sense of my surroundings. Last night comes back to me in waves. The music. The dancing. The girl. *Ellie.*

Which brings me to now. Sitting up, crisp white comforter pooling around my waist, I look around my new apartment. The one I moved into *right before* going out to explore the new city I'll be living in for the next two months.

I drag a hand over my face, still not quite sure last night wasn't a dream. I'm not really sure how it happened. One minute I was exploring downtown, following the sounds of live music up and down the streets, the next I was wrapped around Ellie, her head on my chest, my fingers in her inky hair.

I have never, in all my life, kissed a stranger. But I can't quite bring myself to regret it either.

My phone buzzes on the nightstand with an incoming text.

> Weston
>
> **What time are you coming over?**

I check the clock on my phone, just barely after eight, and tell Wes I'll be over shortly.

My bags are all still lined up in the corner since I chose exploring over unpacking last night. I make quick work of filling the closet and drawers with my belongings before reaching for my camera backpack. I'm assuming Wes and I won't be doing any actual work today, but I rarely go anywhere without it.

Except for last night, of course. Which is a shame, because I would have loved to capture Ellie's smile—the shy one when I first sat down, the sleepy one when I dragged her out to the street. I wish I could have caught the way her dark hair reflected the bright lights. Or the way the striped sweater that she'd tucked into her skirt hung artfully off the smooth slope of her shoulder.

That striped sweater was what originally drew my eye. In a sea of black dresses and cowboy boots, she was the lone pop of color. I can still feel the soft fabric beneath my fingers as we danced slower and slower until we were just swaying, barely keeping each other upright.

Shaking myself from my thoughts, I grab my corduroy jacket, much warmer than the flannel I wore last night, and head out the door.

Ten minutes later, Wes answers before I can even knock on his back door.

His smile is wide and genuine, his arms outstretched for a hug, and although I shake my head at his antics, I realize how much I've missed him being around.

"Does LA suck without me?" Wes asks, turning to head back into the house.

A little, but I'd never tell him that.

CHAPTER TWO

Ignoring his question, I follow him through the house and settle into one of the leather armchairs in the living room. "Where's Lo?" I ask when I don't see his wife.

"She has a doctor's appointment."

My eyebrows bunch together. "Everything okay?"

"Oh, yeah," Wes says, stretching his arms over the back of the couch. "Just her usual check up with her fibromyalgia specialist."

I nod, taking in my surroundings. Weston's house is nice—lived-in and cozy—so unlike his old, bare high-rise in California. Pictures of Wes and Lo from their wedding and from their trip to LA this past summer line the walls, their bright eyes and smiling faces staring back at me. I look away, not liking the way my gut twists at their happiness.

"How was the trip?" Wes asks, dragging me from my thoughts.

"Easy." I shrug. "Got my rental car and got settled in the new apartment without a hitch. Thank you, by the way. The place is great."

"I still don't know why you wouldn't just stay here. It's only two months."

I smirk at him. "You would drive me absolutely nuts if I had to live with you for two months."

He grins and runs a hand through his blonde curls. "That's true."

"Tell Lo thanks for me for finding the place."

"I will. She was glad to help." Wes kicks his feet up on the coffee table. "What's her friend's name—the one who manages the apartments?"

I scratch at the scruff on my chin, trying to remember. "Hm, I don't know. She only emailed me once and then sent all my information over to the leasing agent—Sadie?"

Wes shakes his head. "No, that's not her. That's going to annoy me," he says, his lips tugging up at the corner. "We went to college with her. She and Lo are still pretty good friends, I think."

"I have to take my security deposit to the office when I leave here, so I'll make sure to thank her—whatever her name is."

Wes stands from the couch. "Want a latte? I haven't had any coffee yet today."

I tell him yes and follow him into the kitchen, lowering myself into a barstool. I also won't be telling him how much I missed his lattes. They're better than any I can find at a coffee shop. What a prick—getting me hooked on his espresso and then moving away.

"What did you end up doing last night? I'm sorry we couldn't hang. I forgot we agreed to babysit Lo's niece."

My mind flashes back to warm skin and cool night air and shooting stars. I shift in my seat. "Nothing much."

"Wow, sounds fun," Wes says, smirking at me over his shoulder. "I bet you spent the whole night organizing your underwear drawer and ordering groceries."

He would be absolutely flabbergasted to know how I spent my night. I know I am. When I don't respond, Wes takes my silence as confirmation and laughs loud and long.

"You're the worst," I tell him. "You spent the night changing diapers."

Wes finishes with my latte and slides the mug in front of me. "Yeah, but I came home with someone."

He turns around, starting on his own drink, missing how the words affected me. Something about seeing his life here—with Lo's sweater draped over the couch, their wedding pictures on the wall, and the tight line of stress gone from Weston's shoulders—has my chest tightening uncomfortably.

I know they didn't have an easy relationship—pining after each other since college, living thousands of miles apart for six years, and then marrying for their own personal reasons last summer—but what they have now is worthy of envy. Of the two of us, I never expected *Wes* to be the one to settle down. In LA, Wes had been a chronic casual dater who couldn't help but leave a trail of broken hearts in his wake—not when his own was back here in Tennessee.

But now that he has settled down, I've been questioning *everything* about my own life—namely, what the actual heck am I doing? I'm not twenty-two and making art in the most creative city in the world anymore. I'm thirty and living in a too-small apartment in LA, working with difficult clients who demand the world from me.

Something is missing, and suddenly I'm feeling empty and claustrophobic all at once. I was hoping this time away would help clear my head. But so far, seeing Wes *finally* find peace and happiness with the love of his life, I feel even more scrambled. I'm a soda bottle that's been shaken, and yet no one will take my cap off.

I clench my hands into fists, the sting of my nails pressing into my skin bringing me back to reality. It's fine. I'm fine.

I PULL MY RENTAL into an empty parking spot in front of the apartment complex office and get out. Chilly October air whips at my exposed skin, and leaves crunch under my boots. The world around me is an explosion of color.

My pulse thrums as I take it all in, itching to capture it through the viewfinder. I've missed this in LA—the changing of seasons, the way the world dies and remakes itself year after year. There's beauty in the change, an energy I didn't know my body had been craving.

I'm so lost in my own head that I barely notice the bell above the door jangle as I step inside. There are two offices on the left, separated by a large window in the wall. Through it, I can see a woman sitting at the desk—dark hair hiding her face.

She must not have heard the bell over the music drifting softly from her office, so I make my way to the open door and knock.

She looks up, a bright smile lighting her face, and my heart stops dead in my chest. Suddenly, I remember *exactly* what Lo's friend's name is. "Ellie?"

Three

ELLIE

"Sam?"

Sam's eyebrows bunch together, forming matching lines between them, exactly the way they did last night when he couldn't hear me over the band's loud music. But unlike last night, I can't reach my fingers up to smooth them away. Can't run my hand through his hair and tug his head closer to mine to whisper in his ear.

Whatever comfort and familiarity we had in the dark has been stripped away under the bright fluorescent light of day.

"Sam, what are you doing here?" I ask again.

He seems to finally realize he's been standing motionless in my doorway and moves into my office. His huge body and commanding presence take up all the space in this closet-sized room.

"I'm Cam," he says slowly, enunciating the *C*. "Camden Lane. Wes and Lo's friend."

No. *No, no, no, no, no.*

He can't be—

"I just moved in here yesterday."

My entire body sags like a sack of old potatoes—shoulders slumping, head lolling forward. It's a good thing I'm sitting, or my knees would have given out.

I scrub a hand over my face, no doubt smudging my make-up. And then my neck snaps straight, frantically searching to make sure the office is empty.

"Ellie, are you okay?"

I drag my gaze up to his. I don't allow myself to get tripped up on the hands that were so warm on my neck last night, or the chest that I'd laid my head against for hours, or the lips that tasted like cinnamon and spice and haunted my dreams all night.

I forgot one crucial detail, though. It was his eyes that snared me last night. Such a deep shade of blue, fringed by the most irresistible dark lashes, and so intense and focused that they make my knees buckle.

No amount of fluorescent lighting could dim the effect those eyes have on me.

A car door slams outside, and I look out my window in time to see the only thing worse than the guy I made out with last night showing up in my office—my bosses.

A cold sweat breaks out along my brow, and I jump up so fast that I slam my knee into my desk. Sam—Cam—springs into action, grabbing my elbow with one hand and reaching for my knee with the other. His warm hand massaging the tender skin on my leg is enough to send my heart into a seizing fit, and it *almost* makes me forget that he needs to get out of here. Right. Now.

"You have to leave," I tell him, my eyes no doubt wild and crazed.

His own are confused—concerned—but he nods. "Okay, yeah." He releases me now that I've caught my balance and rubs his neck, looking deeply, heartbreakingly torn. "Is this…are you…?"

I want nothing more than to slide my hand up his forearm, over his shoulder, and into the hair at the nape of his neck. I want those eyes laser focused on mine again, and I want to assure him everything is okay, but I can't. Everything is *very, very* wrong.

"I'll come find you," I tell him instead. Grabbing his arm, I push him out of the office. "I'll find you later, but I need you to go *right now*. Please."

He pauses at the entrance, his searing gaze making me tingle all over—part in anticipation, part in delight, but mostly in dread.

"Ellie, I—"

The door opens, and he cuts off abruptly.

My bosses stand at the threshold, eyeing me suspiciously, and Cam must sense the waves of apprehension coming off me, because he doesn't continue that thought. Instead, he nods in my direction. "Thanks for the help."

And then he's gone.

I don't know how he knew that these people were important, that *those* were the words they needed to hear, but he no doubt noticed the way their expressions smoothed over at his farewell.

That is, until they look at me. Then their faces become nothing but hard masks. It's that look that makes fear wrap tightly around my chest, squeezing until I have no air left.

"Mom, Dad, I wasn't expecting you guys today."

Mom's assessing eyes draw a slow line from my purple suede heels to my bright aqua pants and cherry red sweater before finally securing on my face. Her pale blue gaze is so frigid it could freeze a beach in Hawaii.

"What are you wearing?" My style isn't exactly their definition of professional—or so I've been told.

"Laundry day," I squeak.

"Where's your blazer?" Dad asks, his tall, imposing frame moving past me and into my office, Mom on his heels. I follow after them like a lost puppy.

According to the corporate manual, the dress code for all managers is business professional—and that includes a suit jacket for men and a blazer for women. I just keep forgetting it...at the store.

"Spilled tea on it," I lie through my teeth. I don't know how I even have the mental capacity to keep up with the emotional gymnastics needed around my parents right now. I should be focused entirely on them, but my gaze keeps drifting to the figure walking across the parking lot. "I have to wait for Sadie to get back from her tour before I can go home and get another one."

"What are you looking at?" Mom snaps, and I turn back to them, face heating.

I remember why I was avoiding looking at them a moment ago. Disappointment, anger, and displeasure roll off them in great big heaping waves that threaten to pull me under. Whatever their reason for this impromptu visit, it is *not* good.

My mind drifts again to Cam, but there's no way they could know. Not when I just found out myself. It was an honest mistake, and one I can *never* make again.

"How can I help you?" I ask, hating the way my voice comes out brittle.

"Care to explain what you did last night?" Mom asks, tucking a lock of pale blond hair behind her ear.

It's a loaded question, trying to get me to cough up to more than they know. But the question is...how much do they know? Because unfortunately, kissing my newest resident wasn't the only rule I broke last night.

CHAPTER THREE

"I went out," I manage to say, fighting the urge to wipe away the bead of sweat running between my shoulder blades.

Mom studies me, her stare unwavering, and my stomach knots itself further.

"Cut the crap, Ellie," Dad finally says, pushing a hand through his dark hair and shattering the moment between Mom and me.

I look at him, swallowing hard. I don't even know how to confess to them about Cam. It was a *mistake,* but one I didn't even know I was making.

"We know you went to that resident's show."

I try not to let them see how my shoulders sag in relief. *That's* all they know about. And while it is one of their rules—that we're not supposed to fraternize with tenants outside of work—it's one I've broken more than I can count. My residents have become like family to me, and I could no sooner cut them off than I could my actual family, although the former is much easier to get along with.

"Yeah," I say, trying to sound contrite. "I know, but I—"

"That's enough, Ellie," Dad says, and I'm shocked at the sharpness in his tone. While my father and I rarely see eye to eye on anything, he's never been harsh with me. That role has been reserved for my mother alone.

Before he can continue, though, the bell above the front door jingles, cutting the tension between us. I let out a relieved breath.

Mr. Bart, a middle-aged gentleman who moved in over the weekend, gives me a small smile. "Sorry to interrupt."

"No problem at all," I say and mean it. Anything is preferable to being dressed down by my parents right now.

"I've been trying to get a hold of someone since Saturday, but no luck. The maintenance supervisor hasn't been answering any of my calls, and I haven't gotten a reply to my emails. My heat hasn't been working properly, and it's stuck at sixty-two degrees."

As he speaks, my face slackens, and the relief I felt moments before disappears. I carefully avoid my parents' stares. *Why, why, why today?*

"Is there anything you can do?" he asks.

My dad stands and extends a hand to him. "Daniel Bates. I'm the owner."

"Kristin Bates," Mom says, following suit.

I sit at my desk, boxed out of the conversation. A headache begins to pound behind my eyes, and I rub my temples. At every family function from now until the day I'm laid to rest, it will be brought up that I let a resident go without heat for an entire weekend. "I'm so sorry, Mr. Bart. We will be sure to have this fixed. I'll call maintenance immediately."

The man, no doubt sensing my distress, tries to smile at me. "Thanks so much for the help. And thank you for everything you've done to help me get settled."

I force a pleasant smile. "Of course, and please let me know if there is anything else we can do for you." Mr. Bart leaves and takes all the warm air with him. This place is suddenly the Arctic.

My parents' disappointment is so palpable it's now become a fourth person in this office.

Dad scrubs a hand down his face, letting my name out on a sigh that makes my blood run cold. "Ellie, we've tried this out. It's just not working."

My breath hitches in my lungs. "What?"

"The Flats at Inglewood is one of our nicest complexes, and you're running it into the ground, Elizabeth. Why couldn't he get a hold of maintenance? Why weren't you available? Oh

CHAPTER THREE

yes, because you were out with a *resident*," Mom says, her voice not holding any of the exasperation and weariness in Dad's. Hers is just...stony. And her words are the flint that sets fire to my dreams—everything I've worked so hard for the last few years.

"I wasn't out *with* a resident."

"It doesn't matter *what* you were doing, Ellie. You knew the rules, and more importantly, your job is to be available when the tenants need you."

"But," I splutter, "the residents are happy. The reviews are positive."

"That might be so, but you're causing more harm than good here, Ellie," Dad says, and it feels like a slap in the face.

"What do you mean?" My voice comes out small and shaky. I think I see the stiff expression flicker on my dad's face, but it's there and gone in an instant.

"You constantly forget to turn in your reports on time, you spend more time coddling tenants than actually doing your job, you messed up that listing a few months ago, and we had to give that woman discounted rent, costing us hundreds of dollars *every month*."

What they don't know is that I messed it up on purpose. A single mom with three kids couldn't get approved anywhere else, so I gave her a lower rate and told my parents I'd made a mistake.

They were furious, but it's worth it when she brings in her rent check and homemade cookies for me every month as a thank you. Seeing her boys happy and thriving when I know they were so close to having their entire world flipped upside down is enough to make me not regret that for a second.

"What are you saying?" I ask cautiously.

"We shouldn't have promoted you," Mom says, turning away like she can't bear to look at me. All the air left in my lungs punches out of me at her words.

Dad looks deeply uncomfortable, his head tilted to the side, one hand wrapped around the back of his neck. "Ellie, don't make this more difficult than it needs to be."

They can't be serious. This can't be happening.

I love my job. Growing up, my parents always made it known that they would love for their children to follow in their footsteps, to take over the family business. When my older brothers, Alex and Adam, never showed any interest, I thought this might be my time to shine. I've always been a little too colorful, too quirky, too *much* for my family. My family members are all sophisticated and professional and successful. I'm clumsy and cluttered and emotional.

So I would have worked for them just to make them happy. Loving the job was a pleasant suprise, and the thought of losing it—of disappointing them—is a crushing blow.

"I'll do better," I blurt.

Unbidden, an image of Cam last night, bathed in the glow from the streetlamps, comes to mind. I can almost feel his breath fanning my face, taste his kisses, imagine the way his fingers felt wrapped around my waist.

That can never happen again. It was already so far off-limits that it was almost comical, but now it's absolutely forbidden.

"Ellie…" Dad says, resigned.

Mom gives him a warning look. "We agreed this is for the best, Daniel. We could get hit with a nepotism lawsuit."

"It can't be that bad," I say against the lump rising in my throat.

Dad scrubs his hands down his face. "It's not, Ellie. Not yet. But these things *can't* keep happening."

CHAPTER THREE

"I'll do better," I say again, desperate this time. "Please, give me another chance. Please." It's the waver in my voice that makes the decision for Dad. I can tell from the way the pinched expression relaxes and his breath lets out in a whoosh that he is going to give me another chance. Mom does too, and her sharp jaw ticks.

Standing abruptly, she points one long, elegant finger at Dad. "This is on you. If she breaks any more rules, or costs us more money, or makes us look like idiots to our investors, or we get sacked with a lawsuit, you're the one who's going to clean it up."

Mom strides from my office and out the door, leaving me and Dad alone. Tears prick at the back of my eyes, but I will them not to fall.

"You have until the end of the year, Ellie. Any more mess ups, and that's it."

Swallowing the lump in my throat, I nod. "No more mess ups."

Four

CAMDEN

It takes exactly thirteen steps to walk the length of my new apartment. I know this because I've done nothing but pace it all afternoon.

I'll come find you later.

Yeah, well, that was hours ago. The sky has turned from cloudy and gray to a glittering black, and still, Ellie never came.

After the initial shock of running into Ellie wore off, I was actually excited to see her. I'd lain awake all night wishing I'd gotten her number, and now, by some stroke of luck, she was *right here.*

But she looked so horrified that any thrill I'd felt at seeing her had thickened into a tight ball of dread in the bottom of my stomach.

I'm in the middle of my most recent lap around the apartment when my phone buzzes on the counter. I snatch it up and see my sister's name on the screen.

I consider ignoring it. There's a zero percent chance Hazel won't immediately know something is up, and I don't really want to talk to her about it. But also…there's no way I can tell Weston. I need *someone* to vent to, and Hazel is my only option.

Swiping open the call, I say, "Hey, Hazel. What's up?"

CHAPTER FOUR

"What's wrong?" she asks without hesitation, and I chuff out a laugh and finally slow down enough to collapse onto my new couch. The place came fully furnished, and although it's clean and stylish, it's not the highest quality. The armrest digs uncomfortably into my back, and everything inside of me screams to get up and continue my pacing, but I make myself stay put.

"Who says anything is wrong?"

"You did."

I pick at a fraying thread on the seam of my shirt. "I don't think so."

"You didn't need to," Hazel says, and I hear rustling on her end, followed by a soft thud. I imagine her flopping down onto her printed bedspread, golden brown hair fanning all around her. "Tell me what's wrong."

Pausing, I try to gather my thoughts. One sticks out, though. The same thing that has been running through my mind all day. "I think I messed up. Bad."

"Something happen with Wes?"

"No," I tell her. "I think things are going to be good with Wes. I'm happy to be working with him again, and I think these random acts of kindness videos are going to be much more his style than the old pranking videos we used to do."

Wes had talked to me about his vision before I came to Tennessee, but today we met with his new manager and talked through all the details. The next two months will be busy. We'll be filming a ton of content in advance, but we also built in a lot of time for rest.

I can't even begin to imagine how good that will feel.

"I'm glad you get to work with Wes again. You've been really…aimless since he left."

I scoff, although her words hold a ring of truth. "I haven't been aimless. I had a career before Weston. I was doing weddings and portraits before I quit to work with him full time."

"Yeah, but I don't think it's what you want to do anymore. You've been overworked and underpaid for months. You've been working with all these new famous clients that ask the world of you. You're doing just as much for them as you used to do for Wes, except you've got ten clients instead fo one. You haven't been yourself at all."

"I've been fine, Haze." But I can't help but remember all the long nights I've spent in my little apartment in California, working crazy hours to keep up with the demands of my new clients. I thought when Wes left, it would free up my work schedule to branch out—try new things. Instead, I've been working with one difficult client after another, and I haven't had time to do anything new at all.

"I'm just saying I think this time away will be good for you."

Which is exactly why I agreed to come. I needed *out*, just for a little while. I just need some time to figure out what I want my life and career to look like when I go back to California.

"Yeah, maybe." I adjust my position on the couch so the armrest isn't digging into my back. My phone buzzes in my hand and when I pull it away fro my cheeck, I see a text from one of the demanding clients back in LA, asking me if I'm available for a shoot this weekend.

I shoot back a quick response, reminding them that I'm working out of state for the next two months.

"Cam?" From the tone of Hazel's voice, I know this isn't the first time she's said my name.

"Sorry, I was responding to a text." There's absolutely no way I'm going to give her the satisfaction of knowing she was right about my difficult clients.

CHAPTER FOUR

"I hope you don't think I'm going to forget 'I think I messed up. Bad,'" she says, drawing me back into the conversation.

"I had complete faith in you," I deadpan.

There's silence on the other line, and I smile to myself, trying to guess how long it's going to take her to ask again.

"*Camden.* Tell me what happened!"

I chuckle and recount the story. It takes three times longer than it should to describe my activities since I arrived in Nashville because she keeps stopping me to ask questions and make ridiculous comments.

"So let me get this straight," she says when I finally finish. "*You,* Camden Lane, went out last night?"

"Yes, Hazel," I grumble. "You act like I'm a hermit."

"You're not a hermit. You just hate people and activities."

I think about making a comment about just how much I enjoyed *people* and *activities* last night, but I refrain. "I don't hate people and activities."

"No, but Wes and I had to drag you with us anytime we wanted to go out."

"I have, *sometimes*, in the past, been reluctant to go out," I concede.

But when I got here last night, with no responsibilities looming before me except working with my laid-back best friend again, I felt lighter than I had in months. I wanted to explore—to see this new city and see if I could find some inspiration again.

"Did you at least have fun?"

I can't help the grin that quirks my mouth when I think about last night. About dancing in the dark, Ellie's head resting against my pounding heart. The slope of her hips under my fingertips. A hauntingly familiar fruity, floral smell. Soft lips against mine.

"Yeah, I had fun," I finally answer, and I know Hazel hears the smile in my voice.

"Ew, oh my gosh. Forget I asked."

A laugh bubbles out of my chest.

"Are you going to see her again?" Hazel asks, ignoring my laughter.

"Well, here's the kicker. She's Lo's friend—the one who runs the apartment complex I just moved into."

"She *what?*"

"And she didn't seem very happy about it." My smile dissolves at the memory of the frantic look on her face, the panic in her eyes. She looked like she'd seen a ghost—and that ghost was me.

"Are you going to try to talk to her about it?"

I chew the inside of my lip. "I don't know. I mean, even if she did seem interested, which she definitely did not, I'm leaving. There's no point."

"Cam, you took this job so you could forget your troubles here for a while. If she's willing to try something casual for a few months, I don't see the harm."

"I'm not exactly a *casual* kind of guy," I say, picking at the string on my hem again.

"Camden, I'm going to ask you a question, and I don't want you to overthink it." I roll my eyes and don't answer, but she isn't expecting one. "Did you have fun with Ellie last night?"

"Yes," I say, shocked by how easily the response came. But without a doubt, I enjoyed myself last night.

"And when was the last time that happened in LA?"

Now my mind goes blank, no answer forthcoming. I honestly can't remember. I probably haven't truly had fun since Wes moved. And it wasn't until now that I realized it.

"That's what I thought," Hazel says, her voice quiet and gentle. "If Ellie made you happy, and you were having fun, chase that feeling."

Five

ELLIE

I spend the entire night staring at my ceiling. If my parents show up at the office today, they're going to think I'm high or hungover, and will surely fire me.

Fire me.

The words bounced around in my head all day and night, a pinball stuck in a machine. I never would have expected that working for them could have gone so horribly wrong.

With that warning ringing in my ears and twisting my stomach into knots, I knew I could not go find Cam. Even trying to explain myself was too risky.

So I ghosted him. But it didn't stop me from feeling bad about it. Didn't stop the ache in my chest thinking about his kindness the night before. My perfect night with Cam was a little slice of heaven before I was thrust into my parents' purgatory.

I don't know how I'm supposed to cut off my residents. I've befriended so many of them, and the thought of having to ignore them makes my eyes prick with unshed tears.

But keeping my job is more important, so I have to try harder. Be more professional with the tenants. Get more organized and stay on top of my paperwork.

And stay far, far away from Camden Lane.

I pinch the bridge of my nose and lean my head against the exterior office door. I need to get myself together.

"Morning!" a bright voice says from behind me. Sadie. I turn around and see my best friend and leasing consultant crossing the sidewalk from the parking lot to our office, her short blond hair blowing behind her in the chilly wind.

"Morning," I say back and finally unlock the door.

"Why do you look like you're trying to talk yourself into buying groceries instead of ordering DoorDash every night for dinner?" Sadie asks, following me into the building.

We split up and walk into our respective offices. They're separated by a huge window that takes up the majority of the wall, so Sadie can easily see my tired eyes as I respond, "I'm just tired. I didn't get a lot of sleep."

"Did you stay up watching cat videos on TikTok again? I told you to set a time limit."

I drop my stuff onto my desk and lean a hip against it, smoothing my hands down my fuzzy plum-colored sweater before tapping my fingers on the thighs of my pleated orange pants. Sadie left early yesterday, so she wasn't here after my run-in with Mom and Dad, which I was thankful for. But…I don't know if I want to tell her about it now. Just the thought of letting her know how precarious my situation is has me sick to my stomach.

"No, just couldn't sleep."

Sadie pauses in unpacking her things. "You okay?"

I'm saved from speaking when my phone rings on my desk. Spinning around, I reach for it, thankful for the distraction. Gary, our maintenance supervisor, begins shouting through the speaker as soon as I pick up, and I'm immediately on high alert. I try yelling to get his attention, but he doesn't answer.

"Gary!"

"Oh, Ellie, hi," Gary says, and he must move the phone closer to his mouth because he sounds clearer now. "We've got a bit of a situation down in Building B, third floor. You better get down here."

"Okay, be right there." I slam the phone down and catch Sadie's worried gaze through the window.

"What's wrong?" she asks.

I tug off my teal suede heels and grab the pair of mustard-yellow patent leather flats I keep in my office closet—along with the ugly black blazer I put in there last night in case my parents show up unannounced again. I hop out of my office, pulling the flats on as I go. "It's Gary," I tell her. "He said there's something going on in Building B. I need to go check it out."

"Okay, text me!" Sadie calls after me as I run through the office door. Immediately, I'm hit with a blast of chilly air, and I really wish I'd thought to bring my jacket with me. I tug the sleeves of my sweater over my hands and trek across the parking lot, leaves crunching under my feet.

Building B isn't far, only a short walk from the clubhouse. I climb the stairs quickly, hand wrapped around the cool metal of the railing. "Gary," I holler as I round the corner.

I stop dead in my tracks. There, between Gary at the opposite end of the outdoor hallway and me, is an *armadillo*. A giant, scaly armadillo with beady eyes that stare me down like I'm its next meal. Now, I don't know much about armadillos, but if someone were to ask me if they're dangerous, based on the look on that creature's face, I would tell you they are man-eaters.

I'm hyperventilating. Gary holds his hands up, steadying me. "Ellie, calm down."

CHAPTER FIVE

Breathe in. Breathe out. In. Out. The armadillo takes a step toward me.

I scream and back toward the stairs. My foot fumbles for purchase, missing the step, and before I know it, I'm tumbling down. My head smacks against the wall, and I roll hard until I slam to a stop at the landing.

I don't know if Gary made a running leap over that armadillo, or if he learned to fly, but before I know it, the sixty-year-old man is standing at the top of the stairs. He looks horror-struck. "Ellie!"

I lift a hand and pat my head, looking for injuries. A knot is forming on my scalp, but other than that, I don't notice anything else. "I'm okay."

Gary moves down the steps faster than I thought possible for a man of his age and is at my side a moment later. He helps me to a standing position, and I stare mournfully at the ripped skid mark on the knee of my favorite orange pants. "Ugh," I yell, throwing my hands in the air.

I look up and see the armadillo scurrying its tough body down the stairs. Without thinking, I turn and run down the hall, Gary on my heels. We stop when we reach the other staircase and spin around, out of breath.

"I think we need to work out more, Gary."

"Don't I know it," he says and pats his stomach.

The armadillo stands at the bottom of the staircase, unmoving. "We have to corner it," I tell him, thinking of the hell that will rain down on my head from my parents if this wild animal hurts a resident. I will absolutely, no doubt about it, get fired for that.

"Yeah," Gary says. "Who is going to do that?"

I put my hands on my hips and swivel to face him. "Seriously? I am a small, defenseless woman."

"Didn't you make a platform out of boxes a few weeks ago and stand on top of it, ranting about women's rights?" Gary hooks his hands around his suspenders and eyes the armadillo cautiously as it takes a few steps toward us.

"Irrelevant."

The armadillo moves closer and closer. "Rock, paper, scissors," I tell him. He looks at me with wary brown eyes.

"It's only fair," I say as the armadillo closes in.

"Fine," he huffs. We put our hands in position and count down.

"Rock, paper, scissors, shoot," we yell, and I slap one hand flat down atop my other. His hand is clenched in a fist.

"Ha!" I scream and run down to the first floor, leaving Gary alone with the armadillo. "I'm going to tell Sadie to call animal control!" I crane my neck to yell over my shoulder. Just as I hit the first-floor landing, I run smack into a hard wall. No, not a hard *wall*, but a hard *body,* I realize as warm hands grip my arms. I look up, up into the eyes of none other than Cam.

His hair is sleep-mussed, and I'm transported back to a dark street, with my hands in his hair, making it look that exact same way. "You okay?" he asks, his deep voice sounding as breathless as I feel. I nod, and he releases me. His navy eyes track up the stairs behind me. "Everything okay up there? I heard a bang and shouting." When he looks back at me, concern has replaced his confusion.

I nod, still unable to find the words that are usually bursting from me. The sound of Gary's clanking keys shakes me from my stupor. "Armadillo," I say, and his eyes crinkle, brows bunching together. "There's an armadillo upstairs," I clarify. "Actually, I need to call the office. Excuse me."

CHAPTER FIVE

I expect him to leave when I take a step away and dial Sadie with shaking fingers, but he doesn't move, his steady gaze still fixed on me.

Sadie answers on the first ring. "What was in Building B?"

"An armadillo. I need you to call animal control. The number should be in one of the shared files on the computer."

"On it," Sadie responds, and I hear her typing in the background.

"Want me to come over there after I get off the phone?" Sadie asks. The rattling of keys grows louder, and Gary's stomping feet shake the floor above me. I finally allow myself to look back at Cam. I definitely need backup.

"Yes, please. Bring armor." I hang up and slip the phone into my pocket.

When I turn back to Cam, he's running a hand through his hair, messing it up even more artfully. He's painfully good to look at, especially in the light of day, and I really, *really* need to get out of here.

"So, um, small world, huh?" Cam asks wryly.

The poor attempt at a joke loosens some of the tension in my shoulders, and I find myself smiling, just a little. "The smallest," I breathe.

Cam hesitates for a moment, as if deciding how to proceed. Then he says, "Ellie, can we—"

"I better go," I interrupt him, but he doesn't seem to notice as his eyes track my movements and snag on the rip at my knee.

"You're bleeding," he says, and as I look down, I realize it's true. I shrug, even though now that he's mentioned it, I start to feel the sting of the concrete burn. "Why don't we get you a Band-Aid?" He motions over his shoulder, and my eyes widen when I realize he's pointing at his apartment door.

Absolutely not.

I fumble for an excuse. Under no circumstances should I be alone with this man in his apartment—even if it is strictly for business reasons. "There are no Band-Aids in there," I say. The apartment came furnished, but only with the basics. Unless he brought—

"I packed some," he says, interrupting my thoughts.

When my feet don't move from where they've grown roots into the concrete, he sighs, shoulders sagging. Pushing a hand through his hair again, he says, "Come on, Ellie. Let me just get you a Band-Aid."

I cast a glance back over my shoulder, listening to Gary still jingling his keys and making sure no one else is around. I am all kinds of stupid for doing this, but I'm starting to believe Cam's eyes could convince me to do just about anything.

I nod and follow him inside, taking in the basic furnishings I double-checked the day before he arrived. I immediately spot the differences—the plain white coffee mug sitting upside down on the dish drying mat, the worn flannel he was wearing *that* night hanging on the hook by the door, the masculine scent that's drowning out the smell of bleach from the cleaners.

"You can sit on the couch. I'll be right back," he says and disappears into the bathroom. I'm noticing he doesn't use more words than necessary to get his point across, but he doesn't seem reserved or shy. He exudes the easy confidence of one completely comfortable in their own skin, and I wonder what that must feel like.

I sit still, my heart pounding so loudly in my ears that it almost drowns out the sounds of him rummaging around in his bathroom. I remind myself that I'm not doing anything wrong, even though it may feel like it. Even with my parents' strict rules, I am allowed in a resident's apartment for work reasons, although it feels a lot more personal as he returns, his dark eyes fixed on me.

I expect him to hand me the washcloth, so I'm surprised when he crouches down in front of me. He pauses an inch from my leg and looks up at me from under the fringe of his lashes. "This okay?"

I should say no. I should ask him for the washcloth to clean the wound myself, but I can't speak against the knot in my throat, so I just nod.

He sets the washcloth down on the couch and slowly rolls up the wide flare of my pants, exposing my wound. I try to control my breathing, not wanting him to know how his touch is affecting me.

But I'd be lying if I didn't say it was like all the air was sucked out of the room, leaving nothing but a pulsing electric charge surging between us. I have danced for hours with this man, wrapped around him like he might fly away if I let go. I've kissed him, felt his lips pressed against my own as he guided me in the most expert of ways.

But this is more intimate, by far.

His hand is gentle as it wraps around the back of my calf, and I feel the burn of his fingertips searing my skin. Tenderly, he presses the washcloth to the scrape, and I wince.

He halts his movements immediately. "Are you okay?"

"Yeah, I'm fine," I say, surprised when my voice comes out as a breathy whisper.

If Cam notices, he doesn't say anything, his focus entirely on my wound. I watch, heart pounding erratically in my chest, as he cleans it with precision. He carefully applies antibiotic cream from his first aid kit and then covers it with a bandage.

His fingers grip the fabric rolled above my knee, but he doesn't pull it down. Instead, his eyes travel the length of me, and when they settle on mine, they're as dark as the sky on the night we met.

"Ellie, what happened yesterday?" I shiver at the smooth, deep timbre of his voice.

I'm hit with an overwhelming urge to close the distance between us, to see if he tastes the same as he did the other night, to see if his kisses are still as thrilling when I'm not half-asleep and high on the feeling of being wrapped in his arms.

It would be *so easy* to ignore my parents' rules and give in to this. But it would also have hefty, life-altering consequences.

So I steel myself, straightening my shoulders. When I lean back infinitesimally, he rocks back on his heels, his hands leaving my pant leg where it is. I roll it down, anything to avoid his gaze as I force the words out. "Cam, I...*Spending time,*" I say, emphasizing the words so he knows exactly what I mean, "with residents is off-limits."

"Oh." He scratches at the stubble along his chin with the heel of his hand.

"Yeah," I say, tapping my fingers on my thigh. And then I put my foot in my mouth. "Even if I want to."

Cam's eyes shoot up to mine. "Oh?"

Although I want to slap myself in the face for what I just admitted, I can't help the smile that tugs on my lips. "Do you know other words?"

A slow grin takes over his face, and it's absolutely devastating, forming crinkles in all the places that means he does this often.

"Oh," he repeats, and I can't help the laugh that bursts out of me.

CHAPTER FIVE

I push to my feet and extend a hand to him. He takes it, pulling himself up to tower over me, standing so close I no longer feel like laughing. Instead, I really want to repeat our events from the last time we were this close.

"And this is a pretty hard and fast rule?" he asks, his smooth voice slipping down an octave and sending goose bumps prickling my skin.

"Very hard. Very fast."

His eyes widen at my words, and my face flushes. "Oh, my gosh." I step back, pressing a hand over my mouth. "That was *not* meant to be a line."

Cam stares at me for another moment before erupting in laughter. It's a truly glorious sound, and before I know it, I'm giggling too, my embarrassment fading.

"Ellie?" I hear Sadie's voice in the hall, and I spin around quickly.

"Shoot." I point over my shoulder. "I've got to go. Please don't…" I hesitate. "Can we keep this just between us? All of it?"

He nods, sober again. "Yeah, of course."

I want to hug him. And that just won't do. So I back toward the door, pausing at the threshold. "Thanks, Cam."

I close the door behind me and find Sadie standing in the hall, suspicion written in the pinch of her eyebrows.

"Everything okay?"

I point to the ripped fabric at my knee. "Fell down the stairs."

"Oh, my gosh. Are you okay?" she asks, wariness gone.

"Yeah, I'm fine. Let's go check on Gary," I say and project my voice up the stairs. "Gary, you doing okay up there?"

His scratchy voice booms down the stairs. "All good! She's actually kind of cute."

Sadie rolls her eyes and grabs two huge pieces of cardboard I didn't notice leaning against the wall. I look at her questioningly, and she responds, "You asked for armor."

I take one of the makeshift shields and follow her to the stairs, pausing for a moment to glance back at Cam's door.

"Did you get a hold of animal control?" I ask Sadie when we reach the third-floor landing.

"Critter Gitter is on the way," she responds.

The three of us stand there, staring at the armadillo that Gary somehow trapped in the corner.

"So we just wait?" Gary asks.

I shrug my shoulders. "I think we just wait."

Sadie cocks her head. "You know, you were right, Gary. She actually is kind of cute." The armadillo turns around and looks at us as if it knows we're talking about it.

"How do you know it's a girl?" I ask, holding my piece of cardboard more firmly in front of me in case the thing decides to charge again.

"Look at those hips," Sadie says. "That's a Kardashian armadillo if I ever saw one."

"A Karmadillo, if you will," I offer, and Sadie snorts.

"What's a Kardashian?" Gary asks.

Six

CAMDEN

"Hey, Camden," Lo says, wrapping one arm around me in a side hug.

Wes follows her in, and with a smirk says, "I love what you've done with the place."

I look around the barren apartment. "Interior design *is* my passion."

"We're really glad you're here," Lo says, leaning into Wes's side.

"Eh, the jury's still out," Wes responds and winks in my direction.

Lo rolls her eyes and tucks a strand of her copper hair behind her ear. "I'm glad we were able to find you a place so close, though, since East Nashville real estate is hard to come by. It's so lucky we had an in with Ellie." Lo flicks her eyes up to mine. "Did you get a chance to meet her? She's the best."

Rubbing a hand along the back of my neck, I murmur, "Yeah, we met." I square my shoulders and grab my bag of camera equipment. "You guys ready to go?"

Wes heads for the door, Lo on his heels. "Yeah, let's do this."

When we get buckled in the car and head toward the entrance, Lo says, "Hey, why don't we stop in and say hi to Ellie? I've been wanting to catch up with her. We've barely talked in months."

My stomach sinks like a lead weight as Wes steers into the parking lot in front of the office.

"Is that okay with you?" Lo asks, looking over her shoulder at me in the back seat.

"Yeah, of course," I push out, even though this is very not okay. The *last* thing I want is for Ellie to think I can't leave her alone. Despite Hazel's big talk about me having fun with Ellie, it's not going to happen—not with the rules she mentioned. And that's for the best. For all my actions to the contrary the other night, I don't do *casual*.

The bell above the door jingles, grabbing Ellie's attention. Her eyes immediately lock with mine, widening in surprise as we close the distance to her office. I try to signal with my facial expression that this was *not my idea*. She plasters a smile on her face and turns to face my companions.

"Lo!" Ellie shouts, jumping up from her seat to grab her friend in a hug. "It's been too long." She flashes Wes a grin. "Weston, it's good to see you again."

"You too. Thanks again for setting up the apartment for Cam," he says, giving my shoulder a pat.

Ellie's gaze settles on mine. "No problem. Glad to help."

I swallow as she turns back to face Lo and asks her a question about Wes and Lo's whirlwind wedding a few months ago. Wes joins in, offering up details and cracking jokes. As I listen, I notice that Ellie keeps the conversation focused on them, never once interrupting to share details about her own life.

When she glances back at me and catches me staring, I look away quickly, choosing instead to observe her office. It's an explosion of color and paperwork. She has files stacked precariously on one edge of her desk. A collection of photos is shoved into a tight bunch at the other corner to allow for more haphazardly situated papers and Post-it notes. The wall with the wide window facing the opposite office is painted black, but that's not what sticks out to me. In silver and gold Sharpie, are what looks like…notes.

I squint, trying to get a better look, and see one that says, *We love Ellie! She made us feel so at home! – The Chaperons.* Another reads, *Ellie made this new city feel like home for me. I couldn't be more thankful that this was the apartment complex I found when I moved across the country. – Saylor Smith.*

The whole wall is covered in notes from what must be past and current residents—notes that praise her over and over again. Something in my chest warms, and when I finally turn back to the conversation, Ellie's eyes are fixed squarely on me.

"Aw, this was fun," Lo says. "We should hang out soon."

"Yes," Ellie responds, wrapping Lo in another quick hug. "Call me."

I feel her gaze settle back on me, warming my skin, but I can't bring myself to look. Something about seeing her office, seeing *her* here, makes me feel drawn to her in ways we're not allowed to explore.

"Bye, Weston. Good to see you again." Ellie pauses, and when she speaks again, her voice is soft in a way that forces my eyes back to her against my will. "Bye, Cam."

I swallow against the lump that has begun to form in my throat. "Bye, Ellie."

"You should ask Ellie out," Wes says later, after we've finished filming his tour of Nashville and ended up at a little donut shop between their house and my apartment.

I choke on my donut, coughing so hard that Wes slams his palm into my back and Lo fetches a cup of water. I take a drink, the cool liquid soothing my raw throat. "What?"

Wes and Lo both stare at me with wide eyes.

"What?" I ask again, this time referring to their crazed looks.

Wes takes a bite of his donut and watches me suspiciously. Swallowing, he says, "I said you should ask Ellie out, and then you reacted like you've never met a woman before."

"I choked," I say, although I know the blush searing my cheeks is giving me away.

Lo chews on her lip thoughtfully, her blue-green eyes narrowing. "No, Wes is onto something."

"Wes has never been onto something in his entire life," I retort and shove the whole donut in my mouth, hoping to distract from my scarlet face.

"You like her," Wes sing-songs.

"*Omigah*," I say around the bite in my mouth, then finish chewing before I continue. "You sound like you're in middle school."

"And you're acting like middle school was the last time you kissed a girl."

My face flames hotter, remembering the last time I *did* kiss a girl. Memories flood my mind—of Ellie's fingers scraping my scalp, of her teeth nipping at my bottom lip, of the way she shivered against me when I trailed my mouth along her neck.

Wes points at me. "What are you hiding?" he shouts.

"I'm not hiding anything!"

He tilts his head, scrutinizing me, and Lo watches the entire situation with an assessing look. "You've been seeing someone and not telling me, haven't you? It's Britt, the girl from your apartment building back in LA, isn't it? She's been obsessed with you forever," Wes says.

CHAPTER SIX

"It's not Britt," I finally answer, rolling my eyes.

"But it's someone?" Lo asks.

My face heats again, and I can practically feel Ellie's heart thumping against mine under the multicolored lights of the dance floor.

I open and close my mouth several times, unsure how to respond, but knowing they won't let this go. Finally, I say, "I had an *encounter* with someone recently, but it can't go anywhere."

I take another bite of my donut, pleased with my vague answer.

"So ask Ellie out," Wes says, and I almost choke again.

I watch the dawning pass over Lo's face in the way her eyes bug out and her lips fall open to form a perfect O. Wes looks between us, head whipping back and forth.

I cringe, aware that my ruse is now up.

"You and *Ellie*?" Lo asks. "When? How?"

Letting out a breath and palming the back of my neck, I say, "The night I moved in, I went exploring. I...ran into Ellie. We danced."

"Your face is the color of a ripe tomato because you *danced*?" Wes asks incredulously.

I throw my hands up in the air. "We kissed, okay? Gosh, you're annoying now that you're in love."

Wes flashes Lo a cheeky grin, and she laces her fingers through his. That feeling, that ache deep in my chest that I felt that first day at Wes and Lo's house, is back. I rub at the collar of my shirt as though that may make it go away.

Wes turns back to me, dragging himself out of his silent conversation with Lo. "To be fair, you've always told me that I'm annoying."

"You've gotten worse," I grumble.

"So why can't things go anywhere with Ellie?" Lo redirects the conversation.

I sigh through my nose. "I never said I *wanted* it to go anywhere," I answer, although it tastes like a lie on my tongue. "But even if I *did*, she said it's against company policy."

"I'm pretty sure her parents own the company," Lo says around a bite of her donut. "I bet she would be allowed to bend the rules if she wanted to."

I don't know why the words feel like hand sanitizer in a paper cut, but it doesn't stop the sting. "Yeah, well, she didn't."

Lo seems to realize her mistake. "Sorry, that was insensitive of me."

Wes runs a consoling hand over Lo's back as I say, "No, it's not," though that doesn't feel entirely true. "Even if something *could* happen between us, I'm leaving in two months. There's no point."

Weston's eyes light up, his expression changing in an instant. "You don't have to." I stare at him, lost for words, and he laughs. "Come on. Didn't you have fun today? The boys are back together again."

"Please never refer to us as *the boys*."

He rolls his eyes, chuckling, before turning serious again. "For real, though. It was nice working together again. And you know you'd always have a job here if you wanted it."

I should turn him down immediately, but the words die before I can voice them. I can't tell him I'd rather be in LA, doing what I've been doing the last few months. Not when I know I'd be lying.

If Wes sees the indecision flickering across my face, he's kind enough not to mention it. Instead, he says, "Just think about it, okay?"

"I'll think about it," I agree.

Seven

ELLIE

Sadie walking through the door the next Friday morning pulls me out of a particularly delicious daydream. I'm back in Cam's arms, pressed up against cool brick, his hands burning through the fabric of my velvet shirt, when Sadie bursts into the office.

It's a real mood killer.

She catches me staring as she hefts her giant purse through the door to her office. "What?"

"Nothing," I say, turning back to my desk and shuffling around a stack of papers.

"Why are you blushing?"

"Why *aren't* you blushing?" I ask, trying to throw her off the scent.

She stares at me for a moment before shaking her head. "It's too early for this. I'm going to make coffee. Want some tea?"

"Yes, please," I say, thankful she let the conversation drop.

I work through some emails as she makes our drinks, my eyes snagging on one from Gary. He says something came up and he won't be able to come in until after lunch this morning. My inbox is already flooded with maintenance requests today, and there's no way he's going to be able to finish them all this afternoon.

Positive resident reviews are basically the only thing I have going for me right now. I let my gaze trail over my *Happy Wall*, as I like to call it. When I got promoted and moved to this complex last year, I painted one wall in my office black—something my parents were not very fond of. Anytime a resident moved out or left a good review online, I asked if they wanted to come in and write on the wall.

One year later, there's hardly an open spot left. When I'm feeling crushed beneath my parents' disappointment, I like to look at that wall and know that I'm at least doing *something* right.

But that's not enough, apparently. The last time Gary was unavailable, one of the residents went without heat for a whole weekend, and I almost got fired. So I can't let a single request slip through the cracks today.

I pull a hot pink sticky note from the top of my stack and write down a few of the easy tasks, planning to tackle them when there's a lull this morning. It may make me a little backed up on paperwork, but I can always bring it home with me tonight.

Sadie walks into my office, a mug in each hand. She sets one atop a stack of papers on my desk. "Working on stuff for the harvest festival resident event?"

"No," I respond and pause to take a sip of my tea, the apple cinnamon blend warming me from the inside out. "Gary is going to be late today, so I'm trying to get some of his requests knocked out myself."

"Don't we have a ton to do for the event?"

I wave her off. "It's not for almost two weeks. We'll get it done." Honestly, I'd forgotten about it when I started making a list of my tasks for today. I'll definitely be taking paperwork home tonight.

CHAPTER SEVEN

"So what's on the schedule for today?"

I sort through the mess of files and papers on my desk, almost upending the mug of tea, but I manage to find my list. We walk through the itinerary, coordinating so one of us will be in the office at all times in case of walk-ins.

The bell above the door jingles, and Sadie stands. "There's my first tour."

"Have fun," I say with a wave and turn back to my computer. Her rehearsed speech becomes background noise as I work through emails. I find one from Tyler, the resident in the band I was watching the night Cam and I met. He's inviting me to another one of their shows, and I want nothing more than to send him a response telling him I can't wait to go. Honestly, I'm so proud of him and the band. I've been going to their concerts for a year, and I've watched as they've steadily gained more and more fans.

It's like pressing on a bruise, knowing the night I met Cam is the last of their shows I'll get to go to. I type out an email, congratulating them on booking this gig, but saying I won't be able to make it this time. If my parents are monitoring my work account, I hope they see this and are happy. It's the only thing that would make this ache in my chest lessen.

When I finally emerge from my email hole, Sadie has already left, taking our guests on a tour of the property. I won't be able to start on Gary's tasks until she gets back to man the office, so I dive into paperwork.

I've only made it through a few files when I hear the front door open. Ethel, my favorite resident, a spunky eighty-two-year-old, shuffles in. Her coke-bottle glasses are perched so precariously on the very tip of her nose that a stiff wind would blow them right off.

"Hey, Ethel," I say as she advances slowly into my office.

"Hey, girlie." Ethel lowers herself into one of the chairs across from my desk. "How are you doing today?"

I consider telling her the truth. In fact, a week ago, I probably would have. Sadie is my best friend, and I share almost everything with her, but I keep my deepest secrets for Ethel alone. She's crass and honest and always gives me the best advice. I want more than anything to spill my guts to her about the entire thing right here and now.

But that's the problem, apparently. In my parents' eyes, I should never be close enough with a resident to share the most vulnerable pieces of my heart with them.

"I'm good," I tell her and plaster a smile on my face. "How are you?"

"A little pissed that you're lying to me," she says, crossing one bony leg over the other and pinning me with her milky blue eyes.

I swallow audibly. "I'm good, really. Just a little tired."

From her bunched eyebrows and pinched lips, I can tell we both know I'm lying. I hold my breath, waiting for her to question me further. Ethel is never one to let anything go.

She surprises me, though, by changing the subject. "You got any plans on Halloween? Want to come help this old lady with an order?"

"What's the order?"

"Some bachelorettes want three batches of magnum dark chocolate caramels." She rolls her eyes. "Completely unoriginal."

Some people might find it weird that this elderly woman runs a business making phallic-shaped candies in her retirement, but Ethel has never been one to stick to the beaten path.

"Some people have absolutely no taste," I deadpan, and she nods vigorously.

"So are you going to come help me or not?" Ethel asks.

I chew the inside of my lip, racking my brain for an excuse. I could tell her the truth—spill about the ultimatum from my parents. But she would be outraged and indignant on my behalf. And worse than that, she would tell me to stick up for myself.

That's something I just can't do.

Ignoring the sinking feeling in my stomach, I reach for the first thing to come to mind. "I can't. Tyler's band is playing a show, and he invited me to go watch."

"Well, poo," Ethel says. "I'll just try to give myself some extra time to get it done." She shakily pushes herself up from the chair, and guilt wraps around me, constricting me like a straight-jacket.

I tap my trembling fingers on my thigh underneath the desk. "I'm sorry, Ethel. I wish I could help."

"Nonsense, you go out and have fun. You spend way too many nights hanging out with an old woman anyway. Don't you worry about me."

But as she teeters out of the office, using every available surface for support, I do exactly that. When she reaches the front door, she yells over her shoulder, "Don't think for one second that you're going to get away with lying to me earlier. I will figure it out, young lady."

I don't expect to feel so alone when she leaves, but the ache in my chest spreads, threatening to envelop me whole. Without my residents, my social circle is embarrassingly small. No one at the last complex I worked for wanted to befriend the boss's daughter, and no one knew whether to defer to my authority or the manager's. Coming here, being promoted, has been life-changing. I finally found my *family,* and the thought of having to ghost them makes me sick.

So later, when I'm working through Gary's to-do list and get a text from Lo asking if I want to grab lunch with her and Wes, I practically drop my phone in my haste to respond.

It's not until I arrive that I realize I should have asked more questions.

Lo, Wes, and *Camden Lane* are already seated at a table when I walk into the deli only a mile down the street from The Flats. My heart stops, along with my feet, at the sight.

"Hey!" Lo says with a smile, standing to give me a hug and breaking me from my trance. I hug her back, but I can't tear my eyes from Cam's, which are wide and disbelieving, leading me to think he is just as caught off guard by this as me.

I drag my gaze back to her grinning face, her eyes brimming with excitement. There's no way I can back out now without making the situation more uncomfortable, so I nod and murmur something back before sliding into the booth next to Cam.

He's too big for this seat, and although he tries to plaster himself against the wall, his thigh and shoulder are still pressed against the length of mine. Suddenly, my jacket is *stifling*.

Lo is babbling about something as I try to maneuver out of my coat, but it gets stuck at my elbows. Large hands cinch around the fabric, brushing the exposed sliver of skin at my back where my shirt has ridden up. I shiver so violently at the contact that I almost topple a glass of water on the table.

Cam grips my shoulder with his other hand, steadying me, before slowly pulling the jacket free of my arms. When I meet his gaze, I can't decipher his expression—can't tell if he's as affected by this as me.

I swallow audibly and turn to face Wes and Lo. Their eyes are wide, and I realize that at some point, Lo must have stopped talking, because the tension at the table has become a palpable thing.

Clearing my throat, I flag down a passing waiter. "Could I get a water, please?"

Despite removing my jacket, Camden's leg is still searing mine under the table, and the looks Wes and Lo are giving us are enough to send a hot flush to my cheeks.

The table is silent for another awkward beat as the waiter returns with my glass. I take a long gulp and try to inconspicuously press it against my cheek.

"I'm so glad we could do this," Wes says wryly, and Lo elbows him in the side hard enough to crack a rib.

But his sarcastic remark does the trick, shattering the tension in an instant. Cam's shoulder presses more firmly into mine, as if he's deflating, finally allowing himself to take up the amount of space he requires. I blow out a breath and lean my head against the back of the booth. "Glad to be here," I say with a twist of my lips.

Lunch goes surprisingly well, despite its rocky start. I find myself laughing more than I have in ages, and the guard I'm trying to keep up around Cam slips the tiniest bit. It's dangerous, this line I'm walking, but it also feels too good to stop.

When Cam finishes his food and stretches his arm across the back of the booth, I want nothing more than to lean into him just the slightest bit, but I hold back. There's a difference between lowering my walls and plunging face-first off the top.

As Wes and Lo leave together, Cam and I stand next to our cars, which are parked side by side in the lot. We watch them pull out onto the street and then turn to face each other, that tether between us threatening to tug me right back into his arms.

"I had no idea she was inviting you," Cam says, guilt settling harshly into the lines of his face.

I shrug. "I know."

"Was this...okay?"

Chewing on my lip, I stare up at him and watch his eyes follow the movement, darkening to almost black. I have no idea how to respond, but with his unwavering attention focused solely on me, I want to tell him the truth.

While this entire lunch was *not okay* according to company policy, it was more fun than I've had in months. And I want to do it again—over and over until his expressions are no longer a mystery to me, until I've memorized the sound of his laughter and the feeling of his body pressed next to mine.

I wish so desperately that I could explain that to him.

But I can't.

So I step back, breaking the spell between us. "Not really."

Camden's face falls, and he palms the back of his neck. "I'm sorry. I—"

I reach out, unable to help myself, and grip his forearm. It twitches beneath my fingers, and I drop it like it burned me. "It's okay, really. You don't need to apologize. I just—we just can't do this again."

His denim eyes meet mine again, regret written so plainly in them that my chest cracks in two. "Of course. I understand." He points over his shoulder. "I better go."

It's not until that moment that I realize how chilled I've become. It's like the moment I told him this couldn't happen again, I unwrapped us from the warm cocoon he'd built around us with his laughter and gentle touches.

"Yeah, me too. Bye, Cam."

As I get into my car and crank the heat, I wonder just how many times I'm going to have to say those words to residents in the upcoming weeks. How many times I'll have to blow them off or cancel plans until there's no one left to ask.

It will just be me, alone with my parents' approval and no one to celebrate it with.

Eight

ELLIE

One Sunday a month for as long as I can remember, my family has gone to dinner at the same Italian restaurant near downtown. Tonight is that night—and I'm absolutely dreading it.

There was a time long ago that interactions with my parents didn't leave me wanting to curl up in a ball in my closet, but I can't pinpoint when that changed. The only saving grace about these dinners is that my brothers, Adam and Alex, are great at running interference. One time, Alex pretended to faint to distract my mom while she was criticizing my outfit. He came to asking for smelling salts like a Victorian maiden.

I walk through the front doors and head to our usual table. Mom is very particular about where she sits in restaurants—she wants to be close to the kitchen so our waiter sees us first every time they enter the dining room, but she also refuses to have a bathroom within her line of sight. I can't tell you how many restaurants my family has walked out of because my mother couldn't find a seat to her liking.

When I come around the corner, I see Mom and Dad seated at the table, but my brothers and my sister-in-law aren't here yet. I backpedal until I'm hidden behind a giant fake potted plant and peer through the greenery. Mom's face is painted in displeasure as she talks to Dad, who is calmly ignoring her while scrolling on his phone. No doubt the waiter brought her chilled water instead of tepid or she was forced to stand in the lobby like a commoner and wait for them to prepare our table.

"Whatcha doing?" a voice asks in my ear, and I spin around to find my brother Alex trying to glance through the parted silk leaves to see what's beyond.

"Oh good, you're here," I breathe. He's dressed in fitted charcoal gray slacks and a crisp white button up. His dark hair is styled with some matte pomade. I'm really regretting my clothing choice. I even went for something tamer than usual—a dark teal velvet wrap dress.

I let out a shuddering breath, pushing my insecurities to the back of my mind. "I didn't want to have to sit there alone with them."

His eyebrows inch up his forehead. "Something happen?"

That familiar oily shame coils through my stomach, and I sigh. "We have a lot to discuss."

He links his arm through mine and pulls me toward the table with a wink.

Mom's expression pinches when she notices us. "Elizabeth, what are—"

"I think the moon landing was fake," Alex announces, tugging me down into the chair next to him. "Let's discuss."

Adam and his wife, Kelsey, arrive a few minutes later, prompting Alex to close out of the Google search for images of our flag on the moon and put his phone away.

"You're late," Mom says as soon as they sit down.

"Great to see you too, Mom," Adam says. He checks his watch as they sit down. "We're actually three minutes early."

Mom purses her lips and returns her focus to the menu.

Kelsey smiles at me and gives my arm a squeeze. "I love this dress."

"Is a velvet dress really appropriate for a family dinner, Elizabeth?" Mom asks, glancing up at me. "This isn't one of your app dates."

I give Mom a tight smile. "I've actually never used a dating app."

"This bread is delicious," Adam says loudly.

"So good I might end up choking on it later," Alex whispers and nudges me under the table.

I let out a breath, the tightness in my shoulders loosening.

THE REST OF THE dinner continues much the same way as it started—Mom making passive-aggressive comments, and the rest of us scrambling to change the subject.

When we finally leave the restaurant an hour and a half later, my cheeks hurt from all the smiles I've been forcing. I probably need to schedule a facial. I can just imagine it now.

Why are you here today, ma'am? the esthetician will ask.

No reason. I just pulled a muscle in my face smiling at my mother while she belittled me in every way imaginable. What keeps you awake at night?

Adam, Kelsey, Alex, and I stand in the parking lot next to our cars, watching carefully as our parents climb into their Cadillac and wave goodbye. The second they're gone, we all heave sighs of relief and head back inside.

"You know, I'm really proud of Mom for only sending her meal back twice tonight," Alex says.

Adam hums. "I agree. Really shows growth."

When we get back to our table, there are already four slices of cheesecake waiting for us.

This tradition started a few years ago—once we were all out of the house and I had already started working for Mom and Dad. After one particularly rough family dinner, Alex suggested we go back inside for dessert, and it stuck. Now, every month, after Mom and Dad head home, we sneak back inside and eat the cheesecake we secretly ordered.

It's a good way to decompress.

"I'm exhausted," Kelsey announces after we sit back down. "I don't know how you do it, Ellie."

I laugh it off, but the words stick in my head, echoing and relentless. She's right. While my parents—my mother especially—are hard on my brothers, the last few years I've been the one to bear the brunt of their displeasure.

"So what did we need to talk about?" Alex asks me.

The cheesecake lodges in my throat, and I have to take a sip of water to swallow it down. I tap my fingers against the side of the glass as I set it on the table, trying to figure out how to explain the situation at work. There's no way to sugarcoat it, though, so I say, "Mom and Dad came into the office the other day and told me if I didn't turn things around, they were going to *explore other options*," I say on an exhale.

When I look up, they're all staring at me, Alex with his fork poised outside his mouth. It snaps the tension inside me like a frayed rubber band, and a laugh escapes. Before I know it, I can't stop. I press my hand against my mouth, but it doesn't work.

"El," Alex says, placing his fork back down on his plate. He reaches for me, wrapping me in a hug, and it's only then that I realize my uncontrollable laughter has turned into sobs.

"I just don't know what I did. I thought working for them would make them proud of me. And despite everything, I thought I was *good* at my job." I sniff loudly and hiccup on a shaky breath. "I know I'm not like them—not like you guys. You all have it all together. I know I'm different, but I thought that, despite all that, I was doing a good job."

Tears stain Alex's collar as he holds me to him. "*You* didn't do anything wrong. No matter what they say, I'm proud of you."

Adam's arms wrap around me from the other side.

"Ellie Sandwich," I hiccup.

"Ellie Sandwich," they echo.

When we were kids and I needed affection, I'd find my brothers and make them give me hugs just like this. I always called it an Ellie Sandwich—although they usually called it a Loser Sandwich.

But they did it—every time. And like all those times before, it stitches my heart back together a little. It's still bruised and battered, but it's healed enough for me to keep going.

I pull back, wiping beneath my eyes with the cloth napkin. My mascara smears across the white fabric, and Alex smirks at me. "The cleaners are going to *love* you."

I shove him in the shoulder and reach for my fork, taking another bite of my cheesecake.

They must sense my reluctance to talk about the situation any more, because Alex changes the subject.

"I'm looking at a condo this week," he says.

"To buy?" Adam asks.

Alex nods and swallows the last bite of his dessert. "Yeah, I think this might be the one. It's in a building downtown. Thirty-fourth floor."

"I'm not helping you move," Adam announces.

CHAPTER EIGHT

"What do you mean you're not helping me move?"

Kelsey meets my eyes across the table, holding back a grin.

"I mean exactly that," Adam continues. "Last time I showed up to help you move, you hadn't packed. And then I had to carry your stuff up three flights of stairs to the place you're in now. And you remember what I told you that day?"

"No."

"That *that* was the last time I helped you move."

"I think you said *groove*," Alex says, and I suck in my lips to keep from laughing, knowing where this is going. Anytime Adam tries to make definitive statements on anything, Alex just spouts utter nonsense until Adam is so annoyed that he gives in.

"I didn't say *groove*," Adam says, rolling his eyes.

Kelsey holds up five fingers inconspicuously, and I shake my head, then hold up four. Every time they do this, we take bets on how many things Alex will have to say before Adam loses it.

"Yes, you said you wouldn't groove with me anymore, and I told you that was a shame because I'd just started Zumba classes."

"You've never taken Zumba classes," Adam exhales and presses his fingers to his temples, massaging there.

"I have too," Alex continues. "My teacher told me I had natural rhythm."

"You don't have *rhythm*," Adam argues. "I'm surprised you were able to run cross country in high school without tripping and falling. You're a klutz."

"You're right," Alex concedes and takes a long sip of his drink. "I *am* a klutz."

"Mm-hmm," Adam mumbles around a bite of cheesecake.

"I can hardly walk."

"Yup."

"I really shouldn't be trying to carry boxes up and down my stairs alone then, huh?" Alex asks, his dark brown eyes glittering.

Adam's head snaps up, and I choke back a laugh.

"I'll let you know what day I need help," Alex says with a wink.

"I'm not helping you move."

Alex pushes up from his chair. "I'd love to stay longer, but I have to get going." He leans down, wrapping an arm around my shoulders, and I squeeze his side. "Call me if you need me," he whispers in my ear, and I manage a nod.

He stands up straight and pats Adam on the shoulder. "Bring your truck when you come help me move."

"I'm *not* helping you move."

My phone buzzes on the table, distracting me from their conversation, and I look down to see a text from Gary.

> Gary
> We just got an emergency request, but I can't come in. Can you handle it?

I shoot back a quick text, telling him to forward me the information, and then turn back to Adam and Kelsey. "I've got to head out too."

Adam's gaze tracks over my face, assessing. "You sure you're going to be okay?"

I nod, forcing a smile. As much as I know my brothers will always be there for me, I hate to complain about our parents to them. For some indiscernible reason, my relationship with my parents has gotten more and more unsteady over the years, and I don't want it to happen to them. It's easier if they just don't know the full extent of it.

"I'll be fine," I assure him. "They won't really fire me. They just want me to start making some changes."

I wish I could believe that, but it's too risky to think otherwise.

Adam nods. "You're right."

And that right there is why I don't want to tell them everything—I don't want them to have to question things the way that I do. I don't know if my parents would stoop so low as to fire me, and I hate that I *don't know*. Daniel and Kristin Bates are difficult, but even that's a new level. If I can help it, I don't want Adam and Alex to know how bad things have gotten.

I lean down, giving him a quick hug, and then follow suit with Kelsey. "You won, by the way," I whisper in her ear.

She flashes me a smile, and I think maybe this is enough. Maybe my relationship with my parents is irrevocably broken, but at least I have these stolen moments with Adam, Kelsey, and Alex.

It's enough—it has to be.

Nine

CAMDEN

WATER IS SPRAYING EVERYWHERE and has been for thirty minutes straight. At least it's in the shower, so most of it is going down the drain, but there's still *a ton* of water on the floor, and I'm running out of towels to sop it up.

I hear a faint knocking over the sound of the water spurting from the broken-off shower arm. I glance down at the T-shirt and shorts I threw on after the shower head broke off mid-shampoo. They're drenched, clinging to my body, and dripping onto the floor, but there's nothing to be done about it.

Hopping out of the tub, I head for the door, barely catching myself as my wet feet almost slide out from under me on the vinyl flooring.

I swing open the door, expecting the maintenance supervisor who was shaking car keys at an armadillo the other day, but find Ellie standing there instead. My heart lurches at the sight of her in a mid-length teal velvet dress. She's got on those white boots—the ones she was wearing the night we met—although tonight there are miles and miles of exposed leg that I have to tear my eyes from.

The sound of the rushing water snaps me back to attention, and I grip the door frame harder. "Um, this isn't the best time," I say, trying to force my voice to sound casual.

Ellie catches her bottom lip between her teeth, dragging her hooded gaze down my chest. "You're all wet." When her eyes return to mine, they look clearer. "The shower. You submitted a maintenance request for a leak."

My brows pinch together in confusion. "Yeah."

She shrugs. "Our maintenance supervisor couldn't come in, so I'm here to look at it."

"Oh, um, okay." I open the door wider, and she enters, taking in the trail of water I left as I walked from the bathroom.

She eyes me again, and I notice her gaze lingering on my chest before returning to my eyes. "All this water from a leak?"

"It's a little more than a leak," I say and gesture down the hall.

She walks ahead, heels clicking on the floor. I follow behind, and just as we're about to round the corner, she slips in the same spot I almost wiped out earlier.

I reach forward on instinct, gripping her hips to steady her, and she falls hard against my chest. Her breath leaves her in a whoosh, and she slowly turns her face to look at me.

I wonder if she can hear the way my heart is hammering, if she can feel the way my skin catches flame at having her this close again.

"Thanks," she breathes, and I feel it against my neck.

I expect her to move away from my grasp and continue toward the bathroom, but she hesitates. Her eyes trail down from mine and fix on my lips. The air catches in my lungs, and suddenly, I want to close this infinitesimal distance between us and see if she tastes as sweet as I remember. If her hands will slide up my chest and into my hair the way they did before.

My fingers tighten on her hips, and the spell breaks.

Ellie stands up straight and walks to the bathroom, smoothing her hands down the front of her dress the same way I was imagining them on my chest moments before.

I palm the back of my neck before following.

When I enter the bathroom, Ellie is standing in a puddle, watching the water pour from the broken-off shower arm sticking out of the wall.

"What happened?"

Swallowing, I say, "I was trying to adjust the shower head to a different setting, and the whole thing broke off and started spraying everywhere. It wouldn't stop, even after I turned off the water."

Ellie nods, gaze fastened on the water spraying from the wall. And then she walks into the thick of it and grabs hold of the handle, turning it on and off multiple times. It does nothing, just like I told her.

"What are you doing?" I ask, and she fiddles more with the knob.

Stepping out of the spray, now drenched, she says, "Just checking."

I blink at her. The heavy fabric of her dress is now made heavier with the water and slips down the slope of her shoulder. Her hair hangs in a damp tangle around her shoulders, and there's a smudge of mascara under each dark eye.

"I told you I already tried that."

She shrugs. "I know, but I wanted to check for myself before I turned off the water to the whole building."

Pulling out her phone, she slides past me, her body brushing up against mine in the doorway.

"Where are you going?"

She stops in the hallway, holding up a finger. "Hey, Jackson. This is Ellie at The Flats." I listen as she explains the situation to whoever is on the other end of the line. She nods, listening to his response, then says, "Thanks. See you in a bit."

"That was the plumber," she says to me. "He'll have someone out here within an hour, but in the meantime, we have to turn off the water. It's in your laundry room, behind the washer."

I follow Ellie to the small laundry room and watch as she attempts to lean over the washing machine. Even with her heels, she's too short to reach behind it.

"Here," I say, stepping in behind her. "Let me do it."

"I can reach it," she huffs, trying and failing to reach it again.

Rolling my eyes, I lean forward and grab hold of the nozzle behind the washer and turn it. It's not until I'm done that I realize I'm basically leaning over Ellie, her back plastered to my front.

I step back, slamming into the dryer right as she spins around. I've never noticed how small the closet-size laundry room is until the two of us are in here, the tips of her boots pressing against my bare toes.

"Sorry," I breathe.

Ellie stares up at me, unblinking. The neckline of her dress slips a little more, exposing more creamy shoulder. I want to tug it up and feel her bare skin against my fingertips.

I swallow, and her eyes track the movement. The air between us charges, and I know it would only take one strike of a match to make us combust.

"I better go," Ellie says, shattering the moment.

I blink out of my stupor. "What?"

"The plumber will be here soon, and I need to get the industrial fan to dry the floors before it seeps into the vinyl."

I nod, not moving, and she doesn't either.

Finally, Ellie looks away, her breath leaving on a sigh. "Bye, Cam."

And then she slips past me, disappearing out my front door, and I'm left dazed, staring at the spot she vacated, the lingering scent of perfume the only evidence she was ever here.

"I'M SORRY ABOUT Lo's little matchmaking attempt the other day," Wes says the next day.

We've been working separately in his office for the past few hours, although I haven't gotten much of anything done. My mind has been thoroughly wrapped up in memories of Ellie in my apartment last night. I can still feel the velvet of her dress beneath my fingertips and the heat of her back against my front.

His words shake me from my thoughts, and I wonder if he knows she's all I've been thinking about all day while I'm supposed to be editing videos. I raise an eyebrow at him. "I figured you were in on that."

Wes smirks. "I knew she wanted to do something, but I thought she would be a little more discreet."

"Yes, subtle as a sledgehammer," I grumble, remembering Lo's less-than-covert actions the other day.

His laugh fills the space between us, and I can't help but join in. "She's worried she overstepped," he says a few moments later. "She's all in her head about it."

Shrugging, I respond, "It was fine. She doesn't need to feel bad." It's the truth. I don't want Lo to feel guilty. "Ellie and

I...talked. We're fine, but nothing is going to happen between us."

She made that clear last night. For a moment, I thought she was going to change her mind about us—give in to the tether that keeps pulling us together—but she just *left*.

After the plumber came and Ellie dropped off the industrial size fan for him to set up in my bathroom, I'd stared up at my ceiling for most of the night, wondering if I'd imagined the whole thing. Only the sound of the fan whirring down the hall was enough to convince me it'd actually happened.

"So I should probably tell Lo not to invite Ellie to the Halloween scavenger hunt where she was planning to force you together again?" Wes asks, and my attention snaps back to him.

"Are you serious?"

"She said pushing you guys together is like writing a real-life romance novel."

I heave a sigh and push my shaking hand through my hair. "Yeah, well, maybe she should stick to fiction."

Holding back a grin, he says, "I'll tell her not to invite Ellie."

"She can invite us both, but I'm sure Ellie isn't going to come." *Not after last night.*

Slamming my laptop closed, I push up from the chair. Suddenly, this loft office is making me feel claustrophobic. "I've got to get something from my car."

I snag my keys, although there's nothing I need except fresh air and alone time. My steps thud heavily on the stairs, and the back door clacks closed behind me with a bang, but I don't care when I finally feel the cool air sting my cheeks.

I missed this in LA—the chill in the air and the shifting colors of the leaves. As I stare at Wes and Lo's backyard, I feel an itch to pull out my camera. To capture a moment in time because *I* want to, not because I'm on deadline or someone is paying me.

When a single leaf catches in the breeze and cascades in a gentle slope to land on the hood of my rental, my feet move of their own volition. Unlocking the car, I snatch my camera bag from the back seat and reach inside. My hand stalls on my DSLR, the camera I've used for almost every photo I've taken since college. Instead, I unzip another pouch, one I haven't touched in so long I almost forgot it was there.

Inside is my film camera—the one I learned photography on. I'd found it at a flea market back in high school and took it out to my aunt and uncle's farm, which borders my parents' property. The sky was gray, and the air was crisp, just like today.

It's been so long since I've used it that I know my pictures aren't going to turn out any better today than they did that day. But even that is a little freeing.

I line up my gaze through the viewfinder, not worried about how someone looks at the other end or whether this shot will turn out how I need it to. No, as I release my breath and snap the shutter, it's just me and my camera and the trees.

That ever-tightening band around my chest loosens just the tiniest bit.

Ten

ELLIE

"Wes is planning this super fun Halloween scavenger hunt for his channel. We were planning to invite some friends and maybe get dinner after," Lo says on the phone Tuesday morning. "We'd love it if you could come."

I should be ashamed at the instant relief that floods me at the invitation. After having to turn down both Tyler and Ethel, the thought of spending my night trapped in my apartment with nothing but my disappointment and loneliness to keep me company had my skin breaking out in a cold sweat.

"That sounds *amazing*," I say and hope I don't sound as desperate as I feel.

"I should tell you," Lo says reluctantly, "Cam will be there."

All the excitement dies in my chest. "Oh."

"He seemed to be under the impression that you wouldn't show up if he was there."

My fingers tap out a nervous rhythm on my thigh while I try to figure out how to explain the situation to Lo without divulging how *royally screwed* I am. My heart beats in my throat as I grasp for words.

"Lo, I…"

"No, it's okay," she says quickly. "Don't worry about it. You don't need to explain yourself to me. Whatever is going on is between you and Cam."

I let out a breath, considering my options. But I really only have one, so I say, "Thanks for inviting me, Lo."

We hang up, and I can't help but feel like I'm ending yet another friendship. It seems like that's all I'm doing lately.

The bell above the door jangles, and Sadie comes in. "I finished passing out the flyers for the harvest festival," she says, waving the leftovers in her hand.

I force a smile onto my face, chasing away the intrusive thoughts that won't leave me alone. "Great, thanks." An idea comes to mind, and I jump on it. "Hey, want to have a sleepover Saturday? We could order takeout and watch a spooky movie and pass out candy to all the little kids."

Sadie comes into my office and slumps into one of the seats on the other side of my desk. "I wish I could. I told my sister I would go trick-or-treating with them and the kids. But that sounds fun—next weekend?"

I don't need to check my calendar to know that weekend is *wide* open. "That works."

Her face pinches. "Oh, wait. That's my dad's retirement party, so I'll be at their house all weekend. What about the weekend after that?"

"That's the resident event," I remind her.

"Shoot, you're right."

"The weekend after?"

"That should work!"

The next four weeks stretch out, threatening to suffocate me with loneliness. I try not to let my sadness show on my face and turn back to my computer to distract myself. "Let's go over some of the stuff for the harvest festival."

When Sadie doesn't answer, I look up to find her staring at me, head cocked to the side. "Are you okay?"

I swallow against the lump in my throat. "Yeah, of course."

The squint of her eyes tells me she doesn't believe me, and I tip right on the edge of spilling the truth to her. But I can't. "Really, I promise."

For all my big talk, when Halloween comes around, I am decidedly *not* fine. After scrolling through Instagram and seeing a post of Sadie with her nephews and Tyler backstage with his band, I can't stay in my apartment anymore.

I tug a bright green jacket on and slip my feet into my pink rubber boots. The air is crisp, and the ground is wet from the rain earlier today and littered with fallen leaves. The trick-or-treaters from our complex are just starting to make their way onto the sidewalk, and they all stop to say hi.

Walking past Building D, I glance at Ethel's window. With her curtains open and her lights on, I can clearly see her hobbling around her kitchen in the waning light. Everything inside me screams to go knock on her door when I see her brace a hand on her lower back after she reaches for a mixing bowl from her cabinet.

She's too old and fragile to do these orders on her own, although I would never tell her that. She likes to imagine herself as Wonder Woman. And while her fierce personality and take-no-prisoners attitude could easily win her a role in a superhero movie, she's not thirty anymore—no matter what she thinks.

Shaking myself from my thoughts, I turn back to my apartment. If I keep staring, I'm going to end up going over there and ruin this whole thing. I love my job too much to risk losing it—even if what I love most about it are the things I'm no longer allowed to do.

My apartment feels too small when I let myself back in, my bright, colorful decor doing nothing to energize me like it usually does. No, tonight it feels too stimulating on my frayed nerves. The thought of spending the whole night here alone settles on my shoulders like a much too heavy weighted blanket. But going out alone also holds no appeal. The last time I did led me right to this exact moment.

It's with memories of that night—the one I met Cam—lingering in my mind that I settle onto my teal velvet couch and reach for the remote. I scroll through Netflix, searching for a movie to drown out the sounds of the kids squealing with laughter outside. I click on a movie, but I'm not focusing on it. Instead, I'm remembering being wrapped in Cam's arms. I can almost feel his hand on the back of my neck, his fingers burning through the fabric of my shirt.

I have an overwhelming urge to know what he's doing at this exact moment. I know he's with Wes and Lo, but are they eating dinner, out on the scavenger hunt Lo mentioned, back at their house playing games?

My doorbell rings, and I jump up gratefully at the distraction. I thump down the stairs to my front door and whip it open. Two kids with bright smiles full of missing teeth are smiling at me from behind their costume masks.

"Trick or treat!" they yell in unison, and the tightness in my chest eases a fraction.

I reach for the bowl of candy on the steps and drop two big handfuls into their baskets. Their eyes widen before they thank me profusely and spin back around, rushing to the door on the other side of the duplex.

CHAPTER TEN

Sighing, I trek back upstairs and settle onto the couch once more. I pick up my phone to scroll through Instagram and see a photo of Wes, Lo, and Camden. Wes and Lo are dressed as Black Widow and Captain America, but it's Cam who catches my eye. He's dressed normally, in his jeans that hug him in all the right places, a threadbare gray T-shirt, and his brown corduroy jacket. There's a sticker over the breast pocket that reads *Hi, I'm Dave.*

I actually laugh aloud looking at it. I barely know Cam, but his stupid costume makes me *want to.* I want to know what makes him laugh and how he takes his coffee and if he's kissed a stranger under the stars before, or if he reserved that just for me.

An ache starts beneath my sternum at the thought, and irrationally, I hope I'm the only woman he's done that with.

I stare at the picture until my screen goes dark. And then, without thinking, I swipe it back open and click on Lo's contact. The phone rings in my ear, and a buzzing starts beneath my skin as I wait.

Lo picks up on the third ring, talking loudly over the noise in the background. "Ellie?"

My heart seizes for one wild second, and I think I still have time to change my mind—to make the smart decision, the *right* decision. My impulsiveness makes the choice for me. "Hey, is there still time for me to come tonight?"

Lo is quiet for a moment before saying, "Yeah, of course. But..." She pauses. "Cam is here."

I look around my apartment, feeling that oppressive sense of claustrophobia again. I can't stay here. "I know."

"Is that going to be a problem?"

Lo has no idea how much of a problem it is—no one does. But I can't live like this forever, cutting off every single person who is important to me. If residents are off the table, I need to have someone other than just Sadie to spend time with. I'll go crazy without friends, and Wes and Lo are my best options.

And if my desire to be around Cam again is the driving force behind it, then so be it. It's better that I'm spending time with a short-term tenant who will be gone in two months than one who could be here for years.

"It won't be a problem."

Because no one will *ever* find out.

Eleven

CAMDEN

I HAVE MY CAMERA trained on Wes as he's telling us about the Halloween-themed scavenger hunt we're playing when Lo returns from where she disappeared into one of the shops lining the street a minute ago.

"Ellie's coming," she says, and I almost drop the camera.

Moving it down to my side, I ask, "What?"

She shrugs, looking as confused as I feel. "That was Ellie. She asked if it was still cool for her to come, and I said yes."

My heart beats an erratic rhythm at her words, and I wonder what caused Ellie to change her mind. Whatever it is, I'm thankful for it.

But then a thought occurs to me. "She knows I'll be here, right?"

"She knows," Lo says, and the words are full of meaning.

I'm saved from trying to come up with a response when a deep voice shouts, "LoLo!" I swivel to see a couple dressed as Danny and Sandy from *Grease* walking hand in hand toward us.

A smile breaks out on Lo's face. "Rod, Camilla—hey!"

The woman, Camilla, gives Lo a hug. "It took forever to find you. You were supposed to be two blocks down."

Lo gives Wes a pointed look. "I told him that, but he wanted to have the coffee shop in the background since it's decorated for Halloween."

Camilla laughs, and her eyes settle on me. "You must be Camden. So good to meet you."

Wes introduces me to his and Lo's best friends before returning to his spot in front of the coffee shop. "Let's redo that intro and then get started on this scavenger hunt."

Rod and Camilla are surprisingly easy to talk to. Getting to know strangers has never been easy for me—something that has also made my new career direction the last few months more taxing—but the couple is laid-back and chatty, never allowing for lengthy silences. The way the friend group gently ribs each other painfully reminds me of being back in California with Wes and Hazel. I've been so busy lately that I've barely even had time to spend with my own sister. Watching Wes fall so seamlessly into another friend group makes me both happy for him and sad for the camaraderie I've lost.

Wes has doubled this outing as both a Halloween scavenger hunt and a random acts of kindness video—Lo, Camilla, or Rod will give him a specific costume to look for, and he will find it, chat with the person wearing it, and then allow them to pull out a slip of paper from his plastic pumpkin basket. On the slip of paper is a prize from one of his sponsors, like a coffee gift card or sporting events tickets.

And while it's been fun to record everyone's reactions, my focus has been half on the video and half on the crowd around

CHAPTER ELEVEN

me, looking for one person in particular. And when I finally see her, pushing through the horde of people, my breath stops in my lungs.

Ellie is dressed like her usual self, although a little more wild than the outfits I've seen her wear in the office. Tonight she's wearing red leather pants that make my mouth go dry, a bright turquoise sweater that hangs off one shoulder, and shoes the exact same color. Her hair is pulled back from her face in a red headband, and her lips are the color of ripe cherries. In short, I'm screwed.

Ellie's made it abundantly clear she wants nothing to do with me, but she looks like a present wrapped up in the red bow tied right atop her head. My fingers itch to find hers, to pull her close and see if she would welcome my kiss a second time.

But I know she won't, and it makes my heart sink in my chest.

Her eyes lock on mine, finally spotting me among the throng of people, and a stunning smile slashes across her face. She strides toward me with purpose, not stopping until she's right next to me, slightly out of breath and smelling of that familiar scent I can't quite put my finger on—something fruity and floral.

My gaze snags on her chest, on the name tag stuck there, the one just like mine. Hers reads *Hi, my name is Daisy*.

Reaching a hand out, she says, "I'm Daisy. Nice to meet you."

I wrap my fingers around hers, feeling that same electric zap between us that was there the night we met. "I'm Dave."

I DON'T KNOW WHAT it means that Ellie showed up, that she's called me nothing but Dave the whole night, or that I've followed her lead and referred to her as Daisy, but I don't question it.

That is, until I do.

"Truth or dare," Camilla asks Rod a few hours later. We finished up our filming, ate dinner downtown, and then all wound up back at Wes and Lo's house. Although no longer on camera, Wes can't help but continue to entertain everyone. He found a Halloween-themed twist on Truth or Dare where the dares are inside a pumpkin with the top cut off. If you choose dare, you have to reach inside and pull it from the pumpkin's slimy depths.

"Truth."

Camilla smiles conspiratorially. "Do you like my new hairstyle?"

Rod's easy grin slips from his face.

"Ha ha!" Camilla yells, pointing a finger at Rod. "I knew it!" She turns to Lo. "He's such a liar," she says, wrapping a finger around one of the smooth locks. "He told me he loved it when I came home from the salon, but he looked like a kicked puppy and has *refused* to tell me otherwise."

Rod holds up a hand. "I am under oath here, so I would like to speak my truth."

"We didn't take an oath," Wes reminds him.

Rod shoots him a glare before turning back to Camilla, eyes softening. "I like your straight hair," he says. "I just miss the curls. They remind me of the day we met."

Camilla stares at him for a moment. "Ugh," she finally says. "That's disgustingly sweet. I hate you." But she leans over, giving him a quick kiss before whispering something in his ear.

Rod's gaze swivels to me, and I take a nervous sip of my drink. I really hate Truth or Dare.

"Cam, truth or dare."

"Truth," I respond. There's absolutely *no* way I'm attempting whatever dares *Weston* came up with.

"Do you miss California?"

The question takes me by surprise. I don't know what I was expecting, but it wasn't that. It should be an easy answer—a simple yes or no—but it's not. The fact is, I miss what California used to be. I miss what it used to represent—getting out of my hometown, living in a place full of other creatives like me, getting to try new things. But lately, it hasn't really felt like that. It's become more stifling than anything, and I've become more aimless. I've felt more tethered and grounded here in Nashville than I have in months, maybe years, in LA.

"No," I say, and I can tell they're all waiting for me to elaborate. A small smile tips up one corner of my mouth. "The game is Truth or Dare. I don't have to explain my truth."

"You're the worst," Wes says, laughing, and the others join in.

"You've been telling me that for years." When the laughter dies down, my eyes lock on the one person I've wanted something from all night. I may hate Truth or Dare, but it might be the only way I can get Ellie to truthfully answer the question that's been bouncing around in my head all night.

"*Daisy,*" I say, enunciating the name, and loving the way her lips curve in a smile at it. "Truth or dare."

"Truth," she says without a moment of hesitation.

"Why did you come tonight?"

Rod hisses between his teeth. "Not holding anything back, brother," he says, but I barely hear him over the ringing in my ears.

Ellie's eyes haven't left mine, and it feels like everything in the room has faded away until it's just us. I see her fingers tapping against her cup, watch as she pulls her ruby-painted bottom lip between her teeth, catch the rapid rise and fall of her chest.

The moment is weightless, and I almost regret asking, but I have to know.

She stands, her legs impossibly long in her high-waisted pants, despite her short stature, and takes two steps to the coffee table, where the pumpkin is sitting atop a pile of paper towels. Without hesitation, she pushes up one sleeve of her sweater and plunges her hand in.

There's a loud squelching sound that can be heard over everyone collectively holding their breath. When she pulls out the slip of paper, it's covered in stringy gunk and pumpkin seeds, most likely now indecipherable.

Ellie stares at it for a heartbeat before her head snaps up, her narrowing eyes locking on Lo. Lo, for her part, looks like she hasn't breathed since Ellie stood up.

"What does it say?" Camilla asks.

Ellie's gaze finds mine, her expression unreadable. The moment stretches between us, and every nerve in my body feels on edge, buzzing and humming beneath my skin. Finally, she says, *"Kiss the person who dared you."*

All the air is sucked from the room, and there's suddenly not enough to fill my lungs. They burn in my chest, begging for relief.

"We can skip it," Lo says. "You know what? Let's just be done. We can play something else or watch a movie or—"

"It's fine," Ellie says so quietly that everyone pauses, straining to figure out if we heard her right.

"You want me to kiss you?" I blurt and then want to shove my entire head into that pumpkin.

A hot flush slashes across Ellie's cheekbones, and I stand, moving toward her before I can think better of it. "Sorry," I say, low enough so only she can hear. "I didn't mean it to come out that way. I just meant…we don't have to."

Her eyes meet mine, pools of dark chocolate I could get lost in. One shoulder hitches up, and her sweater slips down it. My hand reaches out, tugging it back up over the smooth slope, my fingers brushing along soft skin.

"It's fine," she breathes. "Just a game, right, *Dave*?"

I nod. "Just a game, *Daisy*." When I move closer, her eyes dart around. She's getting flustered again. It brings the moment back into focus. We're in a room with other people, not alone on a chilly street under a blanket of stars. Whatever spell was woven between us shatters.

When she looks back at me, there's an awkwardness between us that wasn't there before. The palms of my hands itch, and my shoulders feel too tight. I clear my throat. "Ready?"

She nods, eyes wide.

I step a little closer. "Let's pretend I didn't ask that. I wish very much that I wouldn't have."

This earns a small laugh, and I decide then and there that I want to make her do that again. Just not right now.

There's still too much space between us, but I'm painfully aware of the watchful gazes fixed on us.

Reaching up, I brush a strand of hair off her collarbone and slip my hand behind her neck, bringing back memories I've been trying to quash for the last two weeks. Her breath comes in shallow pants, her lips part slightly. My eyes fasten on her mouth, and I want nothing more than to trace it with my own, feel her sigh against me like she did that night.

But there's still this *stiffness* between us, the weight of four sets of eyes zoned in on our every movement.

"Haven't you done this before?" Wes asks, and I stop, my hand clenching at my side.

"What?"

Wes must notice the way my gaze sears him because he raises his hands in a placating gesture. "My bad, my bad."

"I'm not going to lie..." Camilla says. "I feel like I've stepped into a middle school version of *Seven Minutes in Heaven.*"

"It wasn't like this before," Ellie murmurs, her eyes still focused on mine. Her breath fanning against my chest brings me back into our secure bubble.

"What was it like?" I hear Lo's voice through the fog in my mind, but I'm focused entirely on Ellie—on the way her cherry red lip is trapped between her teeth, on the way her hair feels against my fingers, on the fruity, floral smell of her that haunts my dreams.

I'm reminded of cool air and stars, of teasing lips and unhurried kisses. She's right—it *wasn't* like this. Before, it was magic.

I unclench my fist from my side and slide it around her waist, spreading my fingers wide. My thumb presses into the divot above her hip bone as I cinch her to my chest, erasing the last bit of space between us.

Her breath hitches as I lower my head, fusing her mouth to mine. She tastes just like I remembered, but better, like the weeks between this kiss and the last have worked to dull my memory.

Surely it wasn't this good last time. Her hands couldn't have felt like she had lightning beneath her skin as they slid up my chest and into my hair, tugging me down to angle her mouth against mine. There's no way I felt this breathless, this out of control, that night. It's downright impossible that a single kiss made me this weak in the knees.

But it did, and somehow I'd forced myself to forget.

I pull back, my chest rising and falling hard. "That. It was like that."

Twelve

ELLIE

My body is a live wire in the seconds after Cam's kiss, humming and electric.

One of his hands is burning a brand into my hip, and the other is wrapped around the base of my neck, eliciting delicious tingles as he threads his fingers through my hair. Deep blue eyes are locked on mine as he swipes a finger across my bottom lip.

A throat clears behind me, and I remember how very *not alone* we are. I push out of Cam's arms and instantly feel empty and cold, although my cheeks burn. I reach for one of the paper towels on the coffee table, cringing at the string of pumpkin guts that transferred from my hand onto the fabric covering Cam's bicep.

"Like that, huh?" Camilla says, a teasing lilt to her voice. "I can see why you would want to give it a go again."

My face flames hotter, and Lo claps her hands, drawing the attention from Cam and me, still standing way too close in the middle of her living room. I use the distraction to move back to my seat, avoiding Cam's eyes.

"Wes, truth or dare," Lo asks, and I'm grateful she moved on without waiting for me to ask someone. I'm not sure my voice would work properly right now.

A smirk hitches up one corner of Weston's mouth. "Dare, of course."

Lo blanches, her face leeching of color. "Why don't you pick truth instead."

Weston's brow crinkles, already half-off the couch. "Why?"

"No reason."

The gleam returns to Wes's eyes as he stands, hand hovering over the pumpkin. "Why don't you want me to pick a dare, Lo?"

"I'll give you an easy one!" she yells, grasping at straws. "Do you love me?" A moony-eyed look transforms her face. "See, easy enough."

Wes shakes his head. "Nah, I think I'm going to go with dare."

Lo covers her face with her hands as he reaches inside the pumpkin. The situation is so confusing and ridiculous that I almost forget about what just happened with Cam and me. Almost. All the thoughts come rushing back when I catch him watching me instead of Wes.

Those steady eyes focused entirely on me are enough to send my thoughts swirling and my body buzzing. And I'm just not sure what to do about that.

Blinking out of my trance, I look back at Weston. He stares at Lo, eyebrows high on his head. Lo's face is a ripe tomato, blending into the color of her hair.

He reaches into the pumpkin again, plucking another dare from its depths. I have to wonder what was so bad that *Weston* wouldn't do it. I also can't help but wonder if skipping a dare was always an option, because if I'd known, I would have considered it.

With the memory of Cam's lips on mine, somehow even better than that first time, I know my answer—and it's not what it should be.

Weston reads his new slip of paper and then picks out one more. Finally, he looks up, meeting Lo's wide eyes. "*Louise,*" he says, resorting to her full name. "Why do every single one of these papers say the same thing?"

Lo's gaze swivels to meet mine, a pleading, guilty look slashing over her features.

"Wait, what?" Cam asks, his voice dazed, and I wonder if that's from me—if I managed to have the effect on him that he did on me.

"All of these dares say *kiss the person who dared you,*" Wes clarifies, and the room falls silent.

Only to be punctuated by Camilla's booming laughter. "Lo, you didn't," she pants.

Lo looks like she might perish from embarrassment, but soon finds herself holding back a giggle behind her hand.

I just stare at them for a moment, not understanding the joke.

When I do, my eyes lock on Cam's. I can't read his expression—can't tell if he's annoyed or frustrated or relieved by Lo's matchmaking attempt. For my part, I'm not sure how I feel either.

There's no way for Lo to know how much is at stake for me, how much I would lose if anyone outside this room found out about that kiss. But also, with Cam's eyes still fastened on mine, concern in the firm line of his brows, I can't bring myself to regret it. I can't convince myself I wasn't hoping for something like this to happen when I scribbled *Daisy* on a sticker tonight and painted my lips cherry red.

CHAPTER TWELVE

No, as risky and stupid as tonight was, I wouldn't have changed a single thing.

"I THINK WE'RE GOING to head home," Camilla says from where she's snuggled into Rod on the couch hours later. Wes and Lo are at the other end of the large sectional, Lo's head in Wes's lap. I'm pretty sure she fell asleep the minute we turned the movie on.

"Me too," I say, pushing to my feet and gathering the empty bowls of popcorn from the coffee table.

Cam stands, wordlessly picking up the empty cups and following me around the couches into the kitchen.

"Goodnight, LoLo," Rod calls over his shoulder, and Lo mumbles something back, still half-asleep.

I dump the kernels into the trash and set the bowls into the sink. "Is there anything I can do to help before I go?"

"No," Wes answers. "Thanks for cleaning up."

Cam reaches around me to deposit the cups into the sink, and I shiver at the heat on my back.

"It was no problem," I say, and my voice comes out shaky.

Wes glances between the two of us, one eyebrow raised. "You heading out too, Cam?"

Cam clears his throat behind me, and his breath on the back of my neck sends goose bumps prickling along my skin. "Yeah, I'll see you Monday, if not sooner."

"You'll probably be busy tomorrow," Wes says with a smirk, and my face flushes at the insinuation in his words.

My back brushes against Camden's chest as I shift away from the sink, grabbing my huge purse that I stashed on the counter. Cam follows my movements like there's a tether between us.

"Thanks for inviting me tonight. It was fun," I say and feel Cam stiffen behind me, the tension between us becoming a tangible thing.

"Sure looked like it," Wes says, standing and lifting a sleeping Lo into his arms, a grin tugging at his lips.

I can't help but find a small smile of my own as Cam says, "You're a dick."

Weston's laughter follows us out the door.

The air is chilly and damp with the rain that chased us inside during our bonfire. My fingers are still sticky from s'mores, and my eyes are still gritty from smoke, but all of it fades away now that I'm alone with Camden under a blanket of stars again.

A charged silence pulses between us as we walk toward our cars parked side by side in the driveway. When we reach them, I spin to face him, my gaze fastening on the way his skin is burnished gold under the light over the garage.

His eyes are dark, and his bottom lip is trapped between his teeth. I want to reach up, tug it free, and lean in to taste it again. But suddenly, out in the open once more, I'm reminded of how dangerous a thought like that is.

I back up just barely, adding infinitesimally more room between us. My voice is rough and husky to my own ears as I say, "I better get going."

A brief flash of something like hurt crosses his features, but it's gone before I can be sure. Still, the thought of putting it there makes my stomach ache.

CHAPTER TWELVE

Cam moves past me, brushing my shoulder in the process, and I try not to shudder at the contact. He reaches for my door, swinging it wide and grabbing hold of the top.

I don't remember the last time a man opened my car door for me, and what a shame that is.

I pause, one foot kicked up into my floorboard, and meet his eyes. He's got his free hand shoved into his pants pocket, his frame leaning against the car door, his jaw a rigid line in the moonlight.

I wish he would look frustrated or annoyed, but his face is resigned—like this is exactly how he imagined this moment would go, and that causes my heart to crumble just a little more. "Night, Cam."

He murmurs a farewell and shuts me into the car. Through the windshield, I watch him lean his back against his SUV, arms crossed over his chest, like he's waiting for me to pull out of the driveway safely before he gets into his own car.

The gesture threatens my resolve, almost makes me open the door back up and hug him until that severe line above his brows melts. Instead, I fit my key in the ignition and turn.

Nothing happens. The engine tries to start but doesn't turn over.

I meet Cam's concerned stare through the window, but before I can try again, the door swings open.

"It won't start," I say and cringe inwardly at my obvious statement. *Camden, the sky is blue. Fish live underwater. I have no brain cells left when I've been in your presence for this long.*

He glances around the car, eyes assessing. "Do the lights normally come on when you open the door?" he asks.

I grip my bottom lip between my teeth, and my fingers tap out a nervous rhythm against the steering wheel. "Yeah, I guess."

"Probably a dead battery. Is it possible you left a light on?"

"No," I say, searching around in the darkness for another solution. Then it hits me. "Wait." I pause, remembering flipping on the overhead light to apply another layer of lipstick before I went inside. "Actually, maybe."

He stares at me for a beat too long, and a tingle starts beneath my skin. He backs away from the door. "Come on."

My eyes widen. "What?"

"Do you have any jumper cables?"

No. I look around like a set might slither up from the depths of my back seat and save me from having to ride home with him. I can't be locked in a dark car with him and keep my cool. I'm barely keeping it now. With a resigned sigh, I say, "No."

He hooks a thumb over his shoulder, gesturing to his rental. "Neither do I. Wes probably does, but I bet they're in bed. And plus, we would have to wait around or drive it around for a bit after we get it jumped. Why don't you just ride with me, and I'll bring you back tomorrow to get it?"

He seems like he wants to take me back home as much as I want him to—which is to say, not at all. His jaw is clenched tight enough to break a molar, and he still hasn't quite met my gaze.

"Okay," I breathe and grab my purse from the passenger seat. He backs up, giving me a wide berth, and closes the door behind me. Despite his obvious discomfort with the situation, he still opens the passenger door and wraps a hand around my elbow to help me inside.

I don't know how to feel. I'm a chronic people-pleaser and always try to find what would make people happiest and then *do that thing*. But with Camden, I'm not sure what he wants.

I'm afraid it's the one thing I can't give him.

CHAPTER TWELVE

The silence in the car is deafening as I wait for him to get in. He turns on something low on the radio as we back down the long driveway, the tension thick enough to drown in.

His fingers are tight around the steering wheel, turning his knuckles white under the streetlights. The line of his shoulders is rigid, his arms flexed in a way I would appreciate if not for the palpable strain between us.

"What building are you in?" he asks as we pull into the parking lot of The Flats a few minutes later. I'm not sure how we got here; I was so lost in my own head.

"A," I answer and watch as he realizes it's the one directly across from his. That if we looked out our windows at the same time, we could catch a glimpse of one another.

He pulls into an empty spot in front of my townhouse, and I clear my throat. "Camden," I say, and his eyes settle on mine. My heart beats an erratic rhythm, but I gather my courage. "I came tonight because I was lonely and…" I trail off, not sure how I want to end this sentence.

I'm not sure why I say it, but he just seemed so earnest tonight, so sincere, and I feel like I owe him a little honesty in return.

"And?" he asks gently, his voice a warm caress in the dark of night.

I blow out a breath, preparing myself. I don't know the last time I was completely honest with someone, and it scares me, both that I can't remember and that I'm choosing now to break that pattern.

"I was so lonely that night we met. I wasn't supposed to be at that show—you know, *no fraternizing with the tenants* and all—but I wanted to be there. I wanted to support them. You made me feel not so alone. And I guess tonight I wanted to feel like that again."

Slowly, I raise my gaze to meet his. It's even more devastating than I could have imagined, his brows bunched together, forming that crinkle that I want to smooth. Dark eyes threaten to swallow me whole. Full lips turn down at the edges.

"Ellie," Cam says, his voice a low rumble that sends goose bumps skittering across my skin. He reaches across the dash, as if to touch my hands clasped firmly on my knees, but hesitates. He meets my gaze again, questioning. "Is this okay?"

It's just like that moment back in his apartment when he cleaned up my knee. It seems he's always taking care of me—holding me on a dance floor when I'm aching with loneliness, tending my wounds when I'm hurt, catching me on a slick floor when I'm about to fall, comforting me in the dark when I'm vulnerable.

Instead of answering, I reach out, threading my fingers with his, and feel his exhale against my neck.

"I didn't want to say that in front of everyone tonight," I confess.

Cam swipes his thumb across the sensitive skin on the inside of my wrist, no doubt feeling my pulse jumping at his touch. "I'm sorry I asked."

My breath comes out on a shaky exhale. "Don't be. I think it turned out okay."

One side of his mouth quirks up in the slowest of grins, and it sends an electric pulse all the way through me. I could get used to that smile. And that's dangerous.

"Ellie—" Cam says, but he's cut off by the sound of a siren piercing the air. I loosen my grip on his hand and spin around as an ambulance turns into the main entrance, bright flashing lights temporarily disorienting me.

I watch, heart pounding in my chest, as the ambulance stops two buildings down. "No, no, no," I whisper.

CHAPTER TWELVE

"Ellie?"

My throat is thick as they climb out, but I know exactly where they're going. I can feel it like a sick premonition. Dread snakes in my stomach when they head right for the door I knew they would.

Ethel.

Thirteen

ELLIE

ETHEL IS IN THE hospital with a broken ankle, and it's all my fault.

The thought keeps me up, staring at my ceiling, all night. *It was my fault. It was my fault. It was my fault.*

She asked for my help, and I said no, hell bent on following my parents' rules, and she fell.

And I had been kissing Camden Lane on a dare.

My stomach is a tight ball of nerves when I let myself into the office for my Saturday morning shift. I'm dead on my feet and look like I'm sporting two black eyes from the dark circles and tear-swollen lids.

I slump into my desk chair and scrub my hands over my face, all the memories from last night running through my mind on a loop. Sticky fingers and laughter over a fire pit. A scary movie and a warm, heavy throw blanket draped over my thighs. Camden's hand tracing circles on the back of my neck and his lips teasing mine in the most decadent of kisses.

Last night was a mistake. I finally decided to break my parents' rules, but instead of helping Ethel, I ran right to Cam. If I would have been there, she would have been okay.

Now I have to live with the memory of Cam's kiss lingering on my lips like one of those lip stains that promises to be smudge-proof. No matter how hard I try to wipe it from my mind, it stays there.

The bell above the front door rings, dragging me from my thoughts. I look up to see my parents walking through the door. *Of course.*

I'll be surprised if they don't know something is up from the guilt etched into my every feature.

"Mom, Dad, hey," I say, standing and plastering a smile on my face. I know my mother sees the dark rings under my eyes and that she's itching to mention it. I'm just hoping she thinks it's due to the late night 911 incident.

"You look tired," my mom says, and I do my best not to cringe. At least she hasn't commented on my outfit choice—although my mustard-yellow slacks and purple sweater are more in line with their dress code than most things I wear. I was too tired to come up with an elaborate outfit this morning. I'm even wearing Mom-approved flats instead of pointy patent leather heeled boots.

"Long night," I say, and I'm horrified when my voice cracks at the edges.

Both sets of eyes narrow on mine, although Mom's are assessing and Dad's almost look concerned. "We saw the text when we woke up this morning. Is the resident—what did you say her name was—Edith? Is she okay?" Dad asks.

"Ethel," I correct him quietly and settle back into my chair. They sit across from me, all straight backs and folded hands. "She's okay. She should be in the hospital for another few days after her surgery. Luckily, she is in a first-floor apartment, so she won't have to bother with stairs when she comes home." What I don't say is that I've already planned to go over there every day to check in on Ethel and help out as much as I can. Her kids and grandkids are across the country, so she's all alone here. I don't know if they would be okay with it, but I need to do this regardless.

"Good," Dad says with a curt nod. "We actually came in to discuss a few things."

Mom pulls a small notepad from her purse and plucks a pen from the cup on my desk. "First, we forgot to ask at dinner the other night, but you are coming to Thanksgiving this year, correct?"

Unfortunately, yes. I wasn't able to come up with an excuse to get out of it. Last year, I went home with Sadie to visit her grandparents in Ohio. The year before that I went to dinner with my ex-boyfriend's family. I don't think I can bail a third year in a row. "Yes, of course."

Mom checks off an item on her list. "What is your November resident event?" Every month, each complex is expected to throw an event for the residents. Last month, we had a spooky Halloween-themed movie night. "We're doing a fall harvest festival—hayrides around the parking lot, candy apples, hot chocolate, face painting, pumpkin carving—the works," I answer, and I'm surprised when my parents nod in satisfaction.

My mom opens her mouth to discuss the next item when the bell above the office door jangles again and Camden walks in. My heart flips in my chest at the sight of him. That lock of dark hair that falls over his brow. Those perfect lips I can't stop thinking about. Those dark blue eyes that make my pulse race.

But oh no. *Oh no.* He can't be here. Not with my parents two feet away and watching me with laser focus.

I search his eyes, trying to figure out what he's doing here, and then it hits me. Getting my car. In the midst of everything, I forgot.

CHAPTER THIRTEEN

I silently plead with him not to mention it. He flicks his gaze between my parents and me, no doubt remembering them that first day and connecting the dots.

"Is now not a good time for our meeting?"

How he knew my parents would basically froth at the mouth over a business meeting with a resident, I don't know, but I will forever be grateful to him for it. And while they are still facing him, I try to let my gratitude show.

Mom turns around first. "Meeting?"

I quickly work for an excuse. "Yes, Camden is a photographer. He's going to be working with us to get some photos for the fall harvest festival to use on the website and social media." I cringe inwardly that I just offered up his services. I'll take the photos myself so he doesn't have to.

But Cam gives my parents one of those rare, easy smiles that I've noticed he usually reserves for friends. He reaches out a hand. "Camden Lane." He can be quite charming when he wants to be.

Mom and Dad shake his hand, introducing themselves as Daniel and Kristin. Mom looks back and forth between us. "That sounds amazing. I'm surprised Elizabeth came up with it."

I can actually feel myself withering inside.

Camden's eyes narrow. "Ellie has been great to work with so far—extremely professional."

Mom and Dad's gazes swivel to me, eyebrows high on their heads and disbelief clearly written all over their faces.

I want to pull the fire alarm, fake a fainting spell, blow up the whole building—anything to distract Cam from seeing the way my parents look at me.

"That's great to hear," Dad says, and my chest swells. Maybe, just maybe, we're turning a corner. "Well, we don't want to keep you from your meeting." Dad pushes up from his chair and turns to shake Cam's hand.

Nice to meet you," Mom tells Cam as she exits my office.

"Same to you." Cam shakes their hands again before slipping them into his pockets. He leans against my door frame as my parents say their goodbyes and head out. I'm distracted by the way his jacket hugs his biceps, by the long line of his throat and the dark stubble there, by the way his T-shirt, the color of forest moss, stretches across his chest.

By the time the bell above the door jingles, signaling my parents' exit, I've worked myself up. My heart is racing, and my skin feels too tight as I finally look up into Cam's eyes. I still can't handle the way they feel focused on me, like the moment after the first drop on a roller coaster. Weightless and scared and *alive.*

"You okay?" Cam asks, his voice a deep rumble that I swear I feel all the way in my toes.

I shouldn't be so shocked at how easily he can read me—it seems like he always knows when I'm falling apart—but I am. I've spent so long hiding pieces of myself to make others happy that I'm not sure anyone sees the real me anymore. The person I am down in my bones and inside my heart that feels like it's slowly cracking in two.

I don't know how Cam *sees* me, just that he does, and it terrifies me as much as it thrills me.

Stepping out of his space, I retreat into my office, keeping my back to him. "I'm fine. I'm sorry about the harvest festival. Obviously, you don't actually have to come."

"I can do it."

I spin around, my fingers finding my thigh and *tap-tap-tap-ing* against it. "Why?"

CHAPTER THIRTEEN

The tightness in his shoulders loosens, and he runs a hand through his hair, mussing it up. It's then I notice the matching shadows under his eyes, the downturn of his perfect mouth. The lines of his body scream tension, and I was too wrapped up in myself to notice.

"Ellie, is this—" he gestures between us with a finger, "is this going anywhere?"

"No," I breathe before I can think better of it. But all my mind can conjure up is an image of Ethel being wheeled out of her apartment on a stretcher while my lips were still burning from Cam's kiss. I can't unsee the utter disappointment and resignation on my parents' faces while they told me I needed to be more professional, knowing I had just spent the night wrapped in a resident's arms. Cam may be kind and good and so achingly sweet, but he's also a match held over the gasoline, threatening to catch my life in flames.

The hurt on his face is instant and brutal. It shreds at the last threads of my reserve until I'm only holding on by a string. Looking at him is like pressing a bruise, and it takes all my willpower not to turn away.

Cam palms the back of his neck, and my fingers itch to rub away the tension for him, but I hold myself still.

"Okay, I'm sorry. I guess I misread things."

That just won't do. If I have to hide all the pieces of myself from everyone in my life, I want him to at least have the truth.

I move back in front of him, easing his hand from behind his head. His fingers thread with mine, although from the crease between his eyebrows, he's fighting himself about it. I reach up with my other hand, unable to resist finally smoothing my thumb over the line there.

I like the way his body soothes under my touch—the muscles in his face relaxing, his breath fanning my neck, his fingers tightening around mine.

"It's not in your head," I whisper.

His gaze searches mine, deep blue eyes devouring warm brown ones. "I saw the way they looked at you," he says, and I physically recoil.

Cam stops me with a hand to my hip, fingers flexing and bunching in the fabric of my sweater. "I don't like it," he murmurs.

I close my eyes, not wanting to see the look on his face, the pity there. I'm healthy and somewhat successful. I graduated from college with honors and came to work for the family business. And yet, somewhere along the way, I earned their disappointment instead of their pride.

I swallow against the lump in my throat. "If they found out about this, they would never stop looking at me like that," I whisper, and his hand at my hip sags, releasing me.

"So what was last night?" he asks, his voice gentle. The hand that was pressed to my hip instead finds a lock of my hair, twisting it around his fingers.

My breath comes out in a whoosh. "Last night was me thinking maybe I could have something—someone—who makes me happy, just for a little bit. You're leaving soon, and I thought maybe that made you less dangerous."

He's quiet for so long that I crack open my eyes. "Less dangerous?"

"Less dangerous," I repeat.

"Because I'm leaving?"

I nod, and he untwists the lock of hair, his calloused hand instead scraping its way from my collarbone to the back of my neck.

"We could still have that," he says, leaning forward so his voice is a throaty whisper against my skin.

I shiver, my willpower disintegrating by the second. "No."

The word has a physical effect on him—a sigh heaving from his broad chest, a flutter of lashes over midnight eyes, a squeeze of his hand at the base of my neck, a step back, putting space between us.

"Okay, if that's what you want," he says.

I almost tell him *no, it's not what I want. I'd like to finish what we just started, please and thank you.* But I don't, because I can see in the taut line of his muscles and the fever behind his eyes that he's holding himself back.

"I'll get someone else to take me to my car," I tell him, and his gaze flicks to mine.

"We can get it. It's fine."

I shake my head, knowing my self-control is contained to these four walls.

Cam looks like he knows it too. "Still want me to come to the festival?"

Clearing my throat, I say, "If you want to."

He stands up straight, pushing off the doorframe. "I'll be there."

ETHEL COMES HOME FROM the hospital a few days later. It's the first day she's not loopy on pain medication, and she hasn't stopped talking my ear off the whole way home. With every word, the heaviness in my chest threatens to suffocate me.

When we finally arrive at The Flats and I help her get settled on her sofa, I can't take it anymore. "Why aren't you mad at me?" I ask, choking against the lump in my throat.

She stares at me, her pale brows bunching together. "What are you talking about?"

I collapse on the loveseat across from her and drag my hands through my hair. "Why aren't you mad at me for not being there? If I had been there, you wouldn't have a cast on your ankle right now."

"Ellie," Ethel says, her voice firm. "You don't owe me anything. Why would I be mad at you?"

Dropping my hands to my sides, I say, "Because I should have been *here*."

She waves her hand dismissively. "You were at Tyler's show. Do I wish I wouldn't have fallen down? Yes, obviously. But I could have still fallen if you were here."

Guilt and shame coil in my gut. "I didn't go to Tyler's show," I murmur.

Ethel is quiet for a moment. "Okay, where did you go?"

Tears prick behind my eyes, and I force my gaze to the ceiling to try to keep them at bay. "Ethel, everything is so messed up."

When I meet her eyes, she's holding a hand out to me. "Come over here."

Standing, I move to sit next to her on the couch, careful to maneuver around her propped ankle on the ottoman. I lean into her, breathing in her sweet, powdery scent.

"I wish I had a chocolate penis for you," she says softly. "They always help."

I can't help the laugh that bubbles out of me.

Ethel grins, smoothing a hand down my hair. "So tell me what's got you so upset."

I want to tell her about Cam, but I still feel so twisted up over him. I don't know what would have happened if we hadn't been interrupted by sirens. He keeps showing up in my life, making it harder and harder for me to ignore that pull between us.

He's a secret I'm not ready to share yet, so instead, I say, "I need to tell you something. It's about my parents."

Fourteen

CAMDEN

"You've got to be kidding me," Hazel hisses under her breath.

"What?" I ask, sitting straight up from where I'd been snuggled so deep into my couch that I was threatening to become a part of it.

"I got paint on my favorite pants," she whines.

Groaning, I settle back down into the couch. "My gosh, Hazel. You don't have to scare me like that."

"What's your problem?" she asks, and I'm all set to tell her I don't have a problem when the source of my frustrations walks across the parking lot and right into my line of vision.

I push myself off the couch a little so I can see her better.

Ellie looks like a perfect fall day. She's dressed in pumpkin-colored pants that look soft enough to run your hands over and another one of her huge sweaters that slips off her shoulder, this one a deep emerald green and tucked into her waistband.

I wish I had my camera so I could take a picture of her looking like this. She's a photographer's dream study in contrasts. Dark hair and creamy skin, bright outfits and wine red lips.

"I don't have a problem," I tell Hazel. I collapse back against my cushions, watching Ellie walk toward the clubhouse. She's probably going into the office early to get everything ready for the harvest festival that starts in a few hours.

"You've been grumpy for weeks."

"I haven't been *grumpy for weeks*," I retort. I've been *confused* since Halloween. Or rather, the day after—when I talked to Ellie in her office and almost lost my mind. Ellie isn't just a walking contrast, she's a walking contradiction, running hot and cold faster than I can keep up.

Except this time, she was serious. I've only caught glimpses of her in the last two weeks, and I've been going crazy.

"Something is bothering you," Hazel says, interrupting my thoughts.

I palm the back of my neck, considering how much to tell her. I haven't mentioned Ellie to Wes and Lo since they *obviously* cannot be trusted. I've been alone with my thoughts, the way I prefer, but a part of me was also waiting for Hazel to ask.

"I've been thinking about staying here," I finally tell Hazel on an exhale, surprised by my own words.

"Oh," she says, her voice so quiet I can barely hear her.

I catch one last glimpse of Ellie before she disappears into the office. There's an ache beneath my sternum that I can't rub away, no matter how many times I press my hand to my chest.

"Is this about that girl?" Hazel asks when I don't respond.

I don't know quite how to answer her, but I say, "No," and it's the truth, if only partly. "Things with Ellie are…complicated. But working with Wes again is good. And I've been having time to explore with my camera over the past couple weeks. I've just had *time*."

Time I wish I could spend with Ellie, but she hasn't swayed from the decision she made in her office. She's stayed away, and so have I.

"What do you mean *complicated?*"

"I don't think she knows what she wants. Or she does, but she doesn't think she can have it."

"So you haven't been having fun like I told you to."

I think of the kisses, the ones that have been playing on repeat in my mind. I think of her fingers threaded through mine, her face illuminated by a streetlight in the parking lot. I think of Ellie's voice, smooth and sweet as honey, when she said, *it's not in your head.*

"It hasn't been all bad."

Hazel gags. "I'm going to pretend I didn't ask that."

Chuffing a laugh, I say, "You're ridiculous." My mouth smooths back down on the corners, my eyes drifting to where Ellie disappeared. The sun has gone too, leaving the sky a misty gray, almost like she took it with her.

"Nothing is going to happen between Ellie and me," I tell her. "She's made that *very* clear."

"Her loss," Hazel says, but it doesn't feel like it. That hollow spot beneath my sternum definitely feels like it's mine.

MY SKIN PRICKLES FROM the blustery wind as I make my way across the parking lot to the harvest festival. In the few short hours since my phone call with Hazel, the property has transformed into an autumn wonderland.

CHAPTER FOURTEEN

I pause, pulling my film camera from the harness where I have it and my DSLR strapped to my waist. The film photos of tonight will be just for me, a token to remember this perfect night, crisp and invigorating and exploding with vivid colors. I peer through the viewfinder and line up a shot, letting out a slow breath as I snap it.

At the very last second, Ellie enters the frame. The image of her smiling face backdropped with warm russet, bright saffron, and burning scarlet is captured for all eternity.

"Hey," she says, stopping in front of me. I don't miss the way her fingers tap on the side of her thigh, something I've come to realize is a nervous tick. I hate that she feels anxious around me. I want to wrap my hand around the back of her neck and massage away the tension there, but I think that would only make things worse.

Swallowing my desire, I nod in the direction of the festival activities. "It looks really good."

The hesitation lacing her features drops in an instant, replaced by a beaming smile and flushing cheeks. "You think so?"

I watch as she surveys the scene, no doubt just now noticing how perfect it turned out. My mind flashes back to that moment in her office, the way she crumpled at her mother's inconsiderate words. I think Ellie needs reassurance, which is wild seeing as how I've only been here a month and can already tell how beloved she is by the residents.

"It's amazing," I tell her. Lowering my voice, I say, "This place is really lucky to have you."

When she looks back up at me, there's a wetness behind her eyes that cracks my chest right open. She blinks it away and turns back to the festival events. "Thanks, Cam."

Ellie sniffles next to me, and I have the overwhelming urge to comfort her, to wrap my arms around her and tell her over and over again that she's something special, but I know that wouldn't be welcomed. Instead, I lift a hand to give her shoulder a light squeeze. Her sweater has slipped down again, and her skin burns under my touch.

I frown down at her. "Are you okay?" I'd assumed her flushed cheeks were from the cold since she's not wearing a jacket, but she's feverish and radiating heat.

Her eyes meet mine, and I notice the dark circles under them and the fine sheen of sweat lining her brow. "Yeah, totally fine."

"You're sick."

Ellie makes a dismissive sound under her breath. "I'm not sick."

"Ellie—"

She waves me off. "I've got to get back to the event. You're still good to take photos?"

I gesture to the cameras and my waist and notice her shoulders slump ever so slightly, like a weight has been taken off them. "I've got it."

She smiles, and this time I notice how tired it is, how it doesn't quite reach the bruised half-moons below her eyes. "Thanks, Cam."

"Let me know if you need anything."

One corner of her mouth kicks up a little higher. "That's what I'm supposed to say," she almost slurs.

"You're always taking care of everything and everyone. Let me take a turn."

The smile falls from her face, her lips almost forming a frown. "You shouldn't say things like that."

CHAPTER FOURTEEN

I stare down at her, confused. She must see it too, because she murmurs, "It makes it very hard to stay away from you."

My heart beats in my throat at her words. Shrugging one shoulder, I say, "I told you that you don't have to stay away from me, Ellie."

She seems to waver on her feet, and I reach out, gripping her elbow to steady her. I can feel the heat of her skin through her thick sweater, and I want to make her rest—wrap her in a blanket, give her some tea and make her stay there until she's better. I wonder if she's ever let someone take care of her the way she does for everyone else.

Ellie's gaze slowly drags from my hand at her elbow, up my arm and neck, and lingers on my mouth before finally meeting my eyes. "That's what makes you so dangerous." She straightens her shoulders, gathering strength from somewhere deep inside herself, and says, "I've gotta go. See you around?"

"Come find me if you need me," I say. She hesitates for a moment, watching me through her lashes before nodding and heading back into the fray.

Fifteen

CAMDEN

It's not hard for me to get lost in the crowd. It's always been my preference, to be on the outside looking in rather than smack dab in the center of the attention. I think it's why Weston and I work so well together. He can't help but attract the limelight, and I'm happy to stand on the sidelines filming it.

It's also why I think this new direction I've taken in LA isn't working for me. I can't blend into the shadows and capture the little moments no one else sees anymore. I'm suddenly right there in the middle of the action, drawing even more curiosity with the camera glued to my face.

But here at the harvest festival, with kids squealing, parents laughing, and couples leaning on each other, drifting through the madness with their focus only on each other, I can lose myself. The band that's been tightening around my chest for months and loosening little by little since I arrived releases just a little more.

Under the dark purples, vibrant pinks, and burnished golds of twilight, with the stars twinkling their hello for the night, I take my first full breath in months.

It's not until the sun has fully set and people start disappearing back into their apartments, seeking warmth, that I realize I

CHAPTER FIFTEEN

haven't seen Ellie in hours. Sometime after I snapped a picture of her, I lost her.

My heart picks up speed as I search the crowd. I tried to keep an eye on her all evening, watching to make sure she didn't start swaying like before, that the circles beneath her eyes didn't become more pronounced. The thought of her out there feverish and sick makes my heart clench.

I recognize Sadie, the leasing consultant who helped me the day I moved in. She's heading toward me with long, purposeful strides. "Have you seen Ellie anywhere? I saw you guys talking earlier, and she was floating around here somewhere, but I can't find her."

I shake my head, a whirring starting in my ears. I don't know why I think something is wrong, just that I do. It's a sick feeling in the pit of my stomach that I can't rationalize away.

Sadie chews on her lip, eyes darting around in a way that makes me think she's feeling the same as I am. "I need to pay the vendors, but Ellie is supposed to sign off on everything before they leave. Do you have a minute to look around for her while I talk to them, or do you need to get back?"

There's no way I'm leaving until I find her and assure myself that she's okay—and maybe not even then, but I keep that thought to myself. "Of course. I'm going to drop my cameras off in the office, if that's okay, and then I'll start looking around."

Sadie nods and hands me a key ring bracelet that was hanging on her wrist. "The blue key," she tells me before disappearing into the crowd, the lines of worry still etched into her forehead.

I make my way through the waning horde of people and head toward the clubhouse.

The building is quiet and lit with only a few lamps, bathing the office in a warm, almost eerie light. Through the shadows, I almost don't see Ellie as I'm stripping off my camera belt.

My heart seizes halfway through unsnapping the belt. She's slumped over her desk, her hair splayed out around her. I skid into her office and drop my cameras on her desk before kneeling down next to her.

"Ellie," I say, and my voice cracks at the end. I reach for her shoulder, forcing myself to be gentle instead of panicked. Her skin burns under my fingertips, hotter than before, and she lets out a low moan.

The air whooshes from my lungs, and I lean her weight onto me so I can push her hair out of the way. It sticks to her damp forehead in great clumps, and it takes my shaking fingers three times longer to clear it than it should.

Her drooping eyes lock on mine. "Dave, you found me."

I rest my head against hers, trying to steady my breathing. "Yeah, Daisy. I told you I'd be here if you needed me."

"You're really good at that," she whispers, her head falling to the crook of my shoulder. Her breath is warm on my neck, raising goose bumps along my skin. "You always know just what I need, Dave."

Ellie's lashes flutter against my neck, and I fight to hold in a shiver. She pushes herself back to inspect my face, hands braced on my shoulders, head cocked to the side. "Or is it Sam? Cam?"

My voice is rough to my own ears when I say, "I can be whoever you want me to be, Daisy."

The corners of her lips tip up in a lazy smile before falling back down. She leans a little heavier on me, her fingers digging into my shoulders. "I don't feel so good, Dave."

Dave, it is. I'll play along if she allows me to take care of her—or get her to a doctor or urgent care or a hospital if that's what she needs.

I push back a lock of sweaty hair that has fallen in front of her face. "I think we need to go to the doctor. You're sick."

She shakes her head, a sluggish, lethargic movement that almost has her toppling over.

My hands tighten on her waist, steadying her, although I don't even know when they found their way there. She's a magnet that I can't keep from sticking to.

"No doctor," she slurs. "Just a cold."

"This isn't just a cold, Ellie."

"The flu, then."

I nod. "Yeah, probably. So we need to get you to the doctor for some medicine."

"*Istoolate*," she murmurs, her words blending together.

"We can find a doctor that's still open," I tell her.

She shakes her head again and forces herself to sit up, blinking her eyes until they're a little clearer. "Sick too long for the flu medicine."

My blood ices in my veins. "How long have you been sick?"

"Thursday," she mumbles.

"It's Saturday," I say, sharper than I mean to.

"Oh, good," Ellie responds with an indolent nod. "I thought I slept all night."

My worried frustration dissipates, and I give in to the temptation to wrap my hand around the back of her neck. I tell myself it's just to reassure myself that she's really okay, but the truth is, I can't stand to be this close to her without touching her.

Ellie makes a humming noise as I thread my fingers through the hair at the nape of her neck. It's damp from sweat too and reminds me of my purpose here. I was supposed to find her for Sadie, who is equally worried.

"Daisy," I whisper, trying to stay focused as she leans into my touch.

Her eyes flutter shut, and she relaxes against me, bringing her face to my shoulder again. I know I should get up and find Sadie, but I give myself just a moment to indulge in this, to let my beating heart settle now that I know Ellie is safe and okay, if not quite healthy.

"Hey," I say a moment later. "I need to go find Sadie and tell her you're okay. And then I'm going to help you home, okay?"

She nods, and I allow myself one more moment, burying my face in her hair to inhale that familiar scent, the one that lives on the cusp of a memory. I plant a kiss right there, on the spot where her hair meets the skin at her temple. "I'll be right back."

I lean her back against the desk, helping her to prop her arms under her head this time and push her chair in a little more snuggly.

Sadie is with one of the vendors when I finally find her a few minutes later. "She's in her office," I tell her, fighting the irritation rising in my chest. I don't know how Sadie has been working with her for two days and hasn't noticed.

She rolls her eyes, a matching frustration lighting her features. "I *told* her to go home this morning, but she swore she was fine."

"She said she's been sick since Thursday."

Sadie blanches, rubbing a hand over her face. "Our maintenance supervisor called out yesterday, so Ellie and I were in and out of the office all day trying to keep up with his tasks. I've barely seen her since Thursday morning."

CHAPTER FIFTEEN

My exasperation fades. "I'm going to take her back to her apartment."

Sadie's gaze meets mine, assessing. "Why?"

"Because she needs help," I answer easily. From Sadie's distrusting expression, I can't tell if she knows about me and Ellie or not. But I don't know which option would assure her more, so I keep my mouth shut.

She looks like she wants to tell me to go home and that she will deal with Ellie, but then her eyes flit around the festival, and she huffs out a breath. I glance around too. The place is a mess and likely won't be fully cleaned up for another couple of hours—way too long for Ellie to wait for medicine and rest.

"Okay," she says finally.

I spin around, ready to get back to Ellie, but Sadie stops me with a hand on my arm. "Take good care of her, okay?"

The conversation feels weighted all of a sudden, and I think my answer is going to be important to her. "Of course. I promise."

"Thanks, Cam."

Ellie hasn't moved since I left her. She's still hunched over her desk, using her arms as a makeshift pillow, dark hair fanned around her. I squat next to her and reach my fingers out to twist around one of the locks.

"Ellie, I'm back."

She stirs ever so slightly, and I swipe a comforting hand down her back, feeling her rise and fall beneath my touch with steady breaths. It does something to calm the anxiety that's been roiling in my gut for the last few hours.

"Daisy," I say, and she mumbles in response. "I'm going to take you home. Can you walk?"

Ellie lifts her head from her arms and nods sleepily. I push to my feet and slip my hands between hers, gently pulling her up next to me. The minute she's standing, all her weight falls against me, her arms snaking around my middle. Her head rests against my cheek, lashes fluttering against the exposed skin at my collar, just like that first night. I allow myself one moment to linger, enveloped in her feverish warmth and her familiar floral scent.

She nestles further into me and nudges her nose along my collarbone, making every one of my nerves snap to attention. "You feel good," she mumbles.

"Time to go," I force out, pushing her back enough to prop her against my side. "Do you need anything from in there?"

Ellie pats her pockets. "Got my phone and keys. I'm good."

I snatch my camera harness from her desk and hold it in my free hand as we shuffle toward the door.

"Do we need to lock up behind us?"

She shakes her head, lodging herself further into my side. "Can text Sadie."

It's slow moving as we make the trek down the walking trail that leads behind the buildings, trying to avoid the craziness of the parking lot. "How're you feeling?" I ask once we step on the gravel. She slips a little on the loose rock, and I grip her more tightly around the waist. Her sweater bunches in my grip, and my fingers graze the smooth, exposed skin at her side.

She shivers at my touch, and I tug the sweater back in place. "Sick."

"You shouldn't have worked today." I follow the narrow pathway and see her building up ahead.

Ellie sniffles and grabs the front of my shirt in her fist to steady herself. "I've gotta do good," she says cryptically. I want to ask what she means, but I don't know if she's awake enough to answer.

We close the distance to her apartment, and she leans up against the brick wall. "Where are your keys?"

She lifts up the hem of her sweater and tries to pull them from her pocket, but her fingers aren't working properly, her movements uncoordinated. Sighing, she slumps against the wall. "I can't do it."

I grab her elbows and give them a reassuring squeeze. "Hey, it's okay. Do you want me to try?"

She nods, her head just barely moving from where it's propped up against the cool brick. "Please."

The fabric of her pants is smooth beneath my fingers, something soft like velvet, and I can feel the heat radiating from her skin beneath. "You're so hot," I say, a frown tugging at my mouth.

"Thanks, Dave. I'm not feeling up for that right now, though," she mumbles.

I glare at her. "That's not what I meant." Finally, I fish the keys from her pocket and fit them into the lock.

When I turn back to help her through the door, her bottom lip is puckered. "You don't think I'm hot?"

I let out a sigh and roll my shoulders back. "I think I've made my feelings on that front pretty clear."

Her bottom lip is still sticking out almost comically far, and she's staring at me with wide eyes from her spot against the building.

Bending down so we're eye to eye, I say, "Yes, Daisy. I think you're very hot."

"I think you're really hot too," Ellie murmurs, her voice so low and smooth it sends a shiver up my spine.

"Time to go inside. Can you walk up the stairs?"

Her head bobs. "Of course. Just a little cold. Nothin' can keep me down," she says, the words slurring together.

I wrap an arm around her waist, trying to keep her steady as we walk over the threshold. We only make it up two steps before she lets out a whimper. "I don't think I can do it."

If she weren't so sick, I might tease her, but my heart is stuck in my throat watching her barely hold herself upright. I hang my camera belt over a hook next to the stairs and press my forearm under her knees.

"What're you—" She's cut off when I swing her into my arms. Her eyes meet mine, and this close, I can see they're not just brown, but tinged with gold and green flecks.

Despite the state Ellie's in, the air between us still seems to shift, like it does every time she's this close.

"This okay?" I ask, my voice rough to my own ears.

She answers by snaking her arms around my neck and snuggling into that sensitive spot at the base of my shoulder. "Yeah, Dave. This is nice," she whispers, and I feel it against my skin, under it, even, all the way down to my nerves, which seem to hum to life.

I wonder if she can hear my heart pounding so close to her ear, if it sounds different to her this time, now that we're not strangers. If she knows it's beating for her.

"You smell good," Ellie murmurs as I move up the stairs.

"You smell good too," I whisper into her hair, where that familiar scent is strongest.

She mumbles something, but I don't catch it. I stop at the top of the staircase and fumble around for a light switch. Instead of an overhead light, the switch ignites multiple lamps on various surfaces. The warm light casts a golden glow around the apartment.

It's Ellie. It's the first thing I think when I see her space. It's a striped sweater in a sea of black dresses, a ray of sunshine on a cloudy day, a streak of gold handwriting on a chalkboard wall. It's so perfectly *her* it makes my chest hurt.

A patterned pink rug covers the hardwoods, and a teal velvet couch rests atop it. Pillows in every color and pattern are littered across every soft surface. The yellow curtains are open wide, revealing Roman shutters that I know are not standard. I smile, imagining she has a closet full of blinds somewhere in here.

"Where to?" I ask, letting my eyes rove over the stacks of books and empty mugs, the colorful throw blankets tossed over every possible seat, the pictures lining the walls.

Ellie unhooks one of her hands from around my neck and points to an open door down the hall from the living room. The switch in there turns on a star-shaped gilded pendant light hanging from the tall, slanted ceilings. Light filters through the small, star-shaped holes, making the whole room look like a golden version of the night sky.

Somehow Ellie and I always end up under a blanket of stars.

Ellie's bed, covered in a mustard yellow quilt, takes up most of the room. I set her gently down among the sea of pillows, but she seems reluctant to let go. "I have to find you some medicine," I say quietly, and she loosens her grip a bit.

"Please don't leave," Ellie whispers into the crook of my neck, sending goose bumps prickling along my skin.

"I'm not going anywhere, I promise. I'm just going to look for medicine."

"Okay," she says, and finally releases me. "Kitchen cabinet. By the stairs."

I locate the medicine cabinet easily enough and dig through the unorganized mess until I find some expired multi-symptom medicine and a thermometer.

"Ellie, this medicine is expired," I tell her when I come back into her room. I settle on the bed next to her, and she pushes herself up, leaning onto my shoulder for support.

"S'fine," Ellie mumbles.

I frown, but she doesn't open her eyes to see it. "Open up."

She lets me slip the thermometer between her lips, and while it's calculating, I open the box of medicine and fish out two pills from inside.

The thermometer beeps, and I check it. "It's 103.2."

"Not so good," she slurs.

I hand Ellie the pills and repeat, "Not so good." When I'm sure she's not going to drop the medicine, I give her the glass of water she left on her nightstand.

Ellie swallows the medicine, and a little water dribbles down her chin. I swipe it away with my thumb, and her eyes open slowly, catching on mine.

"Will you stay with me?"

I shouldn't. If the state of my heart the last two weeks is any indication, I should stay far, far away. And she will probably regret asking in the morning.

But with those green- and gold-flecked dark eyes fixed on mine and my thumb still rubbing a gentle back and forth pattern on her chin, there's no way I can tell her no. "Yeah, Daisy. I can stay."

I toe off my shoes before settling next to her on the bed, my back against the headboard. Ellie tugs the emerald-green throw blanket around her shoulders and lies down next to me. Her breathing slows, getting deeper and deeper with each exhale. Just when I think she's asleep, she scoots a little closer, lifting her head from the pillow to rest in my lap.

I let out a breath I didn't realize I was holding, feeling a weight lift off my shoulders. When I run my hand through her hair, my fingers slipping through the silky locks, she sighs deeply.

"Cam?"

"Hm?" I ask, my own eyes starting to flutter shut.

"Thank you for staying."

Sixteen

ELLIE

The first thing I notice when I wake up is the way the sheets are sticking to my legs. It's stifling in my room, and the mound of blankets atop me isn't helping. I try to push them off, but my arms ache too badly to move them far, let alone to free myself.

Everything hurts—my head, my throat, my muscles, my stomach. It all hurts. I roll over and press a hand to my forehead, trying to block out the bright sunshine filtering through my curtains.

I gather enough strength to heave the blankets off, and cool air rushes to greet me, instantly chilling the sweat on my lower body. Memories from last night filter through my mind. The last thing I remember is waking up feeling like my skin was melting off my bones. I was in velvet pants and a sweater, my throw blanket carefully tucked around me. I'd shucked it off and retreated to the bathroom to change into shorts and a T-shirt so large it hangs almost to my knees.

I'd stumbled back into my room and found—

I roll over so quickly that my pounding head swims. Camden. He's gone.

It all comes back to me now. My fever finally spiking at the festival. Passing out on my keyboard. Steady arms, soft skin, and gentle hands sifting through my hair.

CHAPTER SIXTEEN

I turn back around and glance at my nightstand. My phone is plugged into the charger, lying next to a cup of water, a box of flu medicine, and a note scrawled in unfamilar handwriting.

I know I should take the medicine first, maybe even check my phone—I'm sure Sadie has been blowing it up. But that's not what I reach for. It's that slip of paper that I know wasn't there last night.

> *I had to go over to Weston's to work this morning. Call or text if you need anything. I can come right back if you need me.*

He wrote his phone number on the back, and I stare at it for much too long.

If you need me. The words are like pinballs in my brain, bouncing around until they break out of the secure box I shoved them into. Just like Cam. He was supposed to be quick and simple, a piece of myself I broke off and gave to a stranger without expecting anything in return. But from that first night, he's just given me back everything I need and more.

I want to take what he's offering now—his comfort, his care, his ability to fix everything I don't know is broken—but I can't. I crossed one too many lines last night. I let Cam come here, into my space, and invade the last little bit of myself I'd been holding back from him.

He's everywhere now—eyes flitting around my office, a warm kiss under a glittering night sky, gentle hands dragging through my hair in my bed, laughter in a booth in my favorite deli. He's everywhere, and I don't know how I will ever erase him.

I reach for my phone, ignoring all the messages from Sadie, and pull up Lo's contact. It's a coward's move, texting her instead of Cam, but I'm worried that if I let my fingers hover over his number, I'd end up calling him and begging him to come back.

> Cam told me he was going to be over there today. Tell him thank you for me and that I'm feeling much better.

I press Send before I can second-guess myself, then set my phone back on the table. It's not long before I'm dragged back to sleep.

THE NEXT TIME I wake up, it's to the sound of someone banging around my kitchen. For a moment, I hope it's Cam, but I squash that hope before it can take root in my chest. There's already an ache building there that I know won't go away easily.

Sadie appears in my doorway, hands on her hips. "You have some explaining to do."

My brow crinkles in confusion. "What?"

She waves her hands around wildly. "I saw you and Cam yesterday."

My pulse quickens as I grasp for what to say. For a split second, I consider confessing everything. But just as quickly, I shut it down. To explain Camden would be to also reveal the whole situation with my parents, and I won't be able to handle her look of disappointment. She wouldn't be mad at me for seeing him, but she's told me over and over again that I am my parents' doormat, and I don't have the energy to have that argument today.

I choose instead to feign confusion. Actually, it's not that hard. I'm so out of my element with Cam that Sadie could probably decipher the situation better than I could. "What?"

"He was in here. It smells like man all over this room."

"Of course he was in here. He brought me back last night." I sniff, hoping to inhale whatever scent she was referring to, but my nose is too congested. Sighing, I ask, "What does it smell like?" I know what Cam smells like—I can't get it out of my head—but I want to find out if it's actually lingering.

Because if it is, then after she leaves, I'm going to stick my face in the pillows and snort until I can catch a whiff of it.

"Like leather and bourbon and everything decadent in this life."

"Mmm." Pillows will be sniffed later.

Sadie comes into the room, the fight seeming to leave her. She perches on the edge of my bed, pressing a hand to my forehead. "You didn't tell me you were sick. I could have handled everything yesterday. Then a stranger wouldn't have had to bring you home."

"He's not a stranger," I mumble.

Sadie arches one perfectly sculpted brow.

"He's a *resident*," I clarify, although that's not what I meant at all. Cam is just Cam, and that happens to make everything more complicated.

Sadie watches me for so long that I start to squirm. "So there's nothing I need to know?"

"Nothing." The words are a punch to my gut, but it *has* to be the truth.

"I've been checking on Ethel," Sadie tells me, and I feel simultaneously guilty and relieved. Once again, I was wrapped up in Cam and neglected her.

I push up off my pillows and try to swing my legs over the bed. "I need to go see her."

Sadie presses a hand to my shoulder. "You are absolutely not going over there. You're sick. In fact, Ethel told me you're not allowed to come back without a doctor's note."

A smile tugs up one corner of my mouth. "Sounds like her."

"Ellie?" Sadie asks, her voice so soft it draws my brows together. When I meet her gaze, she asks, "Why didn't you ask me to help with Ethel?"

I don't have an answer for her. It didn't even cross my mind, but I don't know why it didn't. Sadie may not be as close with Ethel as I am, but she loves her too. She would have jumped right in without hesitation.

"I don't know," I whisper.

Sadie reaches for my hand, giving it a squeeze. "You do too much, El. You have to let people help you sometimes. You're running this place, filling in for Gary, caring for Ethel, and taking on every spare task you can find. What's going on?"

Tears prick the back of my eyes. I want to tell her everything, that since my parents stopped by the office a month ago and told me I needed to stay away from our tenants, I've been so lonely. I've been grasping at anything to fill the gnawing void, the hollow pit that's been carved into my sternum. That the few times I've been with Cam, the only one who really knows what's at stake, have been the only times that ache has dissipated.

I want to tell her every little bit. I want to take Cam from that place of honor and give it to Sadie, but I can't. Besides, I don't think it would work.

"I think I want to rest now," I croak, begging Sadie not to ask more questions. She looks like she wants to, but her lips stay pressed together in a thin line.

"Okay, Ellie," she finally says, tugging the blankets back up around my shoulders. I hadn't realized I'd begun shivering again. "Get some sleep. I'll be here to talk when you need me. Don't forget that, okay?"

She wraps her pinky around mine, a promise.

Seventeen

CAMDEN

I can't figure out why Ellie didn't text me.

After everything last night—fevered confessions, silky hair running through my fingers, whispered pleas to stay—I thought we'd turned a page in our story. I thought things had changed, but just like every other time, the Ellie I get in the dark isn't the one I get to keep in the light.

"Cam?" Weston's voice breaks into my thoughts.

I look at him and notice both he and Lo are watching me with puckered brows. "What?"

"I asked if you were ready to get back to work."

"Oh, yeah." I palm the back of my neck, gripping hard enough to hurt. "Sorry, I didn't hear you." I move behind my camera to continue filming the video where Wes explains the new directions he's taken in his career.

Wes sits back down on the couch and raises his eyebrows at me. I nod, telling him wordlessly to go ahead. My mind is focused anywhere but on his video, though. I zone out as he talks through his plans, face animated, hands moving with every word.

Lo is flipping through a book on the chair beside me, but her eyes keep roaming back to Wes, a smile playing on her lips. It's a quiet, contented smile that makes my stomach twist painfully.

Their happiness has been eating at me all month, and after my night with Ellie, it leaves me jittery in a way I don't want to acknowledge.

"Cam," Wes says, snapping my attention back to the video.

"Sorry, I must have zoned out again." I run a hand through my hair. *I need to get myself together.*

Lo sets her book down on the arm of the chair. "Are you okay?"

"I'm fine," I mutter. "I'm just kind of out of it. I think I'm going to head back home." I reach for my camera, intending to turn it off and pack it up, but my eyes zero in on the indicator light. It's not flashing red like it should be.

Equal parts dread and annoyance snake through me. I pinch the bridge of my nose and let out a deep breath.

"What?" Wes asks.

"I forgot to turn the camera back on, so we didn't get any of that last bit."

Wes shrugs. "No big deal. We can redo it."

Shaking my head, I begin to dismantle my equipment, stuffing it haphazardly into my bag. "I'm sorry. I'm just…" I trail off, not knowing how to end that sentence.

"Hey," Wes says, coming up next to me. "What's wrong?"

"Nothing."

Wes nods at my bag that I just finished packing. It barely zipped without my meticulous organization. "You just shoved everything in your bag," he states like he's the main character in a bad cop drama who just cracked the case.

I inhale deeply through my nose, trying to calm myself down. "Your point?"

"You once made me late for a meeting with my publicist because you refused to pack up your camera equipment without taking it apart and cleaning it first."

"Wes, I'm not really in the mood right now."

"Because something is wrong."

I stare at him, my jaw throbbing from how tightly I'm clenching it. Wes holds my gaze, not budging, and finally, I relent. My shoulders sag, releasing the tension that's been building in them since I lost Ellie among a sea of people last night.

"It's Ellie," I say and collapse into the armchair.

Lo closes her book, and Wes settles onto the couch next to her, his hand finding her ankle and giving it a squeeze.

"What happened with Ellie?" Lo asks.

I push a hand through my hair. "She has the flu, and I stayed over at her place last night to take care of her," I say in a whoosh.

When I look back at them, they both have wide eyes and matching shocked expressions. Lo speaks first. "So what happened between now and then?"

"I came here, and she texted you instead of me."

"Oh," Lo says, almost too quiet to hear.

"That really sucks, Cam. I'm sorry," Wes responds.

"It's fine," I say with a shrug. "I'm not mad at her. I know the rules. But *she* asked *me* to stay, not the other way around. She just…changes direction so fast, and I never know which way we're sticking."

The silence stretches between us, and I can tell they don't know what to say. *I* don't know what to say. This whole situation has me all kinds of scattered.

"Listen," I say, pushing out of the chair. "I'm going to go. I'll see you guys tomorrow."

The sky is gray and moody when I step outside. A drizzle pelts my corduroy jacket, stings my exposed skin, chills me until I feel cold from the inside out.

CHAPTER SEVENTEEN

I'm restless as I drive down the road, flipping the channels back and forth on the radio, unable to find anything that doesn't grate on my nerves. A pulsing energy thrums beneath my veins, making me feel restless and agitated.

I make turn after turn down the rain-slicked streets, unsure of where I'm going. When I stop at a red light and notice a pharmacy to my right, I steer into the parking lot before I can second-guess myself. The cold drizzle turns into a shiver-inducing downpour as I run into the brightly lit store.

Wandering the aisles, I pick up random items I don't need and throw them in my basket. When I round a corner, my eyes settle on cold and flu medicine. I stand at the base of the aisle, unmoving, and silently at war with myself.

Things with Ellie are...complicated. Ellie is complicated, in the most frustrating of ways, but she's still sick. I can still feel her body rack against mine with the force of her coughs last night, feel the feverish heat radiating off her. I can hear her soft whisper on the sidewalk about needing to be good.

It's that last part that makes me sick to my stomach and creates a tender spot under my ribs. It reminds me of why she works so hard at the office, why she takes on more than she should, why she pushes me away.

My fingers graze the medicine, slipping it into the red plastic basket at my side before I can second-guess myself. I stride from the aisle, my body now finding purpose, quelling the restless energy as I search for the rest of what I need.

I stand in line a few minutes later, clenching and unclenching the basket handle, trying not to imagine Ellie sick in bed, all alone. I glance around the bright store, looking for something to distract me, and my gaze snags on a multicolored bouquet of daisies.

I can be whoever you want me to be, Daisy. The words ring in my ears, settle into that hollow spot deep beneath my ribs.

"I can help you now," the woman behind the register says, snapping me from my thoughts.

Before I can think better of it, I snatch up the bouquet and set it on the counter with the rest of my purchases. "Lucky lady," the clerk says, giving me a warm smile.

I paste a stiff smile on my face, unsure of how to respond, but her words haunt me all the way back to my apartment. They replay in my mind with each *tap, tap, tap* of the rain against my windshield.

Ellie's light is on when I pull into the parking space in front of my apartment. I can just make out her silhouette passing by her living room window.

Everything inside me is taut, a bowstring being pulled too tight, as I gather my bags and move in the opposite direction, toward my door instead of hers. My reflection is haggard in the mirror in my entry. Rain has soaked me clean through, making my hair stick to my forehead and my shirt cling to my chest.

I suck in a deep breath as I set the groceries on the counter. Propping my hands on my hips, I stare at the bags, considering. I made a choice in the store, but I don't have to go through with it. I could make the chicken soup for myself, stuff the medicine in my cabinet, and put the wilted daisies in a glass to haunt me every time I look at them.

I can be whoever you want me to be, Daisy. I'm scared that she doesn't want me to be anyone to her. I'm scared of how much that thought scares me.

I don't know why I still go through the motions of heating the stove, cutting up the vegetables, and trimming the chicken. I tell myself to stop as I fill up the Tupperware I

CHAPTER SEVENTEEN

bought at the pharmacy. I beg myself to stay put as I load all my purchases into the grocery bags and cross the parking lot dividing our buildings.

Raindrops pool in the hollow of my throat and catch on my lashes as I stand outside her door, warring with myself. I can't keep doing this, putting myself out there, only to have her turn me away. *This* is the last time.

With that thought ringing in my head, I knock.

Eighteen

ELLIE

At first I think the knock is just my imagination, maybe a clap of thunder, but it comes again, this time softer. I think it must be Sadie, who left her spare key on my kitchen counter this morning.

I peel myself off the couch, where I've spent the last four hours trying to get comfortable. Scooping up the mound of tissues on my coffee table, I drop them in the trash can on my way to the stairs.

"Coming," I yell when the knock comes again, and my voice is a scratchy noise over the sound of the rain. Swinging open the door, I say, "It's really rude to make me—"

The words die in my throat when I see Camden on the threshold. He's soaked, making his clothes cling to him in ways I want to admire. I swallow thickly and try to make myself meet his eyes.

They're the last thing I remember seeing before drifting off to sleep last night, the deep blue of them as he said, *Yeah, Daisy. I can stay.* I can still feel him tucking my blankets a little tighter around my shoulders, feel his fingers dragging through my hair, feel his palm on my forehead checking my fever.

It all comes back with a sickening force, and I have to tighten my hands around the collar of my robe to keep from

CHAPTER EIGHTEEN

reaching for him. "What are you doing here?" I whisper, noticing the bags in his hands.

"I brought you some stuff."

His vague words finally force my eyes up to his. They're almost black in the rain-soaked darkness. "I said I didn't need anything." I expect him to flinch at the words, for them to work the way I intended and make him turn around and leave. Standing here on my doorstep, he is too tempting for me to ignore. I want to lean into him, have him wrap his arms around me and take care of me until I'm better. And then stay after that too.

"I know what you said."

My breaths come faster, panic rising in my chest. I need him to *go*. "Then why are you here?"

Cam doesn't say anything for a long moment, his eyes fixed on mine. I'm distracted by the hard set of his jaw, the tense line of his lips. Cam has never looked at me with anything but fascination, warmth, kindness, desire. Seeing him like this, knowing I put it there, makes a prick start behind my eyes.

He lets out a heavy sigh, his shoulders sagging. "Because, Ellie, sometimes what you want and what you need are two very different things." His gaze pierces mine. "What do you *want*?"

I want this.

I want *him*.

I want him more than I need my parents' approval, more than I crave their validation. I don't need his. He's already given it to me in so many little ways, and I *want* to accept it.

Moving back from the doorway, I open it a little wider for him. Cam stares at me for another long moment, seeming to make a decision for himself. I hold myself still, although I'm dying to reach for him. He gave me the space to make up my mind, so it's the least I can do for him.

I don't have to wait long. I see the moment he decides to come in, the way his eyes somehow darken further, how his shoulders settle, how he finally gives in to that tether pulling us closer and closer until he's standing right in front of me.

The bags gently thump on the floor at my feet, and the breath whooshes out of me as warm arms surround me. This isn't like any of the other times I've been in Cam's arms. It's not like dancing for hours with my head on his chest or kissing him with pumpkin staining my hand or leaning into his touch while he whispers in my ear in my office.

This is different. His arms are big and warm around my waist, his cheek a reassuring heaviness against the top of my head. I wonder if he can feel my heart pounding as I lean into him. I wonder if smoothing my hands up his biceps to wrap around his neck is affecting him as much as it's affecting me.

His breathing settles as he moves his face to my neck. I can feel each inhale and exhale in the crook of my shoulder. I shiver as his lips graze the skin there, not quite a kiss, just a brush of his mouth against my pulse point.

My fingers snake into his wet hair, tugging him a little closer. His whispered words melt into my skin, a deep rumble under his chest that I feel down to my bones.

"Hmm?" I ask, unable to form real words.

His hand comes around my neck, slipping under my hair to angle my ear closer to his mouth, just like that first night. "I said, *you're sick*."

"I don't feel too bad right now."

I feel his chuckle against my cheek. He presses a kiss to my temple. "Come on, I brought you some soup."

CHAPTER EIGHTEEN

Now that he mentions it, the tickle at the back of my throat becomes noticeable again. The ache in the middle of my forehead throbs. My nose drips.

Soup on my couch, my feet tucked under Camden's thighs, sounds really good right about now.

"Okay," I say and kiss the spot on his damp flannel right above his heart. "Let's have soup."

Cam keeps his arm around me, helping me back up the stairs. All the adrenaline I felt at seeing him has dissipated to a low buzz in my veins as my flu symptoms make their reappearance.

When we reach the top of the steps, Cam leads me around the couch, pressing my shoulders down until I'm snuggled among the pillows. He reaches for the throw blanket that pooled on the floor when I stood to open the door and tucks it around me.

"Comfy?" Cam asks, the smooth, low timbre of his voice setting off a hum under my skin.

"Mmm."

His lips quirk in a smile so devastating it's hard to watch. He is a shooting star on a cloudless night, sunrise over a crashing surf, the first flower in spring. He is everything simple and lovely in life, and I can't believe he came back here.

"I'm going to get your soup."

I watch as he fumbles around my kitchen, opening every cabinet and drawer to find bowls and silverware. I expect him to pull out a can of Cambell's to heat on my stove, but he instead lifts out a plastic food container and pours the soup directly into two bowls.

Cam returns, a bowl in each hand, to find me staring at him, confusion lining my face.

"What?" he asks, settling on the couch next to me.

"Where did you get this?" I gesture to the bowls he just set on the coffee table, steam still rising from the contents.

"The soup?" He slips his hand around my ankles, nearly dwarfing them under his palms, and tugs until my feet are under his thigh. I remember sleeping with my head on that thigh last night, firm and steady beneath my head.

"Ellie?" Cam asks, and I realize I got distracted by the feeling of his skin on mine, by the way he read my thoughts on exactly how I wanted to spend my evening.

"Where did you get the soup?"

He shrugs, not meeting my eyes. "I made it."

"You made this?"

His shoulders bounce again, like he thinks it's no big deal, but I see the blush staining his cheeks. He's…nervous, and it makes me feel achingly tender toward him.

Reaching out, I smooth a hand along the slope of his neck, relishing the way he shudders at the touch, his breath leaving him in a *whoosh*. "Thank you for making it for me." I wait until his eyes lock on mine and say, "I'm sorry about this morning."

He stares at me for a long moment before shifting to face me on the couch, his knee coming up to press into the cushion next to my feet. Rubbing the back of his neck, he asks, "Do you want to talk about it?"

A cough rattles in my chest and racks my frame. "Shoot, Ellie. I'm sorry." He snatches my glass of water from the coffee table and hands it to me.

The water soothes my scratchy throat, but my voice still comes out coarse. "Cam—"

He takes the cup from me. "Hey, no. We can talk about it later," he says and pushes a shaking hand through his hair. "I shouldn't have mentioned it."

I reach for his hand, stilling his nervous movements. "I'm okay. I want to explain."

His gaze settles on mine, searching, and I try to find the right words. It's hard to think when he's this close, stealing my every thought before it can fully form.

Camden looks like he always does—his brow crinkled with focus, his lips soft and bracketed by smile lines, his eyes intense. He is attentive, kind, and *good*, and it makes saying what's on my mind a little easier.

"My parents are strict with their rules. They don't bend, and they don't break—especially not with me." I pause, letting out an unsteady breath. "The day after we met, they came to see me at work. They found out I went to that show, and they told me that was my last strike."

Cam's face collapses in confusion, and his hand finds mine, slipping our fingers together. He gives them a gentle squeeze, urging me to go on.

I look away, unable to handle the sincerity in his eyes. "They said if they found out about any more rule violations…they were going to fire me."

When I turn back, Cam's gaze is fixed squarely on our joined hands as his thumb swipes across my pulse point. He no doubt feels the jump there, notices the goose bumps that trail up my arm at the touch.

"I shouldn't have pushed you," Cam says quietly, his voice barely above a whisper.

The words crack open something inside my chest.

"Cam." I give his hand a squeeze, and he meets my eyes. "I'm scared."

Warm hands come up to cradle my face, fingers slipping into my hair. "Hey, they won't find out. I'm going to leave, okay? I won't bother you anymore."

His eyebrows are arched high on his forehead, his eyes earnest, waiting for my response.

I wrap one of my hands around his, turning to press a kiss right in the center of his palm. I tangle my fingers with his again, gripping them tight. "Cam, I'm scared of losing *you*."

He stares at me wordlessly, shock written all over his face. It makes a raspy chuckle burst from behind my lips, the first laugh I've had in days. "Is that so hard to believe?"

"A little, yeah."

His words puncture me, leaving me wondering how he's still here when I've messed things up so badly. I don't know why he still wants me, *if* he still wants me, but I want him. I'm going to make it my mission to prove that to him.

"I didn't want to avoid you. When you walked into my office that first day, I had this fleeting second of happiness and relief that you were there, that you had found me. And then, well, you know the rest. Every time you got close, their words rang in my head until it drowned out everything you were offering, everything I wanted. But Cam, I wanted it. *Want* it. More than anything."

He is quiet for a long moment. "More than anything?" I don't miss the hidden meaning in his words—do I want *him* more than I want their approval?

I search his eyes, my lungs suddenly feeling tight. "I don't—I can't tell them, at least not right away."

I watch him weigh my answer, and my pulse hammers in my throat. "I get that," he finally says, and I let out a shaky breath. His gaze searches mine. "But Ellie, I can't do this back and forth. I need to know..." He hesitates. "I need to know this is going *somewhere*, even if that's all you can give me right now."

I want to offer more, tell him I can give in right here and now, no conditions. But despite how he makes me feel, there's still a niggling worry in the back of my mind, a whisper that tells me I'm making a mistake.

I catalog the deep, piercing blue of his eyes, the gentle slope of his mouth, the fullness of his lips, the hollow of his throat, the feeling of his calluses against my skin, and push the worries from my mind.

"This is going somewhere," I whisper.

He stares at me hard, considering my words, and then his face softens. Inch by inch, muscle by muscle, the lines of tension smooth away, replaced by an easy smile that kicks up one side of his lips and makes my heart hammer.

"I really wish I could kiss you right now."

My skin flushes, and I almost reach forward to snatch the damp collar of his shirt and drag him the small distance between us. "Why can't you?" I ask, and my voice comes out a scratch on vinyl.

His gaze drops to my lips, igniting a fire in my veins. "Flu."

"I think I'm better now."

That heart-stopping grin is back, taunting me with its nearness. "Maybe, but we better play it safe." He sits back, releasing his hold on me and reaches for the bowls on the table. "Time for soup."

Nineteen

CAMDEN

I'm still holding my breath three days later when Ellie is officially fever-free and still hasn't changed her mind. I've gone to her place every night with a different soup to soothe her sore throat after she lost her voice Monday morning, and we've watched movies late into the night. When our eyes are heavy and our bodies are loose and on the edge of sleep, I press a kiss to her temple and retreat to my place.

I still haven't kissed her, and I can't say it's entirely because of the flu. The last two kisses have lingered in my mind, replaying on an endless loop until I was sure they would erase the rest of my memories. But each kiss has set something off in Ellie, a warning bell tolling loudly enough to drown out what she wants.

I'm scared the next one will be the same. Things have been so good the last few days, but I'm still waiting for the other shoe to drop.

I think Ellie can tell.

We're sitting on her couch. There's a spooky movie playing on the TV, empty bowls of tomato bisque on the coffee table, the smell of garlic and basil lingering in the air. My fingers absentmindedly draw circles on her shoulder.

"Hey, Cam?" she murmurs, and I feel it against the bare skin at my collar where her head rests against me.

CHAPTER NINETEEN

I wonder if she can hear my heart beating louder tonight, if she feels how tense I am.

I brush my hand down her arm, relishing the way goose bumps trail in its wake. If nothing else, we at least have this, for however long she will give it to me. I can handle nights on the couch, warm skin, and rumbling laughter at a cheesy movie.

"Cam?" she asks again, this time pushing up so she can look into my eyes.

I get lost in hers, in the color, exactly like hot cocoa. Her brows are bunched together, a lock of dark hair slipping over her forehead. I trace my thumb over the line, smoothing it away, and tuck the hair behind her ear.

I don't want this to end.

Ellie's face softens. "Cam, tell me what's wrong."

It's on the tip of my tongue to say *nothing*, to not tell, in case it reminds her of what's at stake. But I also remember sitting in this same spot three days ago, my heart wrenching at her honesty. She deserves that from me too.

I open my mouth to answer, but she cuts me off. "I think we should go on a date tomorrow."

My worries dissipate under the warmth in my chest, and I can't help the smile that kicks up my mouth. "Oh yeah?"

Her lips curve, and I'm distracted by them. I remember exactly how they tasted, how they felt, how they responded under mine. I want to close the distance between us and try it again, to see if kissing her a third time would live up to the memory of the first two.

She sucks her bottom lip between her teeth, distracting me further, and says, "I—it's going to have to be low key, but I have an idea."

My heart stutters at low key, reminding me just how precarious our situation is. But I meant what I said about taking what she can give me—even if that's already starting to feel like it's not enough.

Her gaze traces my face, as if memorizing what I look like at this exact moment. I can tell because I'm doing the same.

"I've loved this," she says, gesturing to the couch, to the cloud of pillows and blankets we're snuggled into. "But I want more. I want to go do something fun with you."

I don't know how she read my mind; I'm just thankful that I'm not the only one craving more with her. It loosens the band around my chest a little, the one that's still waiting for her to change her mind.

I lean forward, nudging my nose against her cheek, and her breath hitches. "I'd like that."

She exhales, long and slow, her fingers curling into my open flannel, knuckles brushing the fabric beneath. I feel that breath everywhere, right beneath my skin, deep in my chest, at the base of my spine, and the tips of my toes.

I want to kiss her, but I hold back, my hands tightening on the spots they've found at her hips.

I want more with her—a date instead of a night on her couch, wind ruffling our hair instead of a blanket over our laps, dressing up instead of pulling on something cozy to lounge in—and I won't risk a kiss making her remember why we can't have that. I want to show her what we can have if she'll give us a chance.

I brush my lips across her cheek, slow enough to make her shiver, but so light that she doesn't push into me for more. When my mouth reaches her ear, I whisper, "Tomorrow."

CHAPTER NINETEEN

"Something obviously happened with Ellie," Wes says the next morning. He's seated across from me at his kitchen table, our laptops open between us.

I'm exhausted after another late night with Ellie followed by another early morning exploring with my camera. I've been getting up most mornings before the sun, driving all around Middle Tennessee and just stopping when something catches my eye. It's been a salve to my soul that I didn't know I needed.

But I've also been very tired, which is why I can't think of a lie fast enough. Wes is all crossed arms and raised eyebrows waiting for my response. I let out a huge sigh, like he's personally aggrieved me, but I can't help the smile curving my lips. "Yeah, I guess you could say that."

"So it's decided—you're moving here!" he says with a slap on my shoulder.

I stare at him, mouth agape. "Where did you get that idea?"

It's his turn to look confused. "Cam, what's left for you in LA?"

"My job," I answer automatically. "My sister. My entire adult life."

"I offered you a job," he responds, ticking off on his fingers. "Hazel is a grown adult; she doesn't need her brother there to take care of her. And as for your life—you can have a life here if you want it."

It's not like I haven't thought these things myself over the last month, but I also know that Ellie is just starting to come around, just now willing to give me a piece of herself. I'm afraid of how she would react if I suddenly sprang on her that I've been considering moving here.

"Things with Ellie and me are different than they were with you and Lo," I say, running my hand over the back of my neck.

"Oh, I know. By this point in my relationship with Lo, I was already married to her."

I fix him with a glare, ignoring his smirk. "Yeah, maybe I'll move away for half a decade and come back and try with her then," I grumble. Immediately, I feel a punch of guilt to my gut. "Shoot, Wes, I'm sorry. That was a really dickish thing to say."

Wes shrugs and pushes up from the table. I know from the way he's deflecting, putting his hands to work on making a latte, that he's got something he wants to say. Wes can talk to almost anyone about almost anything, but he struggles to say what's deep down.

I've watched him do this same thing hundreds of times before, make this exact same latte when he's had something on his mind—arguments with his old manager, feeling stuck in California, struggling with the direction he wanted to take his career in.

Maybe Wes has more experience with my situation than I've given him credit for.

"I wasted a lot of time with Lo," Wes says as he flips on the espresso machine. "Things worked out for us, but there's so much time I can't get back with her."

Regret, heavy and thick, settles in my stomach.

Wes braces his hands on the counter, shoulders tense. "I don't want that for you. If you think there might be something special between you and Ellie, if you think you could be happy here, don't make the same mistakes I did. Don't go back to LA."

Twenty

ELLIE

Today is the first day I've been allowed to see Ethel. She told me she didn't want to see me until I was fever-free for twenty-four hours. And to bring a doctor's note.

"Come in!" Ethel hollers when I knock on her door. I find her propped against her couch cushions, her injured leg resting on the ottoman in front of her. An irreverent sitcom is playing on the TV, and a particularly impolite joke rings out as I walk in.

"Nothing keeping you down, huh?" I ask, unable to keep the smile off my face. She looks better than she did before I got sick, the tight pinch of pain gone from her features.

"You bring that doctor's note?" she barks when I sit down on the loveseat across from her.

I wave the slip of paper in my hand. "Got Dr. Lonergan to sign it just this morning."

Ethel levels me with a flat glare. "She's a chiropractor."

"You didn't say what kind of doctor it had to be," I say with a cheeky smile. She rolls her milky blue eyes, and I'm glad to see her fully back to herself. "How's the ankle?"

The prick of guilt over my part in her injury hasn't left me, but when I went to see her in the hospital, apologizing profusely, she waved me off with a dismissive hand. She'd been finished with her order for hours and had woken up in the middle of the night wanting water when she fell. So it wasn't quite my fault the way I'd originally thought, but I still should have been there.

"Still broken," she says, turning down the volume on the TV. "You feeling better? I was getting a little worried about you."

I press a hand to my chest, feigning shock. "*You* were worried about *me*?"

Ethel tosses one of her throw pillows at me with surprising force, and I catch it against my chest with a raspy laugh, my voice still scratchy from being sick. "I'm better," I tell her. The memories of the last few days with Cam, the gentle way he took care of me, with gentle touches and warm lips pressed to my temple, bring a soft smile to my face. "Much better."

"What happened?" Ethel's coarse demand brings a blush to my face that she absolutely notices, eyes narrowing with suspicion.

"I don't know what you're talking about," I respond in a very poor attempt to deflect.

"No," Ethel says, and points to her chest. "*I* don't know what you're talking about, but *you* know perfectly well."

I grapple for a response to throw her off. "How do I know that you know what you know?"

"I don't know anything because you won't tell me, but I know there's something I need to know."

"Why do you think I know something that you need to know?"

"Elizabeth," Ethel snaps, resorting to my full name so I know she's serious. "Stop talking in circles and tell me what's got you looking like little heart-shaped bubbles would come out if you farted."

I grimace. "Ethel, you have the worst analogies."

"Don't make me get the spoon," she says, and I shudder. One time, over the summer, the lawn care workers, who are notoriously hot, spent the entire day shirtless while redoing the landscaping outside the office. When Ethel found out I didn't take a picture for her, she got out the wooden spoon and brandished it like the geriatric version of a sword. I had a bruise on my butt for a week after she got a little too enthusiastic.

I hold up my hands in surrender. "No spoon, please." She watches me with wide eyes, waiting for me to continue. I let out a little sigh. "I'm seeing someone."

I'm more than a little shocked when she doesn't respond and instead stares, searching around the mounds of magazines and bonbon wrappers littering her sofa.

"What are you doing?" I ask.

"I'm looking for my phone."

This is not at all the reaction I was expecting. "Why?"

"I want to play that Lizzo song."

I roll my eyes so hard I see stars. "My gosh, Ethel. Can't you just say you're happy for me like a normal person?"

She finally locates her phone with an *Aha!* She must have that song queued up because it starts playing, loudly, within seconds. Flashing me a bright grin, she yells over the music, "You wouldn't love me as much if I were normal."

I yell back, "Your neighbors are going to complain about this noise!"

"Nonsense! Newman hasn't been able to hear since Y2K, and I have to listen to the young couple on the other side have loud, acrobatic sex three times a day. They can listen to my music."

She turns down the music a touch, though. "So who are you dating? Tell me everything."

"Well, it's complicated," I tell her.

She rubs her hands together, sitting up straighter. "The best kinds always are."

A laugh bursts from my mouth. "I don't know about that. It sure has made things a lot more difficult."

Ethel's face turns solemn, although there's still a hint of a gleam behind her eyes. "The best relationships are the ones you have to fight for."

Her words settle beneath my sternum. It feels like every relationship in my life right now is one I have to fight for—including my parents—and I hope she's right. I hope all this *struggle* will amount to something good in the end.

I let out a deep breath. "You're right."

She grins. "Of course I am. Now tell me all about him."

A smile splits my mouth. "Okay, okay. First, I should tell you…he's a resident."

"Where are we going?" Cam asks when I hop in the passenger seat of his car later that evening. I'd given him exactly two directions—dress warm and bring your camera—and stowed the rest of what we needed in a bag in his trunk.

"It's a secret," I tell him, fastening my seat belt and finally looking up into his face. He looks irresistible tonight, with the streetlamps and the glow of the moon casting him in shadows. His dark hair is styled a little more than usual today, the longer wisps pushed back with pomade, begging to be ruffled with my hands. His deep blue eyes shine in the darkness, and I can just make out the fullness of his lips. I want to reach out and trace them, to slide my hand around his neck and bring his mouth to mine and see if they still taste like cinnamon and spice.

I wonder why he didn't kiss me last night. I saw it flicker across his face, a desire that mirrored my own, but he held himself back. I also wonder if he's going to do that tonight. I might actually combust if he does. I am a live wire, ready to catch flame.

"You look beautiful," he whispers, almost to himself, and a hot blush stains my cheeks. I've never had someone look at me like that, with such reverence and fascination, like he can't believe he gets to be here with me. It makes something warm and sticky spread in my chest, filling me up until I feel it like a thick lump in my throat, a flurry of butterflies low in my stomach.

"Thank you," I manage. "You too."

His lips quirk in a smile, and his hand reaches for mine in the dark, threading our fingers together. He lets out a sigh, as if he's been waiting for this all day. I feel it echo in my heart, a skipped beat, before it gets back on track.

Cam brushes a kiss against my knuckles, and his breath fans against my neck as he asks, "Where to?"

I'm distracted as I give Cam directions to our secret location, my eyes drifting from the way his corduroy jacket strains over his biceps to the stubble coating his sharp jaw and drifting down the smooth column of his neck to his hands flexing on the steering wheel.

I'm practically salivating by the time we drive through downtown and end up on the other side of Nashville.

"Which way?" Cam asks as we stop at a red light. He turns, catching me staring, and a grin like I haven't seen before, almost a smirk, lights his face. It's a good look on him.

"Straight," I point ahead, up a gently sloping hill.

"So you got to see Ethel today?" Cam asks, directing the conversation back to where it was before we stopped at the light.

"Yeah, she's doing a lot better."

"Good," he says with a small smile. "I know you were worried about her when you were sick."

"She was in good hands with Sadie. Although I'm not sure how the two of them didn't kill each other. Sadie is Ethel fifty years ago, and they are constantly butting heads."

"Yeah?"

"Constantly. Last year, they got into a fight involving chocolate penises. We were finding them all over the office for weeks."

I told Cam all about Ethel's business during one of our late evenings on my couch this week, so he's not even phased by that line. "Are the candies actually good?" he asks, still following the narrowing road up the hill.

"Oh yeah. Surprisingly so. She uses fair-trade organic chocolate."

"Only the best, I guess," he says with a smile. I decide right then and there that I want to make that smile light up his face as much as possible. Cam is attractive. I noticed it that very first night—all lean lines and sharp angles, dark hair, and midnight eyes—but when he smiles, he's devastating.

"Ellie," Cam says, bringing me back to the moment. "This road is ending."

I look around, noticing our surroundings. "We're here!" I hop out of the car before it's off and run around the front to yank open his door. He stares at me, that almost-smirk back on his face, as I tug him out of the car.

"Come on, come on," I say, pulling him behind me. We stop at the back of his car, and he opens the trunk before I can.

CHAPTER TWENTY

I didn't let him help me load up the supplies, not wanting to ruin the surprise, so his mouth falls open when he sees everything I packed.

"Are we moving up here?"

I nudge him with my shoulder and reach for the giant tote bag, but he grabs it first. He picks up the stack of blankets and his camera pack, which he hefts onto his back.

"You'll be glad for all this stuff soon enough," I tell him, already feeling the urge to tug my jacket closer, to pop the collar against the chill brushing my neck.

I don't know how Cam knows, but after he closes the trunk, he wraps his free hand around the back of my neck, tucking me neatly at his side. His warmth surrounds me, heating me from the outside in. I smile into his shoulder, relishing the way I can do this without fearing someone will see. It's freeing and makes me feel bold enough to slip my hand inside his jacket, feel his heart beating against my palm.

"What is this place?" he asks as we trek up the hill.

"Just wait," I say into the fabric at his shoulder.

I feel his chuckle against my lips, a soft rumble that hums inside me.

When we finally crest the hill, Cam stops, taking in the view. I do too, but it's him I watch instead of the scenery. I watch those photographer eyes assess every slope and valley, every light illuminating the night sky. It's Nashville, in all its beauty, spread out before us, like it was founded just for this night, for two souls to find peace in.

My breath puffs in the air before me. "What do you think?" I can't stop the nervous tap of my fingers on my thigh. He snatches them up, wrapping his big hand around mine.

"I love it."

"Yeah? It's not LA. No City of Angels."

Cam's gaze traces my face in the darkness, pausing on the slope of my nose and the curve of my lips before finally settling on my eyes. "There's nowhere I'd rather be."

My heart swells in my throat, and I swallow against it.

I shudder as his thumb reaches up, swiping at my bottom lip in the gentlest of touches. "Mind if I take a few photos?"

"Go for it."

His thumb glides down my chin, pushing it up infinitesimally. "Stay right there, just like that."

Cam steps back, dropping our things to the ground, and roots around in his backpack. I stand still, chin still raised ever so slightly, watching him out of the corner of my eye. He pulls a camera from his bag, not bothering to loop the strap around his neck. He looks at home behind it, lining up his gaze behind the viewfinder, completely at ease.

A cold breeze kicks up my hair, sending it flying around me. I reach up, intending to tuck it behind my ears, but stop when Cam says, "No, leave it. You're perfect."

His words settle inside me, warm and heavy. Not *it's perfect*, but *you're perfect*. I don't know if he said it on purpose or if it was just a slip of his tongue, if he knew how much those words would mean to me, but no one has ever called me perfect before. No one has ever made me feel as perfect as he does.

Cam lowers the camera, clicking through the photos.

Shaking myself out of my thoughts, I sidle up next to him. He angles the camera so I can see and leans into me. I stare at the photo on the screen, awestruck. Obviously, I knew Cam had to be a relatively decent photographer to make a living at it since graduating from college, but I'm shocked at what I see.

"It's not edited yet, obviously. It will look better when I can adjust some settings," he says.

CHAPTER TWENTY

"It's stunning," I tell him, not embellishing at all. The lights of the city are a blurry, golden glow behind me. My silhouette is just barely visible, my hair whipped up in the breeze, my back arm slightly extended to feel the wind between my fingers.

"You're stunning," he murmurs, warm and low in my ear. I turn to face him, and he's so close, his lips a breath away from mine. He could close the distance between us, seal his mouth to mine. My whole body is poised for it—my fingers ready to curl into his hair, my back ready to arch under his touch, my toes ready to lift me closer to him until there's no space between us.

I'm ready and waiting, but Cam backs up, slipping a palm around the back of his neck and squeezing hard. "What's next for this date?"

I swallow against the disappointment roiling in my stomach. I fight the urge to crumble and retreat inside myself so I can't be hurt. But I can't blame him for being cautious, not after everything I've put him through. I can't close up—the only way to prove myself is to be more open.

I gesture around us, at the vast space at the top of the hill. "I thought we'd have a picnic under the stars. It seems like they've become our place."

A tentative smile blooms on his face, lifting the corners of his mouth in a slow, delicious curve. He reaches for my hand, giving it a squeeze, the earlier awkwardness between us dissipating. "I've been thinking that too."

Grabbing one of the blankets, I spread it out on the ground, listening to it settle against the crunchy grass at our feet. I sit atop it and pull the tote bag into my lap. "I thought since we can't exactly go out to a nice restaurant, we could maybe have a candlelight dinner with the best view in town."

I look into his eyes, trying to decipher his reaction. He sinks onto the blanket next to me, his thigh resting heavily against mine. "I can't think of anything better."

A relieved smile tips the corners of my mouth. "Good."

"So candlelight?" Cam asks, dismantling his camera and loading it back into his backpack.

I pluck several candles from my tote bag, lighting them as I go, and set them in a circle around us. The light casts Cam's tan skin in burnished golds, illuminating the dark fringe of lashes, his full lower lip, and those deep blue eyes that never cease to pull me in.

"Candlelight," I say with a smile. "And I brought something really original for dinner."

"Soup, then?"

I can't help the laugh that rumbles out of me. "I'm really sorry we're having soup again." It's all we've eaten in days, at least the meals we've eaten together. "But it's cold, and this is easy to store. I brought bread too," I say and extract the thermoses and bread from the bag.

"Well, that's new, at least," he says, a grin curving his mouth. "What kind are we having tonight?"

"Butternut squash. I channeled my inner Camden Lane and made it myself."

"That so?"

"You don't want to see my kitchen. It's a disaster." I pause and chew my lip, debating the next part. *Honesty and vulnerability*, I tell myself. Glancing up at Cam, I say, "I just wanted tonight to be perfect."

His eyes soften. "It is perfect, Daisy."

My stomach flips at the nickname, something that started out as a way for me to escape myself, to be someone else for the night. But now it's something more, something just for us.

"You kind of smell like daisies, you know," Cam says, trailing his fingers across my shin.

I shiver at the contact, words scrambling in my mind. I was going to say something, respond, but my thoughts have evaporated under his gentle touch.

He looks up at me through his lashes, a crooked smile on his lips. "Ready to eat?"

It takes a minute for his words to process, but I finally nod, and he opens the thermoses, pouring soup into the lids. It's a good thing too, because my hands are shaking hard enough that I probably would have spilled it.

We spend the evening like that, a blanket draped over our laps, dipping crusty bread in our soup, which turned out better than I could have expected. Maybe those evenings watching Cam cook in my kitchen this week taught me a thing or two.

We stay there for hours, letting the candles drip fat dollops of wax onto the quilt. The tastes of sage, rosemary, garlic, and ginger linger on my tongue. The cool, crisp air whips around us, threatening to blow out the candles, but not a single one does, as if they're glowing just for us. The sounds of the city don't reach us up here, tucked away in our own little bubble. We lie on our backs, pressed together from head to toe, fingers intertwined, staring at a sea of stars, and it's *perfect*.

Twenty-One

CAMDEN

It's the Tuesday before Thanksgiving, and I'm antsy. Wes has wanted to rerecord this same bit three times, and I am *ready to go.* Tonight is my last night with Ellie before I head to my parents' house for Thanksgiving, and we're supposed to be making a dish for her to take to her own family dinner on Thursday.

"Why are you so antsy?" Wes asks right before we're about to start recording for the *fourth* time.

I think about blowing off his question and getting back to work, but I also kind of…want to tell him about Ellie and me. I'm so gone for her, it's disgusting. I think of how sappy and infatuated Wes was with Lo this summer, how much I wanted to laugh every time I saw his moony face. I saw that moony face in my mirror this morning.

I've been silently begging him to bring her up all day, but *of course,* the one time I actually want to talk, Wes has completely missed it.

"I have a date with Ellie tonight," I mumble.

A smirk lights up Weston's face, and he looks pleased as punch. I regret this already. "Is that so?"

He stands from his seat on the couch and moves around all our equipment before heading into the kitchen. I wait silently, knowing his terrorizing is far from over. He takes his time

CHAPTER TWENTY-ONE

meandering to the kitchen and opens the fridge, pulling out two water bottles. "Want one?"

I nod, needing something to occupy my hands, and he tosses it at me. My heart pounds in my chest as I screw off the top and take a long gulp.

Wes wipes at his still smirking mouth with the back of his hand and leans a hip against the counter. "So I take it the other night went well?"

The date the other night went better than *well*. It was the best date of my life. I hadn't wanted it to end. And I'd wanted to kiss Ellie, badly. My body ached with it—my fingers itched to twist in her hair, my lips trembled with the need to find hers, my skin hummed with a frenetic energy—but I held myself back. Then and every day after.

I've wanted to hold out, to show her that what we have can be good, before I test us with a kiss again.

But I feel on the verge of snapping; a rubber band stretched too tight.

"It was good," I tell him, forcing the words through clenched teeth.

"Well, you sure seem like it. You've been a real treat," he says, that infuriating grin never leaving his face.

He makes it so hard to love him sometimes.

I exhale a deep breath, deciding at that moment to be honest. "I'm going crazy, man."

"No," he deadpans. "I couldn't tell."

I resist the urge to chuck my water bottle at his head. Wes must see the stormy expression on my face because he lets out a bark of laughter.

"Dude, calm down," he says, walking back into the living room and settling down in the spot he vacated. "What happened?"

I breathe through my nose and drag a hand through my hair. It's shaking—not a good sign. "Nothing's happened. Things are good—better than good." I've spent every evening at her place since she got sick, making us dinner and then staying over until my eyelids are heavy and my body is limp.

"So you're confused about moving?"

"No," I tell him, and it's partly true. Moving has been niggling at the back of my mind for weeks, but I'm trying to take Ellie out of the equation. Things with her are still so new, so *fragile*, that I can't base this decision on her.

"So you are moving?" Wes asks.

I shoot him a glare. "No, I'm not moving. Forget about me moving for a minute. You're driving me nuts."

He has the nerve to look chastised. *Weston King* looks chastised, hand rubbing at the back of his neck.

"What?" I ask, dread pooling in my stomach.

"Nothing," Wes says, waving me off, but he stands from his seat again and retreats to the kitchen. He's avoiding me, so, obviously, I follow him.

"What?" I ask and settle onto one of the barstools.

Wes leans back against the cabinets, bracing his hands on the counter at his hips. "I don't want to bother you about it, because I actually *don't* want to pressure you into a move."

My stomach flips again, an uncomfortable tumble that leaves me tapping my fingers against the water bottle still in my hands. I recognize the movement as Ellie's, her nervous tap that always prompts me to reach for her.

"It's just that, technically, your job here is done in three more weeks." I hadn't realized how much time had flown by. Despite the ups and downs with Ellie and the constant reminders of what I'm missing whenever I'm around Wes and Lo, things here have been…good. Easy. Fulfilling.

CHAPTER TWENTY-ONE

"My manager wants me to start interviewing people for your job," Wes continues. "And I will if you don't want it. I don't want to force your hand or anything, but I'm probably going to need an answer soon."

I stare at him for a moment, a whirring building in my ears. "How soon?"

He shrugs. "After Thanksgiving. I just—we signed all these new brand deals, and I have all the sponsorships that I need to stay on top of. I can't really go without a photographer for very long. I know your sublet is up in January, so if you plan to go back, that's fine, but I need to find a replacement."

I drag a hand through my hair, a thousand thoughts flitting through my mind. This wasn't how this was supposed to go. I was supposed to come out here for two months, work with Wes and figure out how to proceed when I went back to LA. I was going to take two weeks off to spend with my parents at my childhood home in our little mountain town and get the refresh I needed before jumping back into it. I was *not* supposed to feel even more confused when I got here. I was *not* supposed to meet a girl who flipped my world upside down. I was *not* supposed to want to stay.

"Just think about it. I don't need an answer today or anything."

"Just a week from now," I say, my lips pinching into a thin line.

Wes gives me a rueful smile. "Yeah, a week."

The conversation with Wes is still playing on a loop in my head when I let myself in Ellie's door later. She gave me her spare key when she was sick, skipping fifteen relationship steps, so she didn't have to get up off the couch and walk down the stairs to let me in. I like it, though, our unorthodox take at dating. We're less a guidebook and more a vintage game of Candy Land—missing some cards and having to make up the steps as we go, but still full of color and sweetness, nonetheless.

"Ellie, I'm here," I yell over the music playing through her speakers.

She pops around the corner, standing at the top of the stairs, a smile lighting her face. It's enough to dull the incessant buzzing in my chest since my conversation with Wes. I may not know what I want to do, and I may only have a week to figure it out, but right now, I have *Ellie*.

I take the steps two at a time, reaching her in no time, and stop right in front of her, one step down so we're almost at eye level. Hers are crinkled around the edges, and the light constellation of freckles across her nose distracts me.

"Hey," I say a bit breathlessly.

Before she can respond, my arms are snaking around her middle, my face finding that soft crook at the base of her neck, the one that drives me crazy. That familiar scent is strongest there, like she sprays her perfume in that exact spot. I want to find all the other places she sprays it and nudge my nose along there too.

"Hey." She laughs into my hair, her breath fanning my ear and sending a thrill of awareness through me. I want to kiss her, forget all the consequences.

She leans back, her hands squeezing my biceps. "Come on, we've got a casserole to make."

CHAPTER TWENTY-ONE

I let out a deep breath through my nose as Ellie spins, heading back into the kitchen, the strings of her brand-new apron trailing after her. She bought it over the weekend, when we went shopping at a flea market out in the country. She saw the brightly colored apron covered in daisies and told me she just *had* to buy it now that she was a real cook.

Watching her stand on her tiptoes, trying to reach the baking dish in her overhead cabinet, I don't know how I'm going to leave her to go back to LA in a month and a half. It's too early to be making decisions based on her, especially since she's still so gun-shy about us in general, but I can't picture it. I can't see myself returning to my too-small apartment in LA—staring at my white walls without a speck of color, making dinner for just myself, eating on my couch without her feet tucked under my thigh—knowing she's here and I could have been too.

The thought scares me, sends a zap of fear straight up my spine, but it also feels a little like relief. Like an uncoiling of something in my chest, a weight slipping off my shoulders, a full breath in my lungs. It feels *right.*

"You coming?" Ellie asks, eyebrows pinching together.

I nod, snapping out of my trance, and move to stand behind her, easily picking up the dish she was trying to reach. My chest grazes her back, and I feel her shudder against me, the air between us charging.

I'm reminded of that buzzing under my skin, the one that's been growing more and more persistent over the last few days.

"Thanks," Ellie breathes. I don't move, although I know I should. Or maybe…maybe I shouldn't. I haven't decided to stay, but I feel like I had a major revelation back there. And if Ellie is feeling even a fraction of what I am, a kiss won't derail that, right?

I set the baking dish on the counter and place my hands there, bracketing her hips. I let my head fall into the crook of her neck again, inhaling that fruity, floral scent. I almost don't know if it's familiar, or if it's just *Ellie.* She's been haunting my thoughts for so long it's like I almost can't remember when she wasn't a steady companion in my brain, muddling everything up.

Ellie lets out a shaky breath, her hands pressing to her stomach. I want my hands *right there*, so I don't hold back. I slip mine around her waist, sliding them under her hands, and spread my fingers out across her belly. It jumps beneath my touch, and her heart beats beneath my lips at her pulse point.

I'm driven by need—a need to touch her, to taste her, to see if she feels for me what I feel for her—but it's the way she settles into me, swaying slightly to the sound of the music, that calms me down. She hums under her breath, a sound that thrums in my veins, and her fingers trace mindless patterns on my forearms until my heartbeat slowly returns to normal.

Ellie spins around, her hands gliding up my chest to lock behind my neck. "Hey, you okay?"

I nod and press my forehead to hers. I can wait. I don't want to kiss her again because I can't hold myself back. I want to kiss her again when I know we're strong enough to handle it.

"Good," she says, brushing her lips across my cheek. "I missed you today." I feel the words against my skin, her breath warm on the shell of my ear.

My hands tighten around her waist. "I missed you too." And it's true. When Wes dropped the news on me today, I wanted to talk it out with her, but we're not ready for that yet. *Ellie* isn't ready for that yet. So I wanted the next best thing, to just *be* with her.

CHAPTER TWENTY-ONE

"You ready to make this casserole? Sweet potato is my mom's favorite."

Leaning back enough for Ellie to extricate herself, I nod. "Yeah, let's do it." I spin around, washing up in the sink. "If this is your mom's favorite, why doesn't she make it?"

Needless to say, I'm not a big fan of Kristin Bates. Ellie doesn't talk about her mom much, but I can tell she's a real piece of work. I remember the pinched look on her face when I first met her and the snide comments she made about Ellie's professionalism the next time I had the pleasure of being in her company.

"Mom never cooks her own Thanksgiving dinner. She caters it and expects us kids to bring all her favorite dishes. Adam and Alex always take turns bringing store-bought pumpkin pie that they transfer to a crystal dish and call homemade. And, of course, she *loves* them, so she believes them."

I grip the dish towel in my hands, wringing it between my fists. "And you're expected to bring sweet potato casserole?"

"I've gotten out of bringing it the last two years," she says, pulling ingredients from her pantry. "Last year I went with Sadie to her family's house, and the year before that I talked my ex-boyfriend into inviting me for Thanksgiving."

Something hot and incredibly stupid flares in my chest at her words. We haven't talked about past relationships, but this one must have been serious if she wanted to spend the holiday with his family.

Ellie comes out of the pantry and sees my hands twisted in my dish towel.

"What happened—with him, I mean?"

Her lips quirk in a smile. "Jealous?"

I frown. "No." Maybe a little, but I'd never admit it.

"It's okay if you are," she says, staring down at her feet. I watch as she taps her fingers on the edge of the counter. "I don't really like thinking about you with...other people."

Her honesty buoys something inside me—that piece deep down that is still unsure about how she feels about us, about me. So I decide to be truthful as well. "A little jealous, maybe."

She peers up at me through the fringe of her lashes, a shy smile playing at her lips. "Yeah?"

I hold up my fingers an inch apart. "Just a little."

Her grin splits across her face as she closes the distance between us, a bright slash of pink lighting up her cheeks. "It's okay. I know I'm irresistible."

She has no idea.

Ellie pauses a few steps away, reaching for one of the sweet potatoes and rolling it across the counter under the palm of her hand. "I usually tried to find someone to make it for me—a friend or coworker.

"The year I was dating Jake was only the second year I'd been working for my parents. None of the other employees at that property wanted anything to do with me. I guess they were scared I'd rat on them if they got out of line. So I begged Jake to take me with him to his family's Thanksgiving, and he ended up breaking up with me before dessert. I had to take an Uber home, and I watched movies alone in bed for the rest of the night."

My chest cracks in two, imagining Ellie all alone in her apartment two years ago, watching movies in the dark while her family ate dinner without her. A hard lump forms in my throat, and my hand reaches out for hers. "I'm sorry, Ellie," I say, my voice a raspy whisper.

She shrugs. "It's okay, really. All those moments led me here, right?"

CHAPTER TWENTY-ONE

I nod, not trusting my voice, and tug her hand until her body meets mine. My arms snake around her middle, my chin coming to rest on the top of her head.

"If it weren't for Jake breaking up with me, I wouldn't have ducked my head down and started working so hard. My parents would have never considered me for the promotion to manage this place if I hadn't proven myself there. And if I'd never come here…"

She stops, as if she's not sure how to finish that sentence.

If she'd never come here, we probably wouldn't have met. But if she hadn't come here, we could have stood a chance. We may have still met that night, may have still danced for hours and kissed under the stars. We may have found each other another way and been able to date for real.

That's a lot of *maybes*, and none of them are helpful, so I give her one last squeeze, loving the way she fits *just right* against me, and push back. "Tonight we're going to teach you how to make this dish on your own so you know how to do it next time—with or without help."

Ellie gives me a smile, one that starts slow and eventually takes over her whole face. It's a sucker punch to the gut, and I wish I could take a photo of it and feel this breathless all the time.

I trace my thumb over that smile, unable to help myself. "Hey, thank you for telling me," I whisper.

Ellie shrugs one delicate shoulder, making the sleeve of her sweater slip down the elegant slope. "Thanks for making me feel like I could tell you." She leans forward, pressing her mouth against the fabric of my shirt, right above my wildly beating heart. "Let's make the best dang casserole this kitchen will ever see."

Twenty-Two

CAMDEN

"Cammie!" my mom yells the minute I walk through my parents' front door. Her hands are plunged in the kitchen sink, water up to her elbows. She drops the dishes and runs toward me, wet, soapy hands extended to wrap me in a hug.

I wrap my arms around her middle, relishing in the feeling of being home. "Hey, Ma."

She swats at my side. "You've been living four hours away, and *this* is the first time you could come visit me?"

Rubbing my ribs that she smacked none too gently, I say, "I've been working, Ma. Where's Dad and Hazel? They'll be glad to see me."

"They're down at the farm. Why don't you drop off your bags in your bedroom, and we can go see them?"

My aunt and uncle own an apple orchard and flower farm on the outskirts of town. Since it's on the far side of our property, nestled just past the deep valley that separates my parents' land from theirs, I've spent almost as much time wandering the fields as I have here in my childhood home.

When I walk back into the kitchen after dropping my bags off in my old room, Mom tosses me her keys. I catch them against my chest, and she flashes me a smile. "You're driving."

We ride with the windows down in the beat-up old truck my parents have owned for as long as I can remember, even though the cold air chills me to the bone. I turn my chin up, my hand flexing on the steering wheel, and bask in the feeling of the wind on my face.

"You seem happy, Cammie," Mom says as we bump along the dirt road, her small hand tapping a musical beat against the side of the truck.

"I am happy," I answer easily, and the thought shocks me a little. I'm not sure when my anxiety and listlessness, that itching thrum beneath my skin and that ever-expanding ache in my chest, started to go away. It must have drifted off somewhere under a Nashville sunrise with my camera in hand, or tucked under a blanket on Ellie's couch, or lying beneath the stars with the taste of butternut squash lingering on my tongue.

I'm not sure when it happened—if it was little by little or all at once—but I feel lighter than I have in ages.

"You haven't looked this settled in years."

My brows bunch together, and my eyes flit to hers for a moment before returning to the road. "That's not true," I tell her. It's only been in the past few months that I've started feeling like this, since I branched out and realized I didn't love what I'd found.

Mom clucks her tongue. "Don't act like you know yourself better than I know you. You've never been much for talking; even as a baby you hardly cried. I used to watch your face for every little thing, and you'd get that pinched look right between your eyebrows—yeah, that's the one," she says, pointing at my forehead. "You'd look just like that when you needed something, food or a diaper change or a nap. You didn't cry to tell me, so I had to look close. It's how I've known you've been missing something these past few years."

"*Years?*" I ask, unable to keep the incredulity out of my voice.

She nods. "Years, son. Oh, don't look so bothered. You're just starting to look like yourself again. Something in Tennessee has been good for you. I wish you'd find it here, but at least Nashville is closer than LA. Maybe Hazel will find it next."

Her words set off alarm bells in my head, making me think about my life over the past few years. She's not wrong that Tennessee has been good for me, in more ways than one. It's not just Ellie, although she's played a big part in it. It's the changing of the seasons, the rightness of having my old camera in hand, of having *time* to use it again. It's working with Wes again and falling back into an easy rhythm that doesn't require my entire focus at all times. It's little things and big things, and I don't know how I missed it.

I know, in that moment, that I don't want to go back to LA.

"What is your father doing on a ladder?" Mom screeches as we pull into the farm, yanking me from my thoughts. She's out the door before I get the truck in park, arms flailing as she yells up to Dad, who calmly ignores her as he continues to use a broom to clean out the gutters on my aunt and uncle's farmhouse.

Hazel comes out the front door, a grin lighting up her face when she sees me. She hurries down the front steps and tackles me in a bear hug as soon as I'm out of the car.

"I'm so glad you're here. They're driving me *nuts* already."

A laugh rumbles in my chest, slipping out as I set her back down on the ground. The smile slips from her face, turning into a grimace. "I may have messed up."

"What did you do?"

CHAPTER TWENTY-TWO

She squeezes her eyes shut. "She wouldn't leave me alone about finding a good boy to, and I quote, 'settle down with,' so I may have let it slip that you met someone in Nashville."

I groan, dragging a palm down my face. "Hazel…"

"I know, I know. I'm sorry. But hey," she says, tugging on my hand, and leading me toward the house, where my mom is still screeching at Dad. "Stevie is inside making lasagna. You *love* her lasagna." It's true, I do love my cousin's lasagna, but I hate that Hazel's using it as a distraction.

"This is not the last time we talk about this," I warn.

She pulls me up the stairs, right past our mother, who is now climbing them and trying to pull Dad off the ladder. "Oh, of course not," Hazel tells me, and I roll my eyes.

"Hey, son!" Dad calls down from the ladder. "I'd give you a hug, but I'm trying to clean the gutter right now." He kicks his leg out, evading Mom's hand.

"See you inside!" I yell, right as Hazel tugs me through the door. Really, the women in this family are a force to be reckoned with.

The inside of my aunt and uncle's house is cozy, the golden glow of the lamplight illuminating the old farmhouse decor that hasn't changed in my lifetime. It smells like it usually does, like the scent of the flowers and apple candles that my mom makes and sells in the shop. Although right now there is a distinct smell of garlic and tomato that makes my mouth water.

"Cam!" my Uncle Anthony bellows as we enter the kitchen. He's seated at the table, his leg, wrapped in an ACE bandage and covered with a bag of frozen peas, resting on the chair in front of him.

I stoop down to give him a hug. "Hey, Uncle Anthony. What happened to your knee?"

"Fell off the ladder trying to clean the gutters."

"Ah," I say, right as my aunt circles the island to give me a hug.

She leans back, hands gripping my biceps. "You look good. Nashville suits you."

Hazel, now at the counter next to Stevie, mumbles something under her breath, and they both snicker.

"Thanks, Aunt Jamie," I say, narrowing my eyes at my sister and cousin giggling behind their hands in the kitchen.

Stevie waves her wooden spoon in a circle. "You know, if you don't stop frowning, your face is going to stick like that."

"If I didn't want some of that lasagna so badly, I'd come up with something snarky to say," I tell her, coming around the corner to wrap one arm around her shoulders.

The garlic and tomato scent is strongest here with the lasagna baking in the oven, but it's the fruity, floral aroma of the candle burning on the counter that sticks out most to me.

It smells like home.

WE STAY AT THE farmhouse until long after the sun has set over the mountains, drenching the sky in burnished golds and cotton candy pastels, that I had to snap a picture of on my phone. By the time I end up back in my childhood bedroom, nestled under a ratty quilt that has seen better days, it's well after midnight.

My fingers linger over Ellie's contact. We were texting all night until I told her I was at the farmhouse playing charades with my family. I told her she didn't need to go, but she said she needed to tackle a few of her maintenance workers' tasks anyway since he had called out today.

It's so late now, I doubt she's even up, but I miss her voice. I miss *her*. Tonight is the first night in weeks that I haven't spent curled up next to her on her couch, her feet in my lap and my hand sifting through her hair.

I press Call before I can think better of it. She answers on the first ring, and I can hear the smile in her voice. "Hey, I was just debating calling you."

I settle back against the pillows, warmth spreading through my chest. "I hoped you'd be up."

"Can't sleep," she says. "No one made me tea before bed."

Chuckling, I ask her, "Who made you tea before I came around?"

"Well, I did, but it doesn't taste the same anymore."

"I wish I could tell you it's my special touch, but really, I just add a little honey."

I hear shuffling on the other end, and I can imagine her sitting up in bed, the blankets pooling around her waist. "Are you serious?"

"Yes," I say with a laugh. "The first time I made tea for you, you kept talking about how good it was and how you were going to have to keep me around to make it for you every night." I pause, not meaning to end up where my sentence took me. "I just wanted you to keep me around, I guess."

The line is quiet on the other end for long enough that I feel the need to fill the silence. "I kept adding a little more each day until I was sure you were going to know something was up. I—"

"Cam," Ellie breathes, cutting me off. "That's the sweetest thing I've ever heard."

"Yeah?" I ask, gnawing at my bottom lip. "Not too much?"

"No, it's perfect. *You're* perfect," she says, echoing my words from our first date.

"Good," I say, unable to stop the smile from spreading across my face. "Are you nervous about tomorrow?"

I hear rustling again, no doubt Ellie leaning back against her pillows, shifting until she's comfortable. "A little. I haven't seen my parents since…well, us. I'm worried they're just going to look at me and *know*."

My heart stutters a little at her words. I'm still not entirely comfortable with keeping this a secret, although I understand the reasons for it. I just wish we could be open about it, tell the world, and not fear the consequences.

I think about the revelation I had earlier, about not wanting to go back to LA, and how it was affirmed over and over again with my family tonight. I kept thinking about how anytime I missed them, I could just get in the car and drive the four hours to see them, instead of rationing my money and only flying here a few times a year.

I can't help but wonder what it would mean for Ellie and me if I stayed. If I moved into a new apartment, would she be willing to tell her parents about us? Would we have to fabricate a story so they didn't find out we'd been dating when I lived here?

The thoughts running through my head threaten to burst out of my mouth, but I hold back. Now isn't the time, not with Ellie nervous about seeing her family tomorrow. This isn't a conversation I want to have with her over the phone when I can't see her face and gauge her reaction. I hold back for the same reasons I haven't kissed her again, because I want to make sure our foundation is so firm that these questions won't threaten to break us.

CHAPTER TWENTY-TWO

So instead of voicing what's on my mind, I say, "They won't know. There's no way they could know."

She lets out a little huff of air. "You're right. I'm being paranoid over nothing. I just...I don't know when things got so messed up between us."

My chest aches at her words. "It hasn't always been like this with you guys?"

"No, not always," Ellie says, her voice soft. "I remember when I was a kid, I used to go with them to their office all the time. I'd follow my mom around or read books under my dad's desk. Even in high school, Dad would sometimes pick me up early from school and tell the receptionist I had a doctor's appointment, but he'd really just take me for ice cream instead."

"That sounds really nice," I whisper.

"It was. I wish I knew when things changed. *Why* things changed."

I swallow against the lump in my throat. More than anything, I want to be with her right now. I want to hold her and assure her everything is going to get better. But I can't. And worse than that, I have the potential to make everything *worse*. I can't imagine how bad things would get if they knew about us.

"I'm really sorry, Daisy," I finally manage.

"It's okay," she says, but I hear her sniffle. "I'm trying to do better. I'm going to make things better."

"You shouldn't have to *do anything*, Ellie."

She exhales. "Maybe not, but that doesn't change the fact that I *do*. I'm going to fix things between us. I have to, no matter what it takes."

Her words settle like lead in my stomach, and I wonder how much of herself she's going to have to give up to make them happy. How *much* she's going to have to give up.

"It's going to get better," she says, almost to herself.

"Yeah, Daisy," I say, even though it still makes me sick. "I know it will."

Twenty-Three

ELLIE

"What on earth are you wearing?" Mom asks the moment she opens the door.

I cradle the sweet potato casserole to my chest like a newborn baby. "Happy Thanksgiving to you too, Mom," I say, plastering a wooden smile on my face.

She opens the door wider and spins on her heel before heading back down the long hall to the kitchen. I push the front door closed behind me and lean up against it for support. My eyes flutter closed.

"Hey, loser," Alex's voice interrupts my meditation, and I stand up straight. My smile is genuine this time. "I, for one, like the outfit."

I debated for a long time over what to wear today—the plain white sweater and dark jeans that were completely *fine* and would invite no criticism from my mother, or my red leather pants and an aqua turtleneck with the tags still on it. I ended up compromising and wore purple trousers and a chunky orange sweater.

"Hey, Alex."

Alex wraps an arm around my shoulders and tugs me and my casserole baby into a hug.

"Mom's in a good mood," I say into his shirt before he releases me.

His brown eyes, the exact color of mine, twinkle. "Actually, she seems happy about something, but won't say what it is."

She probably got someone fined by the HOA or got the Girl Scouts to stop *loitering* outside her favorite grocery store.

"Where are Adam and Kelsey?" I ask.

"They had to stop and get ice on the way."

I check my phone screen. I just barely made it here in time. "They're going to be late."

He bumps his shoulder with mine. "At least it takes the focus off us for a bit, right?"

"I need your side dish, Elizabeth," Mom warns from the kitchen.

"We could never be so lucky," I mutter to Alex and head down the hall.

Mom stands at the counter, stirring her homemade cranberry sauce on the stove. It's the only thing she doesn't cater for the holiday. We all hate that sauce, but we have to eat fat dollops of it every year so she doesn't skin us alive and roast us for dinner next Thanksgiving. My mouth is already watering in protest just thinking about it.

The rest of the food is carefully laid out on matching porcelain dishes on the quartz countertops. I plop my bright aqua casserole dish down next to the tasteful array, and Alex chokes on the drink he's just picked up.

I shoot him a glare.

Mom spins around and tuts. "Ellie, please. Can you put it on one of the nice dishes? This isn't a homeless shelter."

My eyes connect with Alex's, and I try not to cringe at Mom's uncouth comment.

"Of course. I was just about to do that," I assure her.

I was, in fact, about to pull out the disposable plastic serving spoon from my bag and shove it into the casserole and call it a day. Alex knows it too. His eyes glimmer conspiratorially, and he opens his mouth to say something, but I chuck one of the dinner rolls at him before he gets a chance.

"Elizabeth!" Mom screeches, and I swivel around slowly, swallowing hard.

"It slipped," I rush to say, but Mom doesn't even seem to notice. Her eyes are fixed on my casserole. "What's wrong?"

"I told you we were having a clean Thanksgiving meal this year," she sputters. I glance around in confusion, and only then do I notice that all the dishes on the counter are vegetables. There are roasted carrots, zucchini, and squash, and what looks to be a beet salad. I don't see a single casserole, pie, or fatty food group represented.

"Your father and I are on a diet."

The three of us stand there in tense silence as I rack my brain for literally any single word in the English language to say in response.

Dad walks into the kitchen at that moment and looks around before frowning at my dish. "Didn't your mom tell you we were having a healthy Thanksgiving this year?"

"You know what," Mom says, and I cringe inwardly because it's *never* good when she starts a sentence like that. "Just leave it. Today is a day of celebration," she says, sharing a weighted look with Dad.

"That it is," Dad responds cryptically.

Before I can ask why they've suddenly turned into Richard and Emily Gilmore when Rory decided to go to Yale, the doorbell rings. Mom and Dad hurry to answer it, leaving Alex and me alone in the kitchen wearing matching confused expressions.

"What was *that*?" I ask.

"Maybe Dad got Viagra," Alex answers. He picks up the roll I threw at him from off the floor and shoves it into his mouth.

I want to claw my eyes out. "Why would you give me that mental picture?"

"Mom does look incredibly satisfied."

"I will throw up on this floor."

Mom, Dad, Alex, and Kelsey all enter the kitchen at that exact moment. "Why are you throwing up on the floor?" Dad asks, eyeing me warily.

I ignore his comment, using my brother and sister-in-law as a distraction. "Adam, Kelsey, you're here!"

"A complete shock, since we were invited," Adam deadpans, wrapping me in a hug.

"Alex thinks Dad got Viagra," I whisper in his ear.

He makes a gagging noise in my ear. "They do seem unusually happy."

I back up, forcing the grimace to stay off my face, and hug Kelsey.

"So what are we celebrating?" I ask when the room falls into stilted silence again.

"Dinner first," Mom says, clasping her hands together. "Make sure to get extra cranberry sauce, Ellie. I know how much you love it."

Okay, so maybe Adam and Alex only serve themselves the tiniest bit of sauce every year. I'm the only one who loads up my plate with it, forces the too-tart sludge down my throat, and raves about it in hopes of winning my mother's affection.

Mom and Dad shoot each other surreptitious glances all throughout the meal, managing to make me so sick to my stomach that I push my food around on my plate rather than eat it. I barely contribute to the conversation, although I do momentarily perk up when Alex tells us he bought the condo downtown.

It's not until the end of the meal that I realize Adam and Alex didn't have to play buffer for me even once, which makes me irrationally anxious.

When my nerves are ratcheted so high I can feel them in my throat, Adam asks, "So Mom, Dad, how's the business?"

Their eyes swivel to me, and I swallow hard, but for once, it's not disappointment lining their features. "We actually have some exciting news," Mom says, her voice carrying the hint of enthusiasm it only does when she's managed to get a free meal after complaining at a restaurant.

"You're pregnant," Alex announces theatrically around a bite of what I think is his fifth roll.

Mom gives him a flat glare.

"No," Dad says. "It has something to do with Elizabeth."

My heart stops in my chest, and a whirring starts in my ears. I have no idea where this conversation is going to go, and it's *terrifying.*

My phone call with Cam last night plays back through my head. I told him I'd do whatever I needed to in order to fix things with my parents, but I'm suddenly scared of what that might require of me.

"What is it?" I ask finally, unable to stand the expectant silence. It feels like teetering on a cliff and willingly jumping as I wait for them to answer.

"Ellie won Property Manager of the Year," Dad says, a smile breaking out across his face.

"I—what?"

Mom nods vigorously, wearing a gleeful expression I haven't seen pointed at me in years.

"Congrats, Ellie," Kelsey says with a proud grin.

Alex squeezes my hand. "That's huge!"

"It's completely anonymous, of course," Mom says, as if we thought she would have picked me otherwise. "It's based solely on numbers and resident reviews. Ellie and The Flats at Inglewood had more five-star reviews than any other property this year."

The words fill me up, crowding into every empty space that has been waiting for their approval and pride for the past few years. I can see it on their faces, in the rosy tint of Mom's cheeks and the crinkles in the corners of my dad's eyes. I can see it, but somehow, it feels a little hollow.

Just the tiniest bit.

This moment should be everything I've ever wished for. It should be validation that I am, in fact, good at my job, despite my more relaxed approach to business. It should be exhilaration at proving myself. It should be so many things, but it's not.

Because there's only one person I want to celebrate with, and he can't be here with me.

I force a smile onto my face. "I can't believe it."

"Neither can we," Mom says sarcastically from behind her hand.

The hit lands, swift and sure, to my middle, although I don't even think she was aiming. Suddenly, the room feels too small. I want Cam here, his hand on my thigh under the table, his voice in my ear calling me *Daisy* and telling me he always knew I could do it.

"Mom," Alex warns.

"What?" She looks genuinely confused, like she has absolutely no idea how her careless words affect her sensitive daughter.

CHAPTER TWENTY-THREE

I look down at my lap, trying to hold the hot press of tears back. I imagine Cam's hand there, anchoring me, but see my phone instead. An idea forms, and before I can think better of it, I say, "Oh, no."

"What's wrong?" Dad asks, his brows pinching together.

"We got an emergency maintenance request, and Gary is off today."

I push back from the table, but stop when Dad says, "We've actually been meaning to talk to you about him. We think you should fire him."

The words lodge in my brain. *Fire him.* "You want me to fire Gary?"

"We noticed he's been calling out an awful lot. You really need a more reliable maintenance worker, Ellie. Remember what happened with that resident's heat?" Mom asks with a knowing look. "Things like this can't keep happening after you're announced Property Manager of the Year. It will reflect poorly on the whole company if your property isn't doing well."

"Maybe we should let Ellie get to that resident's request. Now isn't really an appropriate time to be having this conversation," Adam says gently but firmly, and I shoot him a thankful glance.

"Of course, of course," Dad says, pushing out of his chair. Mom follows, and they each give me a quick hug, something that's few and far between these days. "We're proud of you," Dad whispers.

The words should be everything I've ever dreamed of, but I can't help but notice how cheap it feels. This is the first time in so long that I can remember hearing that from them, and it's only after I won a prestigious award, one that will no doubt reflect greatly on them.

I swallow against the lump rising in my throat. "Thank you."

"We can't wait to present it at the gala," Mom says.

Every year, my parents throw an end of the year gala for all their employees. It's basically an award show and excuse for everyone to get dressed up and have a holiday party. I don't know how I'll make it through this year, listening to them talk about me and knowing they wouldn't say these things if I hadn't won.

"We'll even let you bring a plus-one this year," Mom announces, and it is a treat, since no one is allowed to bring guests to the gala.

It makes me deflate a little, though, knowing the only person I'd want to come with me is the one person who can't.

THERE'S NO MAINTENANCE CALL, obviously, but I head to the office anyway. I can't bear to go home alone, and Ethel's family arrived last night for the holiday, so I can't stop by her place.

The office is quiet, almost stale, like it knows no one should be here today. It's a day for family, for thankfulness, not a day for business.

I log on to my computer anyway and check my emails. I finally get around to organizing my file cabinet and wash the empty teacups littering my desk.

It's not until my phone rings that I notice the time, that the sun set long ago and the office is only illuminated by the glow of my lamps.

CHAPTER TWENTY-THREE

I pick up my phone, seeing it's a FaceTime call from Cam. My heart ratchets in my chest, the feeling calming and exhilarating all at once.

Cam is smiling when I answer, his face only illuminated by his screen in the darkness. "Hey, you. How did it go today?" His brows bunch together a second later. "Are you in your office?"

I want to tell him everything I'm feeling, but I know it won't do any good. Telling him I wanted him to be there with me today, that I wish he could be there with me at the gala, won't change the fact that he can't.

So I plaster on a smile, hoping he doesn't see right through it. "Yeah, I had to stop in here for a bit. But things went really well."

"Yeah? How was the casserole?"

I look at the baking dish on my desk, the one I've been eating from with a plastic fork. "It was perfect." I change the subject before he can ask more about it. "That's not the best part, though."

"What's the best part?"

"Every year my parents host this holiday gala where they give out awards. I won Property Manager of the Year."

Cam's mouth splits in a grin. "Really? Ellie, that's *amazing*."

I tap my fingers on the desk and force myself to keep smiling. "Yeah, it's a really big deal."

"I'm so proud of you."

Somehow, when he says it, it feels like a bandage being pressed over an open wound. It's not healed, not even close, but it will be. That's all I can hope for.

I give him a smile, and although I have to work a little harder for it than normal, it comes easier than it did a few moments ago. "Thanks, Cam. I miss you."

"I miss you too. How was the rest of the day? How were your brothers?"

"They were good. Adam and Kelsey kept the conversation going, especially whenever Alex tried to steer it somewhere controversial. I swear he loves to push their buttons. Twenty-nine years old, and they still don't know what to do with him," I answer with a laugh.

"They sound like fun," Cam says, his mouth quirking in a little grin that makes my heart flip. I wasn't kidding when I said I missed him. I don't know how, when he's only been gone a few days, but I've quickly grown used to having him around. I don't know what I'm going to do when he leaves. I shut the thought down, knowing nothing good can come from me thinking about this when I'm already so raw.

"I think you'd love them." I hesitate for a moment, then say, "Maybe you could meet them sometime."

Cam smiles, this time full and genuine. "I'd like that."

Something chirps loudly in the background, maybe a cricket or treefrog. "Where are you? I thought you were inside."

He flips the camera around so I can see in front of him. He's on a porch that's illuminated under the full moon. In the distance, I can see rows and rows of trees, framed by tall, rolling mountains.

"That's beautiful," I breathe.

He doesn't flip the camera back around, but I can still hear the smile in his voice. "Yeah, it is."

I keep staring at the view, my eyes eating up every inch of the screen. It feels...familiar, homey.

"Hey," Cam says, jumping up. He walks to the edge of the porch and down the stairs, his phone jostling as he goes. "Go outside."

I look around my dim office. "What? Why?"

He flips the camera around so I can see his face in the moonlight. "Come on. Just—oh no, I almost just said *just go with it*." He rolls his eyes heavenward. "That would thrill Wes to no end."

I can't help the laugh that slips out. I love that he can make me laugh and smile, even though that ache is still spreading through my chest. So I stand, walking out of the office, because I know whatever he must have planned will be enough to buoy my spirits a little more.

The wind whips around me as I step outside, and I wish I'd brought my coat. "What now?"

He squints at the screen. "It's too bright in the parking lot. Go around back."

"Is this you finally seizing your chance to murder me? Is someone going to snatch me when I go behind the building?"

"You've got me all figured out. I thought that was going to work," he says, echoing his words from that first night.

"You remember what I said about the canning jars?"

"You remember what I said back?"

He'd told me he doubted there was anything I wouldn't look good in. And just like that night, it sends a shiver through me once more.

"Okay, I'm back here," I tell him when I reach the back of the building.

"Look up," he says, his voice soft as cashmere. When I do, I'm staring at the stars, a black canvas pin pricked with light. They wink at me, making my heart settle the anxious rhythm it's beat all day.

"Wow," I breathe.

"I wish I could be there to celebrate with you." My throat thickens at his words, at how he somehow knew exactly what

I wanted. "I thought maybe we could do this together instead. Me and you under the stars."

I look back up, taking in the view. "Me and you under the stars, Daisy."

Twenty-Four

CAMDEN

My dad is the only one awake when I return to the house from a sunrise photo session the morning after Thanksgiving. He's seated on one of the rocking chairs I was in last night when I FaceTimed with Ellie, a cup of coffee in hand.

He nods to another mug sitting on the table between the two rocking chairs. "Poured you a cup. Figured you'd be wandering back here soon enough."

I settle into the chair, pressing off with my feet, and wrap my chilled hands around the mug. Dad drinks coffee so strong it should probably be illegal, but I'd welcome any warm beverage right about now.

"Where'd you take pictures this morning?"

When I still lived at home, I used to get up most mornings and drive somewhere around town to take photos at sunrise. I loved capturing the way the light hit all the different places in town—the way it crested the hills and glistened on the river, or the way bounced off the shop windows in the square.

My favorite spot to go, though, was right in our backyard. I'd walk through the fields to my aunt and uncle's farm, dew seeping through my shoes and damp fog making my hair curl up on the ends. I took photos of every square inch of that farm, in every light imaginable. It's where I fell in love with photography, where I figured out how I wanted to spend the rest of my life.

It's where I went today when I was feeling confused, where I've been dying to go since everything started feeling so muddled. "The farm."

"Mmm," Dad says, blowing on his coffee before taking a loud sip. "I should've figured."

"Can't stay away for long."

"I'm glad you're back, even if it's only for a little bit."

"Me too," I say on an exhale.

"You liking it in Nashville?" Dad asks, gaze focused on the sun making its way over the mountains in the distance.

I take a sip of coffee, letting it warm me from the inside out. "Yeah, I really do. I, uh." I pause and flick my eyes over to him. "I've been thinking about staying there—not going back to LA."

This gets his attention. "Really?"

I shrug, trying for nonchalant, even though I feel anything but. It's one thing to *know* I don't want to go back, but it's quite another to actually make it happen. "I don't know." I let out a deep breath. "I've just been kind of restless there," I say, and my mind snags on Mom's words from the other day—how she said she could tell I'd been missing something for years. *I didn't realize I'd been missing anything, but I can kind of see it now. It's all I've been able to think about, really.*

"I have to admit, I've wondered why you stayed."

I look at him. "I guess I just didn't realize I wasn't happy anymore." Looking back now, I can see it, even before Wes left. His moving away, pursuing his own happiness, was just the catalyst to make me see my own dissatisfaction.

Dad shrugs like *fair enough*, and asks, "So now that you know, what are you going to do about it?"

CHAPTER TWENTY-FOUR

The coffee cup is almost too warm, burning my hands, but I don't let go. I need something to tether me to this moment when my thoughts, fears, and doubts threaten to pull me under. "I think I'm going to stay—find a new apartment and accept the job Wes offered me." *See what happens with Ellie.* Nashville has a lot to offer, and I want it all.

"I think that's a good idea," Dad says. "Have you told Hazel?"

I turn back to the mountains, to the rolling hills that are just barely tipped with white. "Not yet. I just decided."

"She will be happy for you," he says, but I wonder if he wishes I wouldn't leave her there all alone. "Maybe you can convince her to come too."

I let out a little laugh. "Yeah, maybe."

"It will be nice having you closer." He turns to face me, eyes twinkling. "You can bring that girl to visit."

I sigh, shaking my head. "I'm going to kill Hazel."

"You're seriously going to make me work at the store? On my vacation?" I ask my mom later that morning. We're all seated around the table, plates loaded with pancakes, sausage, eggs, and, of course, cinnamon apples from this fall's harvest.

"It's Black Friday. Of course I'm putting you to work."

"It's Black Friday in *Fontana Ridge*," I clarify. "This isn't New York City. There's not going to be a line of people waiting to get into the store."

Mom gives me a withering look. "Just because you're some big city boy now doesn't mean you get to skip out on our *small-town* event," she says, and Hazel chokes on her orange juice. Mom swivels to face her. "I don't know what you're laughing at. I've got you down for a shift too."

Hazel throws her hands up in the air. "Stevie and I are supposed to meet Wren for coffee! I hardly ever get to see her when I'm in town, and she's been my best friend since kindergarten."

"Tell her to stop by the store," Mom says with a smug smile.

"I would like to circle back to that *big city boy* comment," I say. "You signed me up to play Joseph in the live Nativity scene at Christmas last year, and I was only here for three days. I think that gets me out of my shift today."

Mom pats my cheek. "You made a beautiful Joseph, and you really made quite an impression on Mary. She asked me for your number the day after you left."

"*That's* how she got my number? She wouldn't leave me alone for weeks. I had to pretend like I changed my number."

"Yes, and it really hurt her feelings. She's been avoiding me for months. Used to come into the store constantly," she says, a wistful tone lilting her voice. "Now she never does. Seems like a good place to avoid her…"

I roll my eyes. "Fine, I'll work *one shift*."

I'm deeply regretting my decision later that afternoon. Although Hazel agreed to a shift, she has yet to come relieve me, and the store has been *wild.* This is *Fontana Ridge*. I didn't even think there were this many citizens.

After checking out my most recent customer, I finally catch a break. The store is blissfully empty and a complete wreck. I set about rearranging the scrambled displays.

Mom makes her own line of soaps, perfumes, oils, and candles from ingredients grown on the farm to sell in the shop.

CHAPTER TWENTY-FOUR

They're a huge hit with the locals and tourists, and she's almost run out of stock.

I'm spinning one of the perfume bottles around when the name catches my eye—*Daisy'd and Confused*. Underneath it reads, *subtle notes of daisy, peony, and fresh apples*. I pop off the lid and spritz the air.

Ellie.

That hauntingly familiar scent that reminds me of *home*, it smells like Ellie. Like daisies and peonies in a field, like sunrise peeking through the apple trees.

I stare at the perfume in my hand, trying to shake myself from the trance. It's probably just the name, *Daisy'd and Confused*, that's throwing me off. But no, it still smells just like her when I sniff again. Like that crook where her neck meets her shoulder. I can almost feel her soft skin beneath my lips.

The shop's front door opens, and my head snaps up. Hazel, Stevie, and their friend Wren plow through the door, laughing loud enough to wake the dead. "We're here for my shift," Hazel announces.

I secure the lid back on the perfume and try to pull myself from my thoughts. Ellie's name doesn't stop pounding through me with each beat of my heart.

Hazel stops walking, eyes catching on my face. "Hey, what's wrong?"

"Nothing," I assure her, but it's not quite true.

Daisy'd and Confused, to be sure.

Twenty-Five

ELLIE

Ethel hollers for me to come in before I even finish knocking. I smile to myself and push open the door. She's standing in the kitchen, and phallic-shaped chocolates cover her counter.

"Ethel," I say, my voice stern. "You're not supposed to be up yet."

She rolls her scooter around the island, a pan of candy in one hand. "Pish posh. I don't think those doctors really know what they're talking about. I've been cooped up for three weeks. I can roll around on this contraption just fine. And some bachelorette girlies messaged me on that FaceGram, asking me to make them some chocolates so I thought I'd make myself useful again."

"You were supposed to put on *FaceGram* that you're unavailable until your ankle heals."

She scoots forward, gently pressing a finger to the top of one of the candies to see if it's hardened enough yet. "You worry too much."

"Let's just sit down for a bit," I say, placing a hand on her back and nudging her toward the dining table.

Ethel presses her lips together, blowing air out her nose, but listens to me. Once she's settled with her foot propped on another chair, I head back into the kitchen and start loading her dishwasher.

CHAPTER TWENTY-FIVE

"How was your Thanksgiving?" I ask her.

As I fill her dishwasher and clean her kitchen, Ethel tells me all about having her family in town. The whole family, her great-grandkids included, came to see her since she couldn't make the trip to them this year.

There's an ache in my chest as I listen to her. Ethel has had a full life, one brimming with love and family. I hate that voice in the back of my head that tells me I'm going to have to choose one or the other.

When I finish in the kitchen and settle on the couch across from her, Ethel asks, "How was yours?"

I want to lie and say it was great. I want to tell her about the award and skip the part where I've felt hollow ever since, just like I did with Cam.

"I won Property Manager of the Year for the company."

Ethel's face softens into one of her rare smiles. "Ellie, that's wonderful. Are you happy?"

The question takes me off guard—so direct and to the point and unexpected.

Maybe it's what loosens my tongue and makes the truth slip out before I can consider it. "No."

"Why's that?" Ethel asks.

My fingers find a rhythm against my thigh. I wish I could put what I'm feeling into words, that I knew why this ache wouldn't leave me. "I don't know."

Ethel sits back in her chair. "Did I ever tell you about my late husband?"

I blink at the abrupt change in subject. I expected some wise words or sage advice.

Her lips tip up at the corners, like she knows what I'm thinking. "Have I ever told you about how we met?"

Ethel's told me so many things about Charles—things I *really* didn't want to know. But she's also told me bits and pieces of their love story—what he looked like on their wedding day, how he proposed, what his cologne smelled like, how he made her tea every morning and brought it to her in bed.

I realize, though, that she's never mentioned how they met, so I shake my head.

She crosses one veiny, paper-white leg over her booted foot and brings a hand to her chin. "We had a bit of a forbidden love story," she says, and I find myself leaning forward, eager to hear more. "He was a rich boy from the nice part of town, and I was poor and lived on the wrong side of the tracks. My father actually owed his father some money."

When my mouth falls open at that, she says, "I won't get into all that, but regardless, we were not destined to be together. In fact, it was downright prohibited. I told my mama right when he first started showing interest in me, and she told me I needed to stay far, far away from him."

This story feels eerily familiar in a way that makes goose bumps prick my skin. "What did you do?"

Ethel shrugs. "For a while, I tried. I didn't want to upset them and make more issues for my daddy, so I stayed away." She pauses, her eyes focused on a spot above my head as if she's watching the story play out on home videos on the wall behind me. "But Charles was relentless, and he made me *happy*."

She turns her eyes back on me. "It was just as bad as I imagined it would be," she says simply.

"What was just as bad?"

"When our families found out. It wasn't pretty, and I won't sugarcoat it." Her expression softens, and she leans forward

CHAPTER TWENTY-FIVE

once more, lowering her voice. "There was a long time when all we had was each other."

I'm quiet for a long moment, absorbing her story. "Was he worth it?"

She seems to choose her next words carefully, as if trying to line them up perfectly in her mind. "I think choosing my happiness, and Charles choosing his, was worth it. For us, that happened to be each other. It made every hardship bearable, every trial endurable. When our families finally came around, I was proud of what we had built. We hadn't just chosen each other, we'd chosen to build a life together that we were proud of, even if they weren't."

Ethel finally looks back at me, her eyes boring into mine. "What makes you happy, Ellie?"

Her words rattle through me like pinballs in a machine, shaking me to my core. I hate that I can't answer it. I hate that I don't *know*.

My phone buzzes on the couch next to me, saving me from answering. I look down at the screen and see Gary's name flashing across it.

"I've got to take this," I tell Ethel, and she waves me off. She pushes up onto her one good foot and rolls her scooter toward the bathroom.

Swiping open my phone, I say, "Hey, Gary. What's up?"

"Hey, Ellie. I'm really sorry to do this, but I'm going to have to head out early today. I have a few more requests that I won't be able to get done."

I hold in that sigh that threatens to release from my lungs. I'm tempted, so very tempted, to ask him why. Maybe I should, but I know Gary. He's been here since before I became manager, and until recently, he's always been a reliable employee.

"Okay, no problem, Gary. Email them to me, and I'll get them done."

Today is my day off, since Sadie and I rotate Saturday shifts, but this hopefully shouldn't take too long.

"Thanks, Ellie. You're the best."

We're saying our goodbyes as Ethel returns, scooting through the apartment. "Got to go?"

"Yeah," I say, standing from the couch. "Gary has to leave, so I'm going to finish up a few of his jobs."

Ethel stops me with a hand on my arm. We're both short, just standing a few inches over five feet, but I'm tall enough that she has to look up at me. I can't hide anything from her this way—can't duck my head and hope my hair conceals my expression.

"Are you going to be okay?"

I hate that she asks if I'm going to be okay, that she can tell that I'm not. I feel like I'm wearing my heart on my sleeve, barely protecting it from anyone who may try and injure it.

"Yeah, I'll be okay."

I have to be, even if I don't know how yet.

I'M STANDING ATOP A ladder the next time my phone rings. I pull it from my back pocket and swipe it open without looking. "Hello?"

"Hey," Cam says, and his voice eases a little of the tension in my shoulders. "What are you up to?"

"I'm in someone's apartment changing an air filter."

"Do people really not change their own air filters?"

CHAPTER TWENTY-FIVE

"You would be absolutely *shocked* at the number of things people won't do on their own," I tell him.

"Need some help?"

I almost tip off the ladder. "You're home?"

"Yeah, I'm home," he says, and I can hear the smile in his voice.

"I thought you weren't coming back until tomorrow." I was planning to show up on Sadie's doorstep and beg her to hang out with me.

"I wanted to come back early."

His words rattle through me as I close the air vent. "Any reason?"

"Laundry," he says easily, and I work to hold in my grin. "But I could probably be persuaded to do something else."

I can't help the grin that blooms across my face, the one that warms me from the inside out. "Okay, meet me at my apartment in ten."

Cam is waiting at my door for me after I've returned the ladder to the office, and I hurry across the parking lot to meet him. His broad frame is stretched out, languid limbs and lean lines, as he reclines against my door, scrolling through his phone. He looks up when my feet crunch on the dried leaves, and butterflies cascade through my stomach at the look in his eyes.

They're dark like the most delectable of chocolate and track my every movement as I get closer to him. With each step, I move a little faster until I'm basically running, hurtling myself into his arms.

I'm thankful for the waning late afternoon sunlight, the darkness that has just crept in. Instead of worrying about others seeing my arms snake around Cam's neck or his grip on my waist, I can revel in it. I can breathe in his decadent cologne and push my fingers beneath his collar. Here in the twilight, with the first stars blinking awake for the night, I can just *be*.

"Hey," Cam says into the crook of my neck. His lips brush the skin there, and I shiver. He backs up, hands sliding up and down my arms. "You're cold. Let's go inside."

I'm not cold—in fact, I'm on *fire*—but I don't say that. Instead, I unlock my door with shaking hands, and he follows me inside. I've just clicked it shut when his arms wrap around from behind me, drawing me to his front. I can feel each rise and fall of his chest against my back, each breath against my neck that signals that he's *here*.

"I missed you," I whisper. I didn't realize how much until this moment.

He dips his face to my shoulder and hums, "Me too," and I feel it in my toes.

Spinning around to face him, I realize how close we are. My back is pinned against the door, and Cam leans forward until his elbow hits the wall next to my head. His other hand finds my hip, and his thumb makes a lazy swipe against it. I don't even know if he knows he's doing it.

"Why did you come home early?" I ask, and his finger stops moving.

His gaze focuses on mine, softening into something so sweet and sincere that my breath catches. "I wanted to see you."

I push up to my tiptoes and close the little distance between us, brushing my mouth against his cheek. I don't know why he hasn't kissed me again, but he has his reasons, and I want to respect them, even if I want to press my lips against his until we're breathless.

"That's a good answer," I whisper against his cheek.

"Want to go to a hockey game with me?"

I drop back to the balls of my feet, the back of my head hitting the door as I peer up at him. His hand slips into my hair, massaging the spot without thinking.

"You want to go to a hockey game?" I ask, unable to keep the incredulity from my voice.

His mouth tips into a grin. "I do like sports, you know. I don't normally spend every evening watching scary movies on my couch back in LA."

"Oh," I say. "Well, we could have turned on sports sometimes. If you wanted to watch boys hit a hockey ball into a net, you could have asked."

He sucks his lips between his teeth, fighting a smile. "While that would be incredibly fun, watching boys hit a hockey *ball* into a net in an *arena* would be even more fun."

I drum my fingers up against the doorframe. "That's very…public," I tell him, although I hate having to point it out.

Cam leans back, no longer holding back his smile. "I actually had an idea."

Twenty-Six

ELLIE

"We're at the thrift store," I say dumbly, staring at the sign from the passenger seat of Cam's SUV.

He puts the car in park and gives me a sheepish smile, the glow from the streetlamps illuminating the barest hint of pink flushing his cheeks. "I had an idea, but we don't have to do it if you think it's dumb."

An overwhelming surge of affection for him expands in my chest. Here in darkness, with that stubborn flop of hair falling over his brows, his eyes so sincere as they assess mine, I want to give him anything—everything.

"What's your idea?"

His hands flex on the steering wheel. "I thought we could be Dave and Daisy tonight. We can pick out some disguises for each other." He nods toward the storefront. "Then we can go to the game and not worry about anyone we know recognizing us."

The idea is…terrible. How much can we really camouflage ourselves with thrift shop clothing? But I also can't deny how fun this sounds, how cute it is that he thought of it, or how much I really, really want to go somewhere with him and just be.

His gaze is intense on my face, watching for my reaction, so he smiles when I do—a slow unfurling one that reaches his eyes and makes my heart skip a beat.

Leaning across the console, he presses a kiss to my forehead. "After you, Daisy."

The thrift store smells like they all do—musty, with a hint of mothballs and cigarette smoke—but it feels like a romantic getaway with Cam's hand in mine.

He stops in front of the clothing aisles and flashes me a grin. "Okay, we kind of need to hurry. Let's meet at the dressing rooms in ten with outfits."

I turn toward the women's section, but Cam stops me with his hands on my shoulders, spinning me to face the men's. "You shop for me, and I'll shop for you."

I don't know why that statement makes my skin flush hot and my stomach bottom out, but it does.

"Ten minutes," I repeat, and then we split up into different sides of the store.

I know it's going to be cold in the arena, so I head straight for the coats. Cam's outfit of choice tends to be a Henley that stretches over his chest in the most distracting of ways, dark jeans, and his well-loved corduroy jacket, so I reach for the exact opposite—a leather jacket. It's black and worn in all the right places, soft around the collar and fading at the elbows.

I'm practically salivating imagining him in it.

After searching through the aisles, I locate a black hoodie and black jeans.

Tonight, *Dave* is going to look like a sexy bad boy, and *I am here for it.*

I'm waiting for Cam by the fitting rooms when he finds me a few minutes later. I can't help but laugh at the pile of beige thrown over his arm. His eyes twinkle at me in return.

He reaches out and fits a white beanie with a huge poof atop it onto my head. "What did you pick for me?"

Cam tends to dress in warm colors—moss greens, camel browns, deep navys—and I've rarely seen him in black, so this outfit is particularly different from what he normally wears. He eyes the pieces as I hold them up individually, and he runs his fingers over the smooth leather of the jacket.

"I think I can work with this." His voice is a deep baritone I feel beneath my skin.

I take my outfit from Cam, and duck under his arm as he opens the dressing room for me. His eyes linger on me, standing beneath the fluorescent lighting in a thrift shop fitting room, as he says, "See you on the other side, Daisy."

He closes the door, leaving me alone in my stall. I can hear zippers and rustling on the other side, and *it is distracting*. I can imagine the smooth wall of chest being revealed inch by inch as he tugs the shirt over his head. Can imagine his hands at his belt buckle...

That is enough imagination for today.

I strip out of my outfit—turquoise leather pants and a pink oversize sweater—and stare at the items Cam picked for me. He found a white turtleneck that I would actually wear, probably with some fun patterned pants. Instead, he paired it with beige joggers and a calf-length beige faux fur jacket. He even managed to find white sneakers that are exactly the right size. With the white beanie covering my head and the rest of the hair tucked into my heavy coat, you can hardly recognize me. No one I know would ever expect to find me dressed like this.

"Does it all fit?" Cam asks, and I'm surprised to hear his voice right outside my door.

I swing it open, and I'm completely caught off guard by the sight of him in the outfit I chose. I expected him to look good, but I never could have imagined him looking *this* good. He looks impossibly dark in this outfit, his tan skin and navy eyes accentuating it perfectly. He looks like an angel of death, and I would gladly let him claim me.

"It fits," he says with an easy smile, completely oblivious to the way I've died and come alive again.

"Yeah," I breathe. "Yours too."

He shrugs, the jacket pulling against his broad shoulders. "Jacket is a little tight, but it'll do." He flips up the hood on his sweatshirt. "And I can do this to be even more inconspicuous."

I'm beginning to doubt this plan, because if the goal is for people to *not* notice him, we have failed miserably. Women for miles will not be able to keep their eyes to themselves, and I don't like the pinch that thought causes in my gut.

"You ready?" Cam asks, nodding toward the front. "I figured we could just ask them to ring it up on us and bag our old stuff."

"Yeah, okay." I grab my stuff from the fitting room and follow him to the front. The woman behind the register looks at us with a disbelieving expression, and I don't blame her. The idea of walking out of here in used clothing that hasn't been washed weirds me out a little, but I also know, with Cam's eyes twinkling at mine and his hand somehow burning through the multiple layers of fabric at the small of my back, that I would do almost anything to keep this night going.

The arena is packed when we finally find our seats—nosebleeds, with few others around us—two hotdogs, nachos, and a drink to share in hand.

We sit down right as the game starts, and noise erupts all around us.

"So Dave, tell me all about hockey. Is it like football? I used to cheer for our football team in high school."

"Basically the exact same," he says with a wide grin, taking his hotdog from me.

"Really?"

"No, not at all."

"Well, shoot," I respond, reaching for one of the chips in his lap and dunking it in the artificial cheese sauce.

"How have you lived in Nashville your whole life and never been to a hockey game?"

I shrug, watching big men skate around on teeny, tiny skates on the ice down below. "I don't really like their jersey colors."

Cam snorts a laugh next to me, and I look to see his hand pressed to his mouth, a huge bite of his hotdog bulging in his cheek.

I chew my lip, fighting back a smile. "What? That shade of yellow is atrocious."

He swallows, bumping his shoulder into mine. "So you used to cheer, huh?"

"I know it's hard to imagine," I say sarcastically. "Me in a brightly colored uniform, yelling at people about how great they're doing."

Cam's mouth splits into a grin, and despite the chill, it makes me feel warm, deep in my sternum. "I can picture that perfectly," he tells me.

CHAPTER TWENTY-SIX

I could get lost in his eyes all night and never watch this game, so I force my gaze back to the ice. "Who are we playing?"

I feel his shoulder leaning into mine, feel his weight settle against me in the most delicious of ways. "The Detroit Warriors."

"Are they any good?" I ask. Right now, they all look the same to me as they skate around, spraying ice and slapping their sticks at their feet.

"They got knocked out of the playoffs in the second round last year."

"Oh, sure," I say with a shrug of my shoulders.

I sense his grin before I turn to confirm it. "Yes, Daisy, they're good." He points to one of the giants on the ice. "That guy, Brent Jean, is one of the best offensive players in the league."

"Offense, you say? I've got a cheer for that. *Be aggressive! B-E aggr*—"

Cam stops me midclap, covering my hands with his and bringing his mouth to my ear. "Wrong team," he whispers, his breath warm against my chilled skin.

"Oh, yeah," I say with a sheepish smile.

His eyes linger on my face, as if cataloging this moment, saving it to examine later. "You're really cute. You know that, Daisy?"

I suck in my lips and try to stop the blush that threatens to spread across my cheeks. "You're not too bad yourself, Dave."

We spend the rest of the game like that—eating way too much food, Cam explaining to me why the big men have to sit in the tiny box, and leaning into each other for no other reason than we want to. No one recognizes us, *of course*, because we're not the royal family. I shouldn't have worried about it so much, but it's been kind of fun to be Daisy and Dave tonight, to let go of that gnawing feeling in the back of my head that tries to remind me that this is a mistake.

By the time we pull back into the parking lot at The Flats, I'm pleasantly sleepy, still slightly chilled from the arena, and a little itchy from the unfamiliar detergent these clothes were washed in.

Cam shuts off the car, helps me out, and follows me to my door. I'm still leaning into him, seeking his warmth and steadiness, still unwilling to let the easygoing night come to an end.

My plastic bag of clothes rustles in Cam's hand as he follows me into my apartment. When the door clicks shut behind us, I give in to the urge to close the distance between us. I've been feeling it all night, that tug between us, and I don't want to fight it anymore.

My head lands on his chest, and my arms slide around his waist. He drops the bag of clothes, and they make a soft thud at my feet. Then his hand edges under my hair, freeing it from my jacket and hat, and his fingers trace circles on the back of my neck. He drops his head into the crook of my shoulder, breathing me in, and I shiver against him.

I feel the sharp intake of his breath against my skin, feel the tension between us grow thick and palpable. I want to lean into it. I want to slip my hand beneath his collar and feel his heartbeat. I want to feel his lips and teeth and tongue against

CHAPTER TWENTY-SIX

mine. I want to kiss him, and I don't know what we're waiting for.

"Dave?" I whisper.

His breath fans against my neck. "Yeah, Daisy?"

"Why haven't you kissed me?"

Twenty-Seven

CAMDEN

Why haven't you kissed me?

The words rattle around in my head, and for the life of me, I can't think of an answer. All I can think about is how soft Ellie's skin feels against my fingertips, how good and familiar the spot on her neck smells, how much I want to taste her lips and see if they're just as sweet as I remember.

I know they would be.

Kissing Ellie would be like indulging myself in the most decadent of desserts, the ones you eat slowly to savor them, the ones that are too rich to rush.

And I *want that*.

One word sticks in my brain, though. *Dave.* Not *Cam, why haven't you kissed me?* But *Dave*, and it puts a sour taste in my mouth. I know we've been role playing tonight, being other people so we won't get caught being *us*, but I don't want to kiss her as Dave and Daisy. I want to kiss her as Camden and Ellie. I want it to be real, and I want her to want it like that.

I pull back, my eyes lingering on the pout of her lips, her half-lidded gaze, the way her body sways to fill the space between us.

"Ellie, who am I?"

She blinks up at me, twin half-moons forming between her brows. "What?"

"Who am I?"

"You're Camden," she says, although her voice is uncertain.

I reach up and twist a lock of her hair around my finger, loving the silky, smooth texture of it against my skin. I bet she's soft everywhere. "I am," I say, and my voice comes out a touch gravelly. "And I still will be tomorrow. And I don't want to kiss you unless you're 100 percent okay with that."

Ellie stares at me, confusion lining her features. "What do you mean?"

I swallow, trying to figure out how to articulate the thoughts running through my head, the ones that have become so clouded under the influence of her heady scent. "I'm not Sam, the guy you met downtown, or Dave, the guy you kissed on a dare. I'm Cam, your resident. I'm Cam, the one who makes you tea before bed and watches scary movies with you on your couch. I'm Cam, and I'll still be Cam tomorrow and all the days after. I don't want to kiss you until you know you want *me*, with everything that entails."

I watch her absorb my words. Her throat bobs, her tongue darts out to lick her lips, and her brow wrinkles even further. "Okay."

"Okay?"

"I can respect that," she says with a small nod.

My hands reach for her of their own accord, grasping her arms and squeezing. "Thank you."

Her head comes to rest on my chest, and I feel the heat of her breath through the thin cotton of my shirt. "Hey, Cam?"

"Yeah, Ellie?" I ask, and I can't help but smile at the way the conversation mirrors the one from a moment ago.

"I'm not quite ready yet," she whispers.

My arms tighten around her middle, erasing the space between us. "That's okay."

"I'm sorry."

"Don't be sorry," I say into her hair, loving the way it feels against my lips. "Just know that I want this, and I'm willing to wait for it, but it's up to you to decide when things change between us."

Ellie nods, her nose brushing up against my sternum. "I think that's for the best." She leans back far enough to look into my eyes. "Want to come upstairs and watch a movie?"

My hand slips an inch farther down her back, my fingers unable to stop smoothing against the unbelievably soft fabric of her thrifted coat. "I don't think that's such a good idea."

"Why not?"

"Because my resolve is only so strong."

I watch as the meaning behind my words dawns on her. A pretty blush lights up her cheeks, and her head dips down so her hair covers her face. "Oh. Well, then." She looks back up at me, her bottom lip caught between her teeth.

I want to reach up, tug it free, and suck it between my own.

Going upstairs is *definitely* a bad idea.

I squeeze her waist one last time and lean forward to brush my mouth against her forehead. "Goodnight, Ellie."

"'Night, Cam."

My apartment is dark when I let myself in a few minutes later. I left my blinds open, and through them, I can see the light on in Ellie's window. I can just make out the shape of her through the Roman shades as she walks the length of her apartment and disappears into her bedroom.

CHAPTER TWENTY-SEVEN

I make my way through the shadows and settle onto my couch. There's something I need to do.

Hazel picks up the FaceTime call on the third ring. She flew back to LA this morning, so I can just see the sun setting in the background.

"Hey, you made it back," she says with an easy smile.

I lean back against the couch and turn up the brightness on my phone so she can see my face better. "Yeah, a few hours ago. Did you make it okay?"

"No issues," she tells me.

I let out a deep breath, preparing myself for what I need to say. "Haze, I need to talk to you about something."

Her brow wrinkles. "What's up?"

"I'm going...I've decided to stay. In Nashville," I say, and it feels *right*. When I drove into Nashville this afternoon, when I steered my car into the parking lot, when I heard the crunch of the leaves beneath my feet and felt the chill of the air on my skin, it felt like home. I knew then that I couldn't go back.

Tonight with Ellie, I hoped things would go differently, that she would be all in and I could tell her about my decision. But she decided to wait, so I followed her lead.

Hazel deserves to know, though.

"Oh," she finally responds, her voice a little hollow.

"Are you mad?"

Her head shakes immediately. "No, of course not. I know you mentioned it was a possibility a few weeks ago, but I guess I'm still just a little shocked. Wes was begging us to move all spring and summer, and you turned him down every time."

I push a hand through my hair, the sleeves of the leather jacket pulling tight around my shoulders. "I know, and I had no intention of changing my mind."

"So what changed your mind? The girl?"

"No," I answer truthfully. Being near Ellie is the icing on the cake. If she decides she wants me, that is. But I want to be in Nashville even if she decides this can't work between us. I want to work with Wes again. I want to take pictures of the mist coming off the hills in the early mornings as I wander around with my camera.

I'd like to make tea for Ellie at night and wake up with her next to me.

But even if that never happens, I'm staying.

"No, it's not about Ellie. I just...being here feels *right*. It feels like home in a way California never has."

She's quiet for a long moment, and when she speaks, her voice is quiet, although not unhappy. "I get it. Did you tell Wes?"

"I called him on the way home from Fontana Ridge. I think he cried."

Hazel's laugh echoes through the phone. "I'm sure he did."

I lean back into the cushions, feeling lighter than I have in months. "You know, Haze, the only thing to make Nashville better..."

She laughs. "Yeah, okay."

"You really could move here, you know."

"I..." She trails off. "I'll think about it, but I've actually started seeing someone here." She tilts her head down, trying to hide the blush staining her cheeks.

"Oh?" I ask. "Seems like someone special." I feel a twinge in my chest knowing this is the end of an era. Hazel is five years younger than me, and as soon as she was old enough to move out on her own, she followed me to California. I had just finished college when she showed up on my doorstep and told me she was moving in with me. It only lasted about a year before she got sick of me and found new roommates, but this time, I don't think she's going to come with me.

"Yeah," she says, chewing on her bottom lip. "He is."

"I can't wait to hear all about him. Maybe I can meet him when I come back to pack up my apartment in a few weeks?"

"That sounds great," she says, and I can tell she means it.

"I better go."

"Cam?" Hazel asks, and I pause. "I'm really happy for you."

"Thanks, Haze. I'm really happy too."

Twenty-Eight

ELLIE

"Hey, loser, you going to come help me move this weekend?" Alex asks through the phone on Monday morning.

"How lovely to hear from you, Alex," I say with a roll of my eyes. I grip the phone between my ear and shoulder so I can get back to the mound of work that piled up on my desk over the holiday.

"Bring that new guy you're seeing."

My head snaps up, making sure Sadie isn't back from her tour before I pitch my voice low. "Why do you think I'm seeing someone?"

"I figured that's what your little maintenance call was about at Thanksgiving."

I let out a breath, my heart rate returning to normal. "No, I wasn't leaving to meet someone."

"Oh," he says. "So you actually had to go for a maintenance call?"

"Well, no." I hesitate. "I just wanted to get out of there."

His voice softens. "I understand. Things seemed good, though, right? With the award and all."

"Yeah, it's good," I say, although it still doesn't feel entirely true.

"So you'll come this weekend?" Alex asks, changing the subject.

CHAPTER TWENTY-EIGHT

"Yeah, I'll be there." I suck my bottom lip between my teeth, debating my next words and their possible ramifications. The image of Cam's smiling face on Thanksgiving when I mentioned introducing him to my brothers is what decides for me. "And I'll bring him."

"So there *is* a him?" Alex sounds much too pleased with himself.

"Yes, there's a him," I say on an exhale. "It goes without saying that I don't want you to mention him to Mom and Dad."

"Obviously," he says, and I can almost see his eye roll. He doesn't know the half of it.

"Is Adam coming?"

"Of course."

"So he said no, then?"

"Of course."

I laugh, feeling lighter than I have since Thanksgiving. "Okay, see you *both* Saturday."

An email dings in my inbox as I set the phone down, and I click on it. It's from Cam, and the subject line reads *Harvest Festival Photos*. Eagerly, I open the file. Now that I'm thinking about it, I realize I've never really seen any of Cam's work. I've always assumed he's good, but my jaw drops open as I look at the photos.

They don't just capture moments from the festival. They manage to represent how the entire event felt. I can *see* the joy in a child's expression as they got their face painted. I can *hear* the conversation a couple was having over steaming cups of cocoa, snuggled together on a bale of hay. I can *smell* the damp, earthy scent from the earlier rain and *taste* the rich apple cider on my tongue. I can *feel* the energy, even though I was passed out for most of it.

There are pictures of me too. One where I'm laughing, my hand resting on someone's arm, my eyes and nose crinkled. Another where I'm stooped down, handing a treat to a kid. There's no hiding the fevered flush on my cheeks, but somehow, Cam captured moments of me in my element, and I can't help but stare at them.

Despite my parents' ridiculous rules, I've always loved my job, and in these photos, I look like I was made for it.

There's a twinge in my chest at the thought of losing it, but beneath that, I feel a deeper ache at the thought of losing the one who took these pictures, the one who saw me when no one else was looking.

The bell above the door jangles, pulling me from my thoughts, and Sadie walks in. "Those people had *so many* questions. That tour took ten times longer than it normally would." She stalks into my office and slumps in one of the chairs across from my desk. "What are you looking at?"

I swivel the monitor around to face her. "Cam sent over the photos from the festival."

She leans forward, swiping my mouse to click through them. "Wow, these are, like, *really* good. It's too bad he's not sticking around; he could take photos for all of our events."

The words are a vise to my lungs, suffocating me. Somehow, I'd forgotten that Cam being here was temporary. I'd forgotten that even though he said he'd wait for me, there was an expiration date on his stay. I'd forgotten that even if I did give us a chance, there's another huge hurdle in our way.

Suddenly, more than anything, I want to spill it all to Sadie. I want to tell her everything and have her tell me it will all be okay. But telling Sadie would mean revealing the depth of trouble I'm in with my parents. It would mean asking her to keep my secret and incriminating her if they found out she knew the truth. No, for right now, it's still best to keep it from her.

This weekend, if Cam wants to, I can introduce him to my brothers. And if all goes well, then I'll think about telling Sadie.

"You okay?" Sadie asks, bringing me back to the present.

As I look into her pale blue eyes, I almost blurt it all out right then and there. I really *hate* keeping this from her, and I want to tell her everything—how Cam's laugh warms me from the inside out, how he makes me tea before bed, how I'm terrified my parents will find out and everything will be ruined, how he's the first thing I think about in the morning and the last thing I think about at night, how his smiles have the ability to light up my whole day.

"Yeah, I'm fine," I say instead.

"You didn't tell me your photography is that good," I say later that night. My feet are tucked beneath Cam's thigh on the couch, and a mug of almost too-sweet herbal tea is warming my hands.

Cam rolls his head along the back of the couch, dragging his heavy-lidded eyes up to meet mine. He looks so at home here, his hair ruffled in every direction, his legs stretched out on my coffee table, his fingers tracing little circles on my calf.

"I figured it was kind of self-explanatory," he says with a wry twist of his lips.

I dig my toes into his thigh. "Don't make me regret complimenting you."

His chuckle rumbles in his chest. "Okay, yeah, my bad. Thank you." He throws me a sleepy smile. "That means a lot."

I suck my bottom lip between my teeth. "There were a lot of pictures of me."

Deep blue eyes lock on mine. "You're really easy to photograph."

Scoffing, I ask, "Are some people hard to photograph?"

Cam pushes up on the couch, moving so he's not so sprawled out. "Definitely. Some people are stiff and awkward and hyperaware of the camera. Some people wear colors that don't complement their skin tone and completely wash them out. *Most* people aren't easy to photograph."

"Oh," I say.

"But you," Cam continues, looking away from me, like the words he's trying to find are hidden somewhere around my living room. "You're always dressed in these colorful outfits that make your hair pop and your skin look like sweet cream. Even when you're serious, your lips are curved up, like you could break into a smile at any time."

He pauses, turning back to face me. "And when you do smile, you get these crinkles right here." His fingers reach up to trace the corner of my eye before sliding down the bridge of my nose. "You smile with your whole face, not just your mouth. It's…mesmerizing."

My breath catches in my throat at the look in his eyes. It's soft and indulgent, like slipping between fresh sheets or licking melting ice cream from the cone.

Cam's thumb stalls on my bottom lip, moving in one slow swipe across it. "You, Ellie Bates, are the thing I love photographing most."

I swallow. "More than sunrises?"

"Mm-hmm." He makes the sounds in the back of his throat, his gaze still fastened on my mouth.

"More than the farm?" I ask, thinking of how he told me about waking up each morning to take pictures there while he was home for Thanksgiving.

Cam nods.

"More than..." I pause. "Weston?"

His eyes snap up to mine, and a laugh bursts out of him. I try to hold back my smile, but it slips free anyway.

"Yeah, Daisy," Cam says. "I'd much rather you be on the other side of the camera."

I lean back, sinking into the cushions once more. "Good." I tap on the side of my mug, trying to quell the anxiety that threatens to bubble up with my next words. "I have a favor to ask, and you can say no."

Cam settles back against the couch again too, his hand wrapping around my calf once more. "I'll do it."

One corner of my mouth tips up at his quick answer. "You don't even know what it is."

He shrugs. "I'll still do it."

"Can I at least ask you before you agree?"

"Too late. I've already decided."

I still my fingers against my mug and take a deep breath. "I'm going to help my brother move this weekend, and I was...well, I wanted to know if you wanted to come."

His hand tightens imperceptibly on my leg. "Oh. Well, yeah, of course I'd love to come." After a pause, he asks, "What are we going to tell him?"

Looking at him here, so at home in my space, makes words pop out of my mouth before I can think of the consequences. "I thought we'd tell him the truth."

Cam's gaze fastens on mine. "The truth?"

I start tapping again, but Cam grabs my hand with his, threading them together.

"Yeah," I say, surprised my voice comes out strong instead of breathy. "I think I'd like to tell my brothers. Adam and Alex won't tell Mom and Dad, and if they find out, it's not like they can be fired for hiding it. They're a safe option, and I trust them."

Cam seems to take in my words. I know he can feel how big this is. I'm not quite ready to move a whole step forward yet, but I'm inching closer.

"And you're sure?" he asks.

I nod. "Yeah, I'm sure."

His mouth cracks into a smile that simultaneously cracks something in my chest. Cam is stargazing and too-sweet tea. He is gentle touches and homemade soup. He is all the best things, and I don't know how I got him.

I might not be ready for more yet, but I know I don't want to lose what we have right now.

Cam gives my hand another squeeze. "I can't wait."

Twenty-Nine

ELLIE

My palms are sweating when I hop into Cam's front seat Saturday morning. He doesn't pull out of the parking lot after I've buckled my seat belt, and when I turn to face him, he's already watching me.

"Are you nervous?" he asks. His eyes are serious, but the tiniest of smiles is playing at his lips.

"Not even a little."

His mouth twitches. "You're a bad liar."

I pin him with a stare. "Which is exactly why I'm nervous."

"Oh," he says, and the grin disappears. He reaches for the gearshift and starts to reverse.

I stop him with a hand on this thigh. "Wait, Cam. No, that's not what I meant."

He pauses, eyes searching mine.

"I…well, I'm just not used to being completely honest with my family—as terrible as that sounds. I tell my brothers way more than I tell my parents, but I don't even tell them everything."

"Ellie, I—"

"I'm used to keeping pieces of myself locked away to keep them safe," I continue. My eyes snag on his. "I'm scared to burst this bubble we've been living in and risk it all."

"I don't have to go," he says, his hand tangling with mine again.

"No, I want you to. Really. I'm just a little scared."

Cam runs a hand through his hair, sending the dark locks every which way. "Would it help if I told you I'm nervous too?"

My breath leaves me in a relieved whoosh. "Really?"

"Yeah," Cam says, giving me a boyish smile. A faint line of pink colors his cheeks. "They're your brothers, and I want to impress them. I figure telling them I've been dating their sister in secret isn't going to make the best first impression."

I squeeze his fingers, and his rough calluses scrape against my palm in the most delicious way. "To be fair, they've met our parents. They understand the need to keep things from them."

"Yeah, I guess," he says, although he doesn't sound convinced.

"Cam," I say, making sure to enunciate his name, to let him know I mean *him* and no one else—not Sam or Dave—just Cam. "You make me happy, and they'll see that. That's all that's going to matter to them."

He lifts his eyes to mine, as if checking for sincerity. "Yeah?"

I nod. "Yeah, of course."

His lips split into one of those devastating smiles now, the one that makes butterflies take off in my stomach. "Okay, let's go."

CHAPTER TWENTY-NINE

"I MEAN THIS IN the nicest of ways," Cam says, hands clasped together behind his head. "Your brother should have hired movers." His chest rises and falls with his labored breathing, causing his shirt to stretch tight over his muscles.

The man is...hot. He's so hot, it's distracting.

Cam smirks, pointing to his face. "Eyes are up here, Daisy."

A hot flush stains my cheeks. "What were you saying?"

"Alex should hire movers next time he moves."

"Alex isn't moving again for many moons," Alex says as he and Adam ascend the last flight of stairs.

"You neglected to mention that Alex lives on the third floor of an apartment complex with no elevator."

I flash a cheeky smile at Cam. "Must have slipped my mind."

Adam grabs ahold of Cam's shoulder. "You're going to get so much free pizza out of this."

Cam's chuckle reverberates down the open hall as they head back into the apartment.

Cam and my brothers hit it off better than I could have expected. Something gooey filled my chest at how easily they all started joking with one another. It started with Alex asking if Cam felt guilty about sneaking around with me, which caused Cam to blush such a deep red that even his ears were tipped in it. But then Alex and Adam had broken, their laughs punctuated with stories of all the things they've kept from Mom and Dad over the years.

It was good. It *is* good.

It makes me a little nervous how easily he fits in here. It's like maybe if he didn't, then when this thing has to end, I won't be left with the memories of Cam wiping tears from his eyes at one of Alex's ridiculous anecdotes.

But it also gives me hope—that sticky feeling that has been spreading through me—that this might all work out. That maybe I can make my parents love Cam the way my brothers seem to.

All the introspection has made it really hard to work. So hard, in fact, that I haven't moved a single box downstairs. I've made an excellent overseer, though, so I think that should count for something.

"There are plenty of boxes left in there," Adam says, hefting two large boxes toward the stairs.

"Thank you for letting me know," I respond, not moving from my spot leaning up against the wall.

Adam rolls his eyes and disappears. Cam and Alex come out a second later, arms full.

"Don't push yourself too hard, Ellie," Alex grunts out.

"Supervising is a tough job, but someone's got to do it."

Alex follows Adam down the stairs, but Cam stops in front of me. He leans in until his breath tickles my ear, and I struggle against a shiver.

"If you help, I'll make you more of that tomato bisque tonight."

"Deal."

"So this is the place?" I ask, staring in wonder at Alex's new high-rise condo. The floor-to-ceiling windows allow for an unhindered view of downtown, and it's breathtaking.

Alex stops, hands on his hips as he surveys the space, and I think I see a hint of pride reflected in his expression. "This is it."

"Wow," I breathe.

"My bachelor pad," Alex says reverently.

I roll my eyes. "You ruin everything."

"What?" He spins to face me.

"Here I was, so proud of you for buying your first place, and you call it your bachelor pad with the same hushed admiration as someone uses when they see the *Mona Lisa*."

"Oh, this condo is much prettier than the *Mona Lisa*."

"Those are bold words, my friend," Cam says.

"She doesn't have *eyebrows*," Alex responds, as if this should be obvious. "That would be like having this place without the windows."

"Well," I say, "to be fair, the windows would probably be the eyes. And she has *eyes*. Curtains would be the eyebrows of this room."

"And you don't have curtains," Cam adds helpfully.

"So basically," Adam says. "This place is your *Mona Lisa*."

"It would look so much prettier with eyebrows," I say wistfully.

Alex glares at the three of us. "You guys are *not* going to start referring to my condo as *Mona Lisa*. I want to make that clear now."

"Thank you for buying Mona," I say around a bite of pizza a few hours later. Cam and I are seated next to each other on Alex's couch, our shoulders brushing every time we take a bite. The taste of rich tomato sauce and garlic lingers on my tongue, and melting cheese keeps stringing from my mouth to my plate.

Alex rolls his eyes. "This little nickname isn't going to stick."

"I bet ole Leo thought the same thing," Adam adds.

Alex ignores him and turns to focus on Cam, who is pulling the pineapples from his pizza to put on mine. The gesture makes me feel a little floaty since I know he likes the pineapple, but he knows I *love* it, so he gives it to me anyway.

"So Cam," Alex says, and it pulls me from my sappy thoughts. "When are you planning to go back to California?"

Cam stiffens next to me, and his eyes briefly swivel my way before turning back to Alex. "My temporary job here is over next weekend, and then I'm taking a few weeks off to spend the holidays with my family."

The pizza sinks like a rock in my stomach, spreading until my appetite is all but gone. Obviously, I knew my time with Cam was coming to a close, but I didn't realize *just* how quickly it was going to be over. Yes, we could still stay together—try long-distance—but I wouldn't get nights with him on my couch anymore. I wouldn't get my feet tucked under his thigh or too-sweet tea before bed. I wouldn't get forehead kisses or homemade soup or stolen moments under the stars.

I feel like I've been hit by a freight train.

Alex is talking again, but for the life of me, I can't focus on what he's saying. The only coherent thought in my head is that Camden is leaving, and I don't want him to.

CHAPTER TWENTY-NINE

"Do you want me to come up?" Cam asks as we pull into The Flats parking lot a few hours later. The sun has just begun to set, casting him in pastels and golds.

He looks irresistible, but I shake my head anyway. It's gotten hard to think when he's around, and tonight, I have a lot to consider.

"No, I'm going to hang out with Ethel for a bit. I haven't seen her much this week since her family was in town."

I don't miss the crestfallen look that settles over his features. We've been spending every evening together, and normally I would invite him over after I checked on Ethel.

He parks the car and turns to face me. "Is everything okay?"

No. "Of course."

I can tell he doesn't believe me, and that he wants to press for more. I want to *tell* him more, but I don't quite know how to articulate what I'm feeling.

"Is this about what Alex said?"

I avoid his eyes, gathering my purse from the floorboard. "Alex said a lot of things today."

Cam runs a hand through his hair. "About me going back to LA."

"No, of course not. It's—"

"Because I wanted to talk to you about that. I—"

I cut him off with a wave of my hand. "Cam, it's fine. I knew you weren't going to be here forever."

"Ellie—"

"Can we talk about this later?" I ask, hating the way my voice trembles. "I really need to go check on Ethel."

Cam looks like he wants to press the issue, but I watch as resignation settles over him—shoulders slumping, hands flexing on the steering wheel, jaw clenching and unclenching. Under different circumstances, I would enjoy the view, but right now, it's taking everything in me to maintain eye contact.

"Yeah, we can talk about it later."

I reach for the door handle and pause. "Are we still going Christmas tree shopping for my apartment tomorrow?"

"I still want to go if you do."

"Yeah, I want to." I suck my bottom lip between my teeth. "I'll talk to you tomorrow, okay?"

"Okay, Daisy. Talk to you tomorrow."

I barely make it out of the car and into my apartment before the tears start to fall. I'm hit with the full force of how much I don't want Cam to leave while also equally terrified at the prospect of him staying.

I should change out of my dusty moving clothes, maybe take a shower, but I want to talk to Ethel *right now.*

The chilly air bites at my skin as I trek across the property to her apartment. She's sitting on her couch when I let myself in. When her eyes lock on mine, she immediately asks, "What's wrong?"

Instead of sitting on the loveseat across from her, I settle next to her on her floral sofa. Her thin arms come around my shoulders, tugging me close. We sit in silence for a long moment. Her embrace is maternal, and it makes my heart ache.

"I don't want Cam to leave," I murmur.

Ethel's frail hands swipe down my hair and over my back. "Maybe you should tell him that."

"I can't ask him to stay."

"Don't ask him to stay. Just make sure he knows there's something here for him if he decides to."

"It's just…I don't know how much I can offer him."

CHAPTER TWENTY-NINE

Ethel sits back, pushing my hair from my face. I'm not surprised to find it's damp, with clumps of hair sticking to the wetness. "I think you need to figure that out, girlie. I know you love this place, and you love all of us, but The Flats can only give you so much."

"But my parents..."

A hard look steels her eyes. "If you want my opinion, your parents can go screw themselves for all I care."

I can't help the choking laugh that comes out of me.

"Tell me something. Have your parents ever made you feel about yourself the way that Cam does?"

No. The answer hits me like a ton of bricks, and honestly, I don't know how to feel about it. Even when they told me they were proud of me, I still felt empty. But Cam...from the beginning, Cam has seen me and wanted me just as I am. It scares me more than I'd like to admit.

"I'm not saying you need to come clean to your parents right away, but I do think you need to consider what's most important to you here. If you want Cam, figure out a way to make your parents okay with it. You've been with him all this time, and you still won Property Manager of the Year. It obviously hasn't affected your job performance. And if he moves into another complex, the conflict of interest is gone."

I know they won't see it that way, that even if they don't fire me over this, I still won't be able to keep their approval, respect, or pride.

But...are stolen moments under the stars and almost too-sweet tea and nights on my couch worth it? Is *Cam* worth it?

I think he is.

Sitting up, I square my shoulders and wipe the lingering tears from my eyes. "I've got to go."

"Are you going to strip naked and beg him to stay?" Ethel asks, her chin resting on her fist like she's watching her favorite part of her favorite movie.

I roll my eyes. "Oh my gosh, no. I'm going home."

"Home?" She sounds incredulous. "What are you going to do there?"

"I'm going to make some tea, maybe heat up a can of soup, and sit on my couch alone." I'm going to remind myself of exactly what I'll be missing if Cam leaves, if I let him slip through my fingers.

"That sounds horrible."

I let out a deep breath. "Yeah, it really does."

Thirty

CAMDEN

I NEED TO TELL Ellie about my decision to move to Nashville.

That was made abundantly clear after yesterday, but when I tried to talk to her about it in the car, she didn't seem to want to hear it. That conversation replayed through my head all night as I tossed and turned, twisting my sheets into a tangled mess at the foot of my bed.

I just need her to know that I don't expect anything from her, that this isn't my way of pressuring her into moving forward. And I'm not sure how to do that, which is why I've continued to keep it to myself.

But after seeing the way she changed after Alex's question yesterday—the stiff set of her shoulders, the downcast tilt of her lips, the furrow between her brows—I know I need to tell her.

I just need to figure out when. And how.

I knock on her door the next morning, and all the thoughts vanish from my mind when the door swings open. "Hey," Ellie says, a little breathless.

She's dressed in a bright red sweater and a fitted pair of ripped jeans. Her lips are painted the exact same color as her top, and it takes everything ounce of strength I possess to pry my gaze away from them.

I don't know what I was thinking, telling her I wanted to wait to kiss her until she was ready. Right now, all I want to do is press her against the wall and bury my face in her neck, where that daisy and apple scent is the strongest. I want to breathe her in until I can't smell anything else ever again.

"Hey," I manage.

"You ready to go?"

Whatever tension was between us last night has disappeared under one of Ellie's easy smiles.

"Yeah, let's go."

She grabs her coat, the furry beige one from the other night, and pushes her arms through it. "This is very much not my vibe, but I'm a little obsessed with it."

I can't help the grin that quirks my lips. "I'm glad."

"You did good," she says, pulling her door shut and locking it behind her.

The drive to the tree farm, which is about thirty miles outside of Nashville, is unusually quiet, although not uncomfortable. I think we both have things on our minds, and neither of us knows how to voice them.

"Do you want to come over tonight?" Ellie asks as we pull into the farm's parking lot. "Help me decorate the tree?"

I pull into an empty spot and turn in my seat to face her, feeling like a giant weight has been lifted off my shoulders. "Yeah, I'd love that."

Her cherry red mouth splits open in a grin. "Good, me too."

I debate whether to say the next part. It's probably too vulnerable, too desperate, but I find myself wanting to say it anyway. "I didn't like spending the evening alone last night."

Her smile disappears and her hand finds mine. "I didn't either," she says, and her voice is uncharacteristically solemn.

I give her hand a squeeze. "Is that a bad thing?"

She drags her gaze up my chest, and I feel everywhere it touches, like a finger on my skin. "No, I don't think it is."

My breath hitches in my lungs. Maybe telling her I've decided to stay won't scare her off. Maybe…it will be a good thing. I lift our joined hands to my lips and press a kiss to her knuckles. "Let's get you a Christmas tree."

Her smile is a slow, distracting curve of her mouth. "Let's do it."

We hop out of the car, and I retreat to the trunk.

"What are you getting from back there?" Ellie asks, her shoulders bunched up against the cold as she waits near the front of the SUV.

I reach for my camera and slide the strap around my neck. "I brought my camera."

"To the Christmas tree farm?" she asks, looking amused.

I wrap an arm around her shoulders and steer her toward the entrance. "Every time we're together, I always wish I had it, but I usually don't."

"And why's that?"

I lean my head down, nuzzling my nose into Ellie's hair so I can speak directly into her ear. "There's always a moment I wish I could stop time and take a photo of you."

She looks up at me, and we're so close I can count the faint constellations of freckles across her nose. "I'm really glad you sat at my table one night in October, Camden Lane."

It's not a declaration of love, but my heart hammers as if it is. So often, I feel like Ellie is falling for me, despite herself. Like if she could force herself not to, she would. But this right here, this little moment in time, tells me she doesn't regret it, that she wouldn't change it.

"I am too, Ellie Bates," I say, breathing in that scent of her, the one that reminds me of home.

As we enter the farm, I reluctantly let go of her, only for her to find my hand seconds later. She gives it a squeeze, and I have to tell myself to stop internally squealing over it like a middle school girl.

"So what kind of tree are you thinking?" I ask, trying to calm myself down.

She hesitates for a moment, then says, "Don't laugh."

I look down at her, unable to hold back my grin. I never know what is going to come out of her mouth. "I won't laugh."

"I want a blue spruce."

I immediately start walking toward the blue spruces. "Why's that?"

"I think it would look best with my couch." I can't help it, I laugh. Ellie elbows me in the ribs. "I told you not to laugh."

I grin down at her, loving the way she looks here, surrounded by trees, the gold tinting her cheeks and the tip of her nose pink. "It's just so you."

"Oh, great," she grumbles with a roll of her eyes.

I tug her to a stop in front of a copse of trees. "No, that's a good thing. You are an explosion of color in a dreary landscape. You're a striped sweater in a crowd of black dresses. You, Ellie Bates, are the statement piece the whole house is designed around."

Ellie stares up at me for a long moment, her lips slightly parted. "You always say the right things, you know that?"

Her words affect me slowly—a warmth spreading through my chest, an itch beneath my fingers to reach for her, a tug low in my stomach.

I reach for my camera hanging near my waist. "Stay right there."

With that look on her face, the one I can't quite name, and her sweater standing out among the green of the trees, she makes a perfect picture.

I step back, and when I look through the viewfinder, she's brushing her fingers across the branches, glancing at me over one shoulder.

The shutter clicks, snatching this moment from the universe and securing it for eternity.

"Which playlist—Classic Christmas Tunes or New Holiday Favorites?" Ellie asks a few hours later. We've hauled her tree into her living room, and she's busy lighting every pine or sugar cookie candle she owns, which is a truly surprising amount.

"Classic," I say easily and get to work untangling the bundle of lights for the tree.

The beginning notes of Nat King Cole's "The Christmas Song" float through the speakers, and I flash Ellie a smile. "This is my favorite."

"I had a feeling," she tells me, crossing her legs and sitting down on the floor next to me. She turns on a recorded fireplace on Netflix, and the sound of crackling birch fills the room.

"Oh, yeah?" I ask. I watch out of the corner of my eye as she begins pulling ornaments and ribbons from dozens of random grocery bags and gift boxes.

"You're definitely a Nat King Cole kind of guy." Her eyes twinkle. "Guess my favorite Christmas song."

I rub my hand along the scruff on my jaw, thinking. I know it won't be an oldie, that would be too ordinary. It will be something happy and upbeat—probably a modern rendition of a classic.

I name off the few newer songs I know, and she just keeps shaking her head, pulling out ornaments and littering them all over the carpet. They're every color imaginable and not in any particular style.

Finally, I lean my back against the couch. "I give up."

She flashes me her brightest smile. "I stumped you."

I stare at her for a moment, a grin touching my lips. I doubt she realizes that she's been stumping me since the day we met. "Yeah, Daisy, you stumped me."

She sits back, a satisfied smirk on her face. "'Please Come Home for Christmas' by the Eagles."

"Really?" I would have never guessed. It's so opposite of her—slow and sentimental. It's more like me than her.

Ellie shrugs. "Yeah, I don't know why, but I just love it."

I bump her shoulder with my own. "If you help me decorate this tree, I'll make you homemade peppermint hot chocolate."

"Don't tease me," she says, pressing a dramatic hand to her chest.

I roll my eyes and tug Ellie to her feet. Her soft laugh fills all the empty spots in my chest, and I think to myself that I could listen to her forever.

We work through stringing the lights on the blue-green branches. I stay quiet for the majority of it, while Ellie sings along with the songs on her playlist or stops to tell me a holiday memory. Before too long, the tree is full of her hodge-podge assortment of ornaments.

CHAPTER THIRTY

"Where is this one from?" I ask, hanging up one that looks like an armadillo. I've taken to asking her about each ornament and listening as she explains the story behind each one.

Ellie comes around to my side of the tree and asks, "Which one?" When she sees the ornament in my hand, she squeals and claps her hands together, bouncing on the balls of her feet. "You found Karmadillo!"

My eyebrows inch up my forehead. "Karmadillo?"

Leaning around me, she snatches the ornament from my hand and moves to place it on the front side of the tree—a place of honor for only her most special of decorations. "Remember the day after you moved in? When I fell down the stairs chasing the—"

"Armadillo," we say at the same time, and she gives me one of her crinkled nose smiles.

"Right," Ellie continues. "Well, Gary and Sadie and I really fell in love with her. We were sad to see her go."

"Naturally."

"So Sadie surprised us last week with these armadillo ornaments she found online." Ellie pulls me so I'm standing next to her, facing the front of the tree. "Isn't she cute?"

I stare at the little glass armadillo covered in glitter. It looks remarkably like the real thing and is just as ugly. I'm saved from responding, though, when the song changes and the distinctive notes of "Please Come Home For Christmas" fill the room.

Ellie's face brightens, and in that moment, my heart stops in my chest. With the lights from the tree reflecting on her skin, her dark eyes sparkling, and a smile forming on her perfect lips, she is absolutely beautiful.

My voice, normally so smooth and steady, comes out in a gravelly murmur as I ask, "Want to dance with me?"

Her gaze softens and she steps closer, leaving almost no space between us. "I'd love to." My hands find the smooth slope of her hips on instinct, and I drag her the final few inches separating us. Just like that first night, we fit together like we were made for this.

With every gentle sway to the music, Ellie settles a little heavier against me. I'm hit with the overwhelming need to tell her I'm staying. This might not be the best moment, but with her fingers tangling in the hair at the nape of my neck and her head resting over my wildly beating heart, I can't stand for another minute to go by without her knowing.

"Cam," Ellie says before I get a chance to tell her my news. She slows and leans back so I can see her face. "I've been thinking." She hesitates, chewing her bottom lip. "About us."

My heart, which was beating so out of control just moments before, stops dead. "What about us?"

"I know you're going back…"

I should correct her, tell her now, but I want to hear what she has to say next too much to interrupt.

"I was thinking maybe we could keep trying *this*." She reaches between us, fingering one of the buttons at my collar. Her throat bobs in a swallow. "I think I still need some time before I tell my parents, but…I want there to be an *us* to tell them about."

Ellie finally looks back up at me, the black of her eyes nearly encompassing the dark brown. "That is, if you do. I know I've messed things up a lot in the past, so I understand if you—"

"I'm not going back to LA."

She steps back half an inch, her hands splayed out across my chest. "What?"

I swallow and tighten my hands on her waist. "Wes offered me a permanent job, and…I took it."

"You're staying?" she asks, and I can't read the emotion in her voice.

I nod. "I didn't want you to feel pressured, so I didn't tell you earlier, but—"

Ellie silences me with her pointer finger pressed to my mouth. "I want to hear all of this later, but right now, I just really want to kiss you."

My breath lets out in a whoosh, all the air I no longer need, because Ellie will be my oxygen. I breathe her in, slanting my lips across hers.

Two months ago, I tasted Ellie for the first time, and I thought it couldn't get better. Weeks later, I did it again and thought no kiss would measure up.

I have never been so happy to be wrong in my entire life.

Ellie is both soft and firm against me, smooth as silk but demanding and hungry, like she's wanted this for a long time too.

My hands, no longer content to stay at her sides, slide up into her hair. I trail my mouth along her jaw, pausing at her ear. This was where it all began, my hand beneath her hair and my lips at her ear.

I press a kiss there, hot and slow, and she makes a noise in the back of her throat like she remembers it too.

My nose nudges down the slope of her neck, looking for that one spot where her scent is the strongest, and I breathe her in. "You know this spot has always driven me crazy?" I say, and my whisper disappears into her skin.

Ellie shudders against me, her nails scratching against my scalp. "Is that so?"

"You smell like daisies and apples," I say, kissing back up the line of her neck.

"It's my perfume," she tells me, her voice a breathy murmur.

"I want some. I'll spray it on my pillow and never sleep again."

Ellie's laugh rumbles through her. "Okay, I think I can make that happen."

Warmth spreads through my chest at the sound. I like that we can do both—that we can be breathless one moment and then laughing the next. I want her laughs in my ear and her moans against my skin. With Ellie, I want it all.

"Hey, Cam," Ellie says, her fingers threading through the hair at the base of my neck. I fight against a shiver, but when she smiles, I know she felt it.

She pushes to her toes and sets her cheek against mine. "I'm glad you're staying."

I scrape my lips against Ellie's jaw, and now it's her turn to shiver. "I am too."

"About my parents—"

"We don't need to figure it all out tonight."

She settles back on her feet, staring up at me, her lips quirked in a grin. "Good, because I can think of much more useful ways to spend our time."

Thirty-One

ELLIE

I WAKE UP ON my couch. Cam is on the other end, where he must have fallen asleep last night while we watched a movie. The apartment still smells like Christmas—like pine candles and the gingerbread cookies we made sometime around midnight.

My gaze follows the rise and fall of Cam's chest, the lock of dark hair across his forehead, the hand resting on his abdomen. He's mesmerizing, and I want to wake up to this view every day.

His eyes flutter open, locking on mine, and a slow smile curves his mouth. That smile makes butterflies take flight in my belly. I remember feeling it on my neck last night, tasting it on my lips.

"Morning," he says, his voice gravelly with sleep.

"Morning," I echo.

His hand finds mine, tugging me until I'm leaning over him, and then his lips are on mine. There were a lot of kisses last night—slow, drugged kisses; frenzied, exploring kisses; happy, sloppy kisses—but this one is my favorite. This unhurried, sleepy good-morning kiss will go in the books.

I pull back, unable to contain the stupid grin on my face. I am disgustingly, deliriously happy. "I need to get ready for work."

"I think you could wait," he says, trailing his fingers up and down my arms.

"What time is it?"

Cam peers around me, glancing at the clock in the kitchen. He hesitates before answering. "You have plenty of time."

"So I'm already late for work?"

His eyes trace my face. I know I must look a mess, my hair matted and my sweater all bunched up and hanging off my shoulder, but Cam looks like he wants to sear this view into his brain. "What answer will make you stay a little longer?"

I shove off him with a laugh and stand up. I turn around to check the clock, and I am, in fact, late for work.

"Shoot, I've got to get ready."

Cam snags my hand before I can rush to my room and pulls me down to him once more. "One last kiss for the road, Daisy."

When he says stuff like that, in that raspy morning voice, there's no way I could say no.

A few minutes later, when I am *thoroughly* awake, I pull back, feeling dizzy. "I really, really need to get ready."

One corner of his mouth tips in a lazy grin. "Sorry about that. I got a little carried away."

He looks perfect lying here on my couch, his hair mussed from sleep and my hands, his body resting amid a sea of pillows and blankets. If I don't get up right now, I'm never going to make it into work.

"Getting ready now," I say finally.

I can feel his eyes all the way to my bedroom door.

There's no time to shower, and I barely have enough time to throw on another oversized sweater and pair it with some purple velvet pants. When I hurry out of my room and into the bathroom, Cam is there, holding my perfume.

"Perfect," I say, snatching it from his hand. I spritz it on both sides of my neck, and when I turn back, Cam looks like he's been hit by a truck. His eyes are fastened on the crook of my shoulder.

"*Daisy'd and Confused*," he says so quietly I almost think he's talking to himself.

I hold up the perfume bottle, label facing out. "Yeah, isn't it amazing? That's actually where I came up with the name Daisy for my Halloween costume. I sprayed on my perfume and thought *Daisy* seemed cute."

"Where did you get it?" Cam asks, sounding a little strangled.

My head tilts to the side, confused at his reaction. It was just last night that he told me this very perfume drove him crazy, so I'm not sure why he's acting like this about it.

"I actually have a cool story about this," I tell him, giving the bottle a little shake. "In college, a couple of my girlfriends and I rented a little AirBnB in this mountain town in North Carolina. One of my friends found it on a Pinterest article about day trips from Nashville or something."

I wave my hand in the air, dismissing that unimportant detail. "Anyway, we went to this farm, and they had a little shop. I found this perfume, and I swear, it smelled exactly like the fields. I *loved* it, so I bought basically the entire line. It's made in-house. Now, whenever I run out, I order it online from there."

I press my fingers into the bridge of my nose. "Gosh, I wish I could remember the name of that town. It was so—"

"Fontana Ridge," Cam breathes.

I stare up at him. "That's it. How did you know that?"

"That's my hometown," he tells me, and my brows climb up my forehead in disbelief. "That's my aunt and uncle's farm. And my mom makes all the stuff in the shop."

My eyes widen in shock and disbelief. "Really?"

"Yeah, Daisy," he says, his lips quirking in a smile. "I kept thinking you smelled like home, and now I know why."

Something warm and sticky spreads through my chest at his words.

"Small world, huh?" I ask, echoing our conversation outside his apartment the morning we found Karmadillo.

The grin he gives me lets me know he remembers too. "The smallest."

I lean forward and press my mouth against his, loving the way his hands slip beneath my hair. His thumb drags a slow line from my ear all the way to my throat, and I shiver against him.

Backing up, I reach for my toothbrush, knowing I'm going to have to take this to the office bathroom if I want to make it to work on time. "I've got to go, but feel free to take that back to your place and spray it on your pillow," I say with a wink.

And then I spin around and dart down the stairs before Camden Lane can find a more reliable way to distract me.

Sadie is already in the office when I arrive, and I am suddenly hit with an overwhelming amount of guilt. I drop my stuff, toothbrush included, onto my desk and go over to hers.

"Cutting it a little close," she says, tsking, but I can see the smile on her face.

CHAPTER THIRTY-ONE

"Overslept," I tell her. "Hey," I say, and she looks up at me from her computer.

"What's up?"

I blow out a breath and tap my fingers against my thigh, trying to steady my nerves. "Can we get dinner tonight? Just me and you?"

"Yeah," she says with an easy tip of her lips. "I'd love that. I feel like we haven't gotten to hang out in weeks."

It's true, and after tonight, when I tell her the truth about Cam and my parents, I'll be able to spend time with her without the guilt that's been gnawing at me.

The bell over the door jangles, and Sadie and I turn in unison to see a young couple walking into the office. "My tour," she tells me. "Talk to you in a bit."

I smile and introduce myself to the couple before heading back into my office. I listen as Sadie chats with them while taking their information. She gives me a wink as they walk out to go visit their potential unit.

My heart lightens a little at the gesture. It's all going to be okay. Sadie might be upset with me when she finds out how much I've kept hidden from her the last two months, but she will come around.

The bell rings again, but this time it's not a stranger walking in to tour an apartment, but my dad, and he looks resigned. It sends a chill up my spine and causes goose bumps to break out along my skin.

"Hey," I say as he enters my office. "I didn't know you were stopping by today."

My feeling of dread worsens when Dad pushes the door closed behind him and the snick echoes through the room.

"Ellie, we need to talk," he says, settling into one of the chairs across from my desk, and a heavy, oily feeling settles in my gut.

I swallow against the lump rising in my throat, my mind whirling with possibilities. "Okay."

"There was a domestic dispute here yesterday afternoon, so we were required to review the security footage for the last twenty-four hours."

My heart beats erratically in my chest as I try to remember the events of last night—hauling my Christmas tree from the top of Cam's SUV, laughing at a joke he made, feeling his lips press to my temple before we carried the tree inside.

"You know what we found," Dad says, his voice stoic. For the first time, maybe ever, I notice he looks haggard. His hair is a mess, his eyes underlined with dark circles. I can only imagine the conversation he had with Mom when they found the footage. Her words from months ago echo in my mind. *This is on you. If she breaks any more rules, or costs us more money, or makes us look like idiots to our investors, or we get sacked with a lawsuit, you're the one who's going to clean it up.*

And now he's here to clean it up.

"Dad, I'm sorry. I—"

"We had to turn in the footage to the HR department. Your mom is discussing options with them now, but I wouldn't expect it to be good."

A scratchy feeling tears up my throat. "But I won Property Manager of the Year," I say dumbly, grasping at straws.

He runs a hand through his hair. "Yeah, I know, but this was a breach of contract, Ellie. It was unethical and puts us at risk of a lawsuit."

"Cam wouldn't sue us."

"That's great that you think that, but we have no way of knowing for sure, which is why we have these rules in place. If we need to evict him or take legal action against him for some reason, it's a conflict of interest."

"I know, but he's moving out in a week. He only signed a two-month lease."

"It doesn't matter if he's no longer a resident, Ellie. He can sue at any time for anything that happened while he was living here. When you break up, he could lie and come up with any reason to sue."

"It was just one date." The words tumble out before I can consider them. They taste bitter in my mouth, but when I see the way my dad perks up at them, I know it's my best course of action. "It was a mistake. I thought it was okay since he was moving out next week, but I should have waited."

Dad lets out a breath and pushes his hands through his hair. "Okay, I'll see what I can do."

I feel his disappointment wrapping around me, suffocating me and threatening to cut off my oxygen. I don't know what to say to make it better. I don't know how to fix it. "I…" I trail off when no words come to my mind.

Dad leans forward, resting his elbows on his knees. "We have to suspend you until we figure out how to proceed."

The air hitches in my lungs. *Suspend me. Figure out how to proceed.*

"Is there a chance for me?" I ask, and it comes out strangled.

Dad shrugs. "I don't know, Ellie. I really don't. We own the company, but you know it isn't really up to us. We've got investors and HR." He pauses. "And your mom isn't exactly ready to go to bat over this. She thinks it will refelect negatively on us if we try to make excuses for you."

One time in the third grade, I was racing with my brothers on our bikes. My bike had the prettiest tassels in every color imaginable, and I loved watching the way they blew in the wind. I remember looking up from those rainbow tassels to see that I'd veered into the center of the road and there was a car coming straight at me. I swerved, barely missing the oncoming car, and landed flat on my back on the street.

I feel like that now—like I've just slammed hard onto concrete and had the wind knocked out of me.

I don't know why I expected my mom to fight for me on this, but it stings, nonetheless.

Clearing my throat, I say, "I understand."

Dad's mouth turns down in a frown, and his knuckles turn white from how tightly his hands are squeezed together. "You know your mom."

"Yeah, no. I get it." I need to get out of here before I lose it. "Is my suspension effective immediately?"

Dad nods and motions to a briefcase I hadn't noticed him carry in. "I'm going to set up shop here for the day."

My head bobs, not quite trusting my voice. I stand on shaky legs and manage to grab my bag before I walk through the door. I look straight forward, knowing that if I move my eyes even a fraction, the tears I've held back will slip free.

Sadie is walking up the sidewalk with the couple when I exit, but I continue right past her, my back stiff as a board, my shoulders so tight I'm convinced they're the only things keeping me upright.

"Ellie?" Sadie asks, and I hear the concern in her voice, but I don't acknowledge it. I can't acknowledge it.

I just keep walking—keep putting one foot in front of the other until I'm in my apartment. Just last night I'd stood here, letting Cam kiss a trail up my neck. I'd laughed against his lips and fallen asleep with my feet tucked under his thigh on the couch.

I'd woken up this morning and stared at my ceiling and thought I could end up loving this man.

But now the black hole in my heart is threatening to consume every good feeling until I collapse in on myself like a dying star.

Wrapping my arms tight around my legs, I attempt to fold myself into the smallest ball I can manage. And then I finally cry.

Thirty-Two

CAMDEN

"I finally told Ellie I'm staying," I tell Wes late Monday morning.

He looks up from his computer, eyes wide. "Really? How did she take it?"

I smile at the memory of her lips crashing against mine.

"That good, huh?" Wes says with a smirk.

I try to glare but know I'm failing miserably.

The smile doesn't leave his face as he turns back to the task on his computer. "Good, I'm glad."

"Me too," I say and return to the blank screen I've been staring at all morning. There's no way I'll get any work done today.

"So what's the plan for the next few weeks? When are you going back to LA to pack?"

I push a hand through my hair, trying to clear my mind enough to recall all the schedules I've been sorting through since Thanksgiving. "I'm going to finish up things here this week and still take the holiday break to visit my parents. But instead of staying two weeks there, I'm going to stay one week and then head back to LA to pack up my apartment."

"You know you're welcome to stay here until you find a place, right? You can store your stuff in our garage."

CHAPTER THIRTY-TWO

I shrug. "I'll probably donate most of it so I don't have to pay to ship it here. And thank you, but I think I already found a place."

Wes props his hands behind his head, leaning back in his chair. "Wow, where?"

"It's just a few miles from here. I'll probably sign a year lease and save up to buy something."

"Somewhere with more room?" Wes asks, grinning.

I roll my eyes, but the thought lodges in my head, and I know it won't go away anytime soon. "It's too early to think about that," I tell him.

He sits up, going back to work on his computer. "Yeah, maybe. But don't forget what I said about not wasting time."

I CONSIDER LEAVING WESTON's early, but Ellie won't be off until five, and I know I'll just pace my apartment waiting to see her. The hours pass by slowly. Ellie doesn't respond to any of my texts, but I also remember how quickly she left this morning and wouldn't be surprised if her phone is stuck in one of her couch cushions.

"Just go home," Wes says, fighting a smile, when I check the clock one more time.

It's four forty-five, and as long as Ellie doesn't have to stay late tonight, she should be getting off work right as I'm getting back. I stand, gathering my things. "Okay, see you tomorrow."

Wes just grins at me, reclining in his chair again. "Hey, Cam?"

I turn around, already halfway out the door.

"I'm really happy for you, man."

I pause, thinking about how I really owe all of this to him and his annoying, unrelenting efforts to get me out here. I owe him more than I could ever repay. "Thanks, me too."

And then I'm gone.

I pull into the parking lot a few minutes after five and don't even bother going back to my place when I see Ellie's light on upstairs. My heart hammers in my chest at the thought of her, and I hope I never outgrow this feeling. I hope every time I see Ellie I feel *just like this*—frenzied with anticipation, overwhelmed with longing, and absolutely bursting with joy. It's ridiculous, but I never want it to end.

I knock on Ellie's door, but when she doesn't answer, I let myself in, like she instructed me to do weeks ago. "Hey, Ellie!" I call up the stairs. "You here?"

The sounds of the TV drown out any response, so I doubt she heard me. I climb the stairs, and when I reach the top, I see her sprawled on the couch, and something inside me warms at the sight.

This is what I want to come home to every day. The thought hits me like a punch to the chest, stealing the air from my lungs, but I know it's the truth.

Seeing her here like this, everything is exactly right.

"Hey," I say, unsurprised at the way my voice comes out raspy and strangled.

Ellie sits up, and as soon as she turns to face me, I know something is very, very wrong. Her face is tear-stained and splotchy, and her hair a disheveled mess. She's wearing an oversized black sweatshirt that stands out against her skin, making her look deathly pale and so unlike herself that I almost don't recognize her.

CHAPTER THIRTY-TWO

My feet move of their own volition, propelling me forward until I'm in front of her, knees sinking into the plush rug covering the hardwood. I curl my hands around the side of her face, assessing every piece of her.

"Daisy, what's wrong?"

Ice splinters through my veins when her hands come up to wrap around my wrists and pull. She loosens her grip immediately, and my arms fall onto the couch cushions at her side.

"Cam, I messed up."

I resist the urge to reach for her again, although every nerve in my body is screaming for me to. "What happened? Whatever it is, we can fix it."

"Us," she answers, her voice raw and raspy as she stares right into my eyes.

If I thought I was breathless before, I am absolutely suffocating now. "What? Why? Tell me what happened."

"They found out."

She doesn't have to clarify. A sick feeling starts in my gut and spreads until it's all-consuming.

"It's okay. We were going to tell them anyway. It's okay, I promise."

"Cam, they may *fire me*."

My heart wrenches at her words. I know how much this place and these people mean to her—they're everything. "They won't fire you," I say, but even I know it's not something I can guarantee. "I can talk to them."

She shakes her head. "It's not just up to them. They have investors and the entire HR department on this. If they say I'm out, then I'm out. And my mom…" She pauses, looking away from me. Something inside me cracks when she sniffles, and I can't stop myself from reaching for her hand. My fingers thread through hers, and she doesn't let go.

Ellie turns haunted eyes back on me. She looks so empty that I want to cry. "My mom isn't fighting for me."

An overwhelming urge to locate Kristin Bates and give her a piece of my mind surges through me.

I force the urge down and focus on Ellie instead. *This* is where I'm needed right now; not out seeking revenge on her mother. "Ellie, it's going to be okay."

"I just messed everything up. I told my dad it was a mistake, a one-time slip-up, but I don't know if he believed me."

Her words hit me like shards of glass. "Is that how you feel?"

Tortured eyes fix on mine. "No, of course not."

I stare at her, wishing I didn't feel like I was being ripped in two. "Then why say that? Why not just tell them now and explain the situation?"

"Cam, I can't do that right now. They'll fire me if they know I've been seeing you for months. They'll never trust me here again."

I try to ignore the frustration coiling inside me, but it's useless. "Would that be so bad, Ellie?" I snap. "You *hate* working for them. You're miserable here, and you're forced to give up every single thing that makes you happy."

"I'm not *giving you up*. I'm just asking to keep this a secret a little bit longer."

I push back onto my heels, disentangling my hand from hers to push through my hair. "So when do we tell them?"

Ellie chews her bottom lip, eyes drifting around the room. "I don't know. Maybe a few months? Then we could tell them we reconnected?"

CHAPTER THIRTY-TWO

I stare at her, unblinking. "So we're going to hide our relationship for months and then lie to them about how we got together—forever? That's the plan?"

She sinks back against the couch, and I watch as her fingers tap against the cushions. Everything inside me screams to reach forward, clasp them between mine, and assure her everything will be okay.

But it doesn't feel okay—none of it—and I don't think I can promise her it will be.

"I don't know, Cam. It's all happening so fast, and I feel like I'm letting everyone down."

My heart cracks a little at her words. "You're not letting me down," I say on a huff of air. "But Daisy, I can't…I can't keep doing this. The back and forth is killing me."

A single tear drips down her cheek. I want to drag my thumb across it, wipe away the wetness, and make sure she never cries again.

But I don't. I clench my fists at my sides to hold myself back.

"I think maybe you need to figure out what you want," I tell her. "I know what I want. I want *this*. I want *you*, Ellie, but not like this." I suck in a breath. "I *can't* have you like this—no more secrets, no more lies."

Pushing to my feet, I stand on shaky legs. I can feel Ellie's stare on my back as I walk to the stairs. I turn around at the top and open my mouth to say something—anything—when her front door opens. Swinging my gaze back down the stairs, I see Sadie there.

I head down, not looking back, and see the confusion lining her features. "I was just leaving," I say, and let myself out.

The tears come before I even hear the snick of the door closing behind me.

Thirty-Three

ELLIE

I'm shaking on the couch when Sadie sits next to me, her hand immediately finding my back. She rubs slow circles there, and it's the only thing grounding me enough to keep me from completely losing it.

We sit in silence until I'm unsure of how much time has passed. It could be minutes or hours, days or weeks. There's nothing inside me to mark the passing of time—no tears drying on my face, no pangs of hunger in my stomach, no sleep tugging at my eyes. I am empty.

"Ellie," Sadie says, her voice low and concerned. "What happened? Your dad told me you'd been suspended, but he wouldn't tell me why."

I sniffle, trying to sort through my thoughts. "I've been seeing Cam, and they found out."

Sadie's hand stops moving on my back, and the little piece of my soul left unharmed starts to crumble. What if she's mad at me for not telling her? What if she can never forgive me for keeping this from her?

I can't bring myself to face her, to see the disappointment sure to be on her face.

"Why didn't you tell me?"

I raise my eyes to hers at the gentle tone of her voice, no condemnation to be found. And suddenly, I don't know how

CHAPTER THIRTY-THREE

to answer. What were my reasons for keeping this secret from my best friend for months?

"I messed up," I say, not missing the way my words echo what I said to Cam earlier. I've messed up *so often* recently, and I can't pinpoint where everything went wrong.

"It's okay," Sadie says. "Just tell me what happened."

I stare up at the ceiling, willing the tears to stay at bay. "I was going to tell you tonight at dinner, but I should have told you sooner. I should have told you about everything from the start, but I didn't want you to get in trouble if they found out. I didn't want you to have to lie for me or risk your job like I was."

"Risk my job?"

My breath leaves me in a whoosh. "Yeah, I didn't tell you about that either, but my parents approached me in October and told me if I didn't start making some changes around here, they were going to have to start exploring other options."

Sadie is quiet for a moment. "Exploring other options?"

I can't fight the redness that stains my cheeks, the hot lick of embarrassment at having to admit the level of dysfunction between my parents and me. "Fire me. They were going to fire me if I didn't turn things around. They told me to stay away from the residents and make sure to get my reports in on time. Keep our numbers strong and our reviews good. Be *better*."

"Ellie, you won Manager of the Year."

The memory feels like a kick to my stomach. "Yeah, and they were proud of me. They were finally proud of me, and I messed it all up."

"With…Cam?"

I nod, although that answer doesn't feel right. My time with Cam didn't feel *wrong*. "I was irresponsible, and I put the company at risk of a lawsuit. I made my parents look dumb in front of their investors and their employees."

"He's moving out this week," Sadie says gently. "You won't be forbidden from seeing him anymore."

"They'll fire me if they know this has been going on for months. They'll say I'm untrustworthy and a liability."

Sadie is quiet for a long moment, and I know it's because she can't refute my statement.

"The only way to make this work is if I tell them it was a one-time slip-up. I told my dad that Cam *just* asked me out and I thought it would be okay since he was moving out next week. I just have to convince them it's the truth," I say aloud, but it's more to myself than Sadie.

Sadie nods. "You're right." She hesitates. "But…what about Cam? Are you okay ending things with him?"

Tears prick the backs of my eyes—ones that feel equally sad and furious—because *no*, I am most definitely not okay with it. "I asked him if we could keep it just between us a little longer, and he said no."

Sadie is quiet so long that I turn to face her. Her bottom lip is trapped between her teeth, her eyebrows furrowed.

"What—you agree with him?" I ask.

She shrugs one shoulder. "Ellie, I don't know if I *agree* with him, but I see where he's coming from. What are you supposed to do—lie forever? What if things get serious between you? Are you always going to keep it a secret how long you've been together? As bad as things can get between you and your parents, you guys are still a close-knit family."

I hate how similar her words are to Cam's, how it feels like she's taking his side in this.

Pushing up off the couch, I walk into my kitchen and turn on my tea kettle.

"Ellie," Sadie says, following me. "I'm sorry. Now is *not* the time for this conversation. I just wanted to be here for you if you needed me."

I drop a tea bag into my mug and brace my hands on the counter. "I think…I think I just need to be alone."

Sadie looks like she wants to press the issue—keep cranking my jack-in-the-box handle until I explode and tell her everything on my mind—but she just blows out a breath and says, "Okay, yeah. I can do that. I'll handle checking on Ethel for the next few days."

"Thank you," I whisper.

I listen to her pad down my stairs and hear the door clicking shut behind her. Then the tears fall. They splash on the counter as I pour the water in my mug and let the tea steep. Through bleary eyes, I see the bottle of honey sitting on my counter, the one that has rapidly diminished since meeting Cam.

I just wanted you to keep me around, I guess.

I can hear his words like an echo in my apartment, like a whisper against my skin.

Ignoring the honey, I take a sip of the scalding liquid, not even noticing how bitter it tastes.

I DON'T HEAR FROM my parents until Wednesday morning when they call me into my office. I spent all of Tuesday pacing my apartment, wondering what their decision would be. I almost picked up my phone to call Cam at least a hundred times, but every time I did, I remembered his words—*not like this*—and that I still don't have a solution.

Anxiety twists in my stomach as I stand on the stoop outside the office. There are two cars in front of the building—my parents' SUV and an unfamiliar sedan. I can't imagine a scenario where I get to keep my job.

The thought of packing up my apartment, of having to say goodbye to my team and the residents here, threatens to release the dam on my emotions all over again. Thinking of having to start all over, find another job, makes me queasy. No respectable property management company is going to hire the daughter of their competitor, so I'm going to have to look in a different field. And also explain why I got fired in the first place.

Tears threaten to fall, but I shove them down and open the door. My dad is seated behind my desk, working on something on my computer.

He looks up when I come in, and I notice how tired he looks. Guilt, thick and hot, courses through me at that. I can't imagine the work I've created for them or the fights I've caused my parents. Mom has always accused Dad of being too easy on me, and I've always tried my best to prove her wrong.

"Morning, Ellie," Dad says, standing as I draw near. "We're meeting in the conference room."

The conference room almost never gets used because it's...well, it's icky. The fluorescent lights flicker, and the carpet has mysterious stains, and there are no windows, so you feel like you're in a prison. I have a brief moment of panic that it hasn't been cleaned. I can imagine a dust bunny landing on my mom's pressed pantsuit or a spider scurrying across the floor. I honestly don't know which one would be worse.

Mom and an unfamiliar man are seated around the table when we enter, folders open in front of them. Dad ushers me forward and motions to the lone chair across from the three of them.

"Ellie, this is Dakota, one of our HR reps," he says as he settles into the chair next to Mom. "We thought it would be best to have him present for this conversation."

My mind is suddenly dragged back to a memory from elementary school. I'd accidentally broken a jump rope on the playground when my friend and I decided to play an impromptu game of tug-of-war. The jump rope snapped, and we were both sent to the principal's office.

I remember the principal had looked so big and intimidating, sitting up straight in his chair with his unwavering, disappointed gaze fixed on me. I feel like that now as I adjust in my seat and it creaks loudly beneath me, the sound echoing in the windowless room.

"Hi, Dakota," I squeak out.

He gives me a closed-mouth smile, and my gaze fixes on the way the fluorescent light shines on his bald head.

"Ellie, we called you in here to discuss the situation with the resident," Mom says, bringing me back to the moment.

"It's over," I blurt out, and her gaze narrows on me. "It…" I hesitate, the words sticking in my throat. "It was nothing—just a one-time mistake."

Dad clears his throat. "That's good to hear, but it doesn't negate the fact that you had an inappropriate relationship with a resident."

My heart stutters at those words, and a thousand tiny moments flash through my mind—Camden making me soup when I was sick, smiling at me in the dark on top of the world, FaceTiming me and telling me to look at the stars, adding a little more honey to my tea every night until I was addicted to it. No, nothing with Cam was inappropriate. It was magic.

"After discussions with the HR department and with our investors, the board has decided that you may keep your job under certain conditions," Mom says, and my eyes snap to hers.

"I'm not fired?"

"The fact that you won Manager of the Year was taken heavily into consideration," Mom tells me. "You have otherwise proven to be a decent employee." I can't read the look in her eyes to determine whether she means what she's saying, or if it's all for Dakota's benefit. I remember her in my office, threatening to hold Dad accountable if I didn't clean up my act, but I also remember her at Thanksgiving, finally telling me she was proud. I don't know which version of my mother I'm going to get when we're finally alone, and it causes a shiver to rack my frame.

"What are the conditions?" I force myself to ask. If they want me to strip naked and run around the property, I'll do it as long as I can keep my job.

Dad looks to Dakota. "Dakota is going to come work on-site for the foreseeable future. He's going to monitor the situation and make sure things here are running properly."

My eyes flick to Dakota, who looks bored more than anything else. I wonder how he feels about coming to babysit his bosses' daughter, and if he would have rather fired me and gotten it over with.

"Okay," I manage. I honestly can't believe that I'm getting off this easy.

"That's it," Dad says, standing, and Mom follows suit. They go about gathering their things, and I can't help but think about how quickly this was resolved. It feels like my heart has been cleaved in two, but they're able to act completely unfazed.

I wish they would look at me—acknowledge me—but it's like the moment they were done with their meeting, they were also done with me. Here in this conference room, I cease to be their daughter. I'm just another employee, one who they, unfortunately, had to stop in to formally reprimand on their way to the office.

"About Saturday...?" I ask as they head toward the door.

Mom arches an eyebrow, looking like she's already moved on from the meeting. "Saturday?"

"The gala. Am I...should I still come?"

"You are still Manager of the Year. You're expected to be there to accept your award."

I swallow and nod. "Thank you."

I wonder how it will feel—if that award will make it all feel worth it, or if I'll still feel this gnawing emptiness inside of me.

THE NEXT FEW DAYS pass in a blur. Dakota is always there, hovering in the background, and I can tell he's driving Sadie nuts. There's a tick in her jaw whenever he's around—or maybe that's for me since we still haven't talked about the situation in my apartment the other day.

The whole thing has caused a sick feeling in my gut that won't go away. I think that feeling is what distracts me enough to forget what day it is. That is, until Cam walks into the office Friday morning.

Suddenly, I know exactly what day it is—his move-out day.

He looks as wrecked as I feel, and I want to smooth that crinkle between his brows, push my hands up his chest and into the hair at the nape of his neck, and kiss him until he's smiling again. I want to feel that hitched grin right against the crook of my shoulder.

When I got ready for my meeting Wednesday morning, I noticed my perfume was gone, and I remembered tossing it at Cam and telling him to take it and spray it on his pillow. I wonder if he did, and I wonder if he's as haunted by our memories as I am.

I stare at him, and I'm reminded once again of how beautiful he is. With that lock of hair that never stays back and the sleeves of his corduroy jacket straining against his biceps, he would make anyone look twice. My stomach bottoms out at that thought.

"Hi," I whisper.

His eyes dip to my mouth, where I've sucked my bottom lip between my teeth, and fix there. For a long moment, I stand there and feel his gaze like a caress. I remember every moment of his mouth being on mine, of his breath fanning my cheeks, of his hands slipping beneath my hair. I remember it all, and it threatens to pull me under.

"Hey," he says back, finally making eye contact again.

Dakota comes out of the bathroom at that moment and assesses the situation. He stares at me with wide eyes, and I clear my throat, turning back to Cam.

"Can I help you with something?" I ask Cam.

I don't miss the flash of hurt that crosses his face, but it's there and gone in an instant. "I'm just here to return my keys."

He moves forward until he's standing right in front of me. With him staring down at me like that, I think I may never breathe again. He drops the keys into my waiting palm, his fingers brushing against me, and I fight against a shiver that trails up my spine.

"Thanks for everything, Daisy," he says, low enough that only I can hear. One corner of his mouth tips up in the barest of smiles. "It was all worth it to me."

Then he turns and lets himself out, and I'm left staring, pondering his words. Despite everything, I think he's right—I think it was worth it.

Thirty-Four

CAMDEN

I don't remember much of the drive to Fontana Ridge. One moment I'm sitting in Nashville traffic, and then next I'm passing the rickety welcome sign in my hometown.

When I get to my parents' street, I hit the brakes and stare down the gravel driveway at their house for a long moment before continuing on. I don't think I'm ready to see them yet, to have them ask me what's wrong and have to come up with a way to explain it.

No, I need some time alone in the fields with my camera.

The sun is just beginning to dip behind the mountains when I pull into the empty parking lot at the farm. Somehow, even with everything dying off for the winter, it still smells like Ellie—like daisies and peonies and sun-kissed apples.

Leaves crunch beneath my feet as I take off into the rows and rows of trees. Around every bend, after cresting every hill, I tell myself to pull out my camera. The light through the trees is breathtaking. The splashes of color are a dream. The last of the dying leaves float in the breeze like they're dancing just for me.

But I don't reach for my camera. For the first time in a long time, I've found a moment I don't want to remember. Despite the beauty all around me, I don't want to steal this moment from space and time and have a tangible way to look back on it. I don't want a reminder of how my heart feels like it's cracked in two or how my lungs feel like they can't catch a full breath.

I would do anything to *forget* this moment in time, to close my eyes and have my world right side up again when I open them.

"Hey," someone calls, and I turn to see my dad standing among the trees. "I thought I saw you drive by."

I search my mind for something to say, for a reason to explain why I'm here in the orchard instead of sitting around the fireplace at my parents' house, but I can't think of anything.

"Wanna sit?" Dad asks, nodding toward one of the trees to our left. It's got a wide trunk, perfect for leaning against.

I nod, and we settle next to each other, our backs reclining against the old tree. Something about it makes me feel anchored, like even though my world feels like it's crashing down around me, there are still the trees. No matter what is going on in my life, these trees will still be here. Their roots will continue to grow deeper and deeper into the soil, weathering the storms and drought and disease, and will still be able to produce new fruit each year.

"You headed back to Nashville early at Thanksgiving. I was kind of expecting you to hold off on coming back," Dad says, his eyes fixed on the horizon.

"I thought about it," I answer honestly.

I had considered it that morning when I woke up on Ellie's couch to find her warm, brown eyes staring back at me. Watching her run around her apartment, trying to get ready for work, the thought of leaving her for two weeks seemed unfathomable. It still does.

"What made you decide to stick to your original plans?"

I swallow and track the sun as it slips behind the mountains, bathing the world in pinks, oranges, and purples. "Things changed."

Dad finally turns to face me, and I stare into his eyes that are so similar to mine, notice the lock of salt and pepper hair that falls over his forehead. "Is it something you want to talk about?"

I let out a deep breath and brace my elbows on my knees. "Not yet, but maybe later."

Dad's hand comes to rest on my shoulder, giving it a comforting squeeze. He doesn't say anything, just turns back to watch the sky once more.

We sit there until the sky turns black and glitters with stars.

Saturday morning, I wake up to soft, golden light filtering through the curtains of my childhood home. After watching the sunset with my dad last night, I came back to the house, and Mom made us all hot cocoa before turning on a holiday movie.

I couldn't tell you what we watched, since my mind was focused elsewhere. When the two hours were up, I had stared at the end credits and realized I hadn't noticed a single second of what was on the screen.

I can't spend this whole week in a fog. I pull myself up out of bed, knowing I'll need to keep myself busy today or get sucked into my thoughts and never come back out.

CHAPTER THIRTY-FOUR

After showering and changing into warm clothes for the day, I head into the living room. Mom is sitting on the couch, wrapped in a blanket, watching the news, a book in her lap.

"Morning, Cammie," she says, giving me a warm smile. "Coffee's still warm."

"Morning," I say and shuffle into the kitchen, my eyes still a little bleary. "Did Dad already head into work?"

Dad owns a trail guide company that caters to tourists and locals alike. While he doesn't actually guide many hikes or camping trips himself anymore after hiring my cousin Stevie, he still has a lot of work to do in the office and attached general store most days.

"Yeah, he has a big group that came in for a winter camping trip today. Stevie is heading it up and should be back early next week."

"Cutting it pretty close to Christmas," I say, pouring coffee into one of the cracking mismatched mugs in the cupboard. Mom has never learned that some things aren't microwaves safe, so all our mugs are cracked and chipping after years of her reheating her coffee every morning.

Mom shrugs as I head back into the living room. "You know Stevie. She's out of here any chance she gets."

"I've never understood why she's stayed here so long." I settle onto the soft, worn sofa that's been here for as long as I can remember.

"I think she would feel too guilty leaving her parents to run the farm by themselves."

"They have Wren," I say, referring to Hazel and Stevie's best friend, who happens to be the farm's only unrelated employee.

"I know that, and you know that, but I think Stevie is too worried about disappointing them—although they never would be."

Her words are a strike to my chest, hitting a little too close for comfort. I fix my eyes on the TV and take a sip of my coffee, hoping it will be enough to distract me from thoughts of Ellie.

The woman on the screen talks about the surprisingly good conditions in the mountains today, clear skies and without any chance of snow. I knew it would be, since Dad would never allow Stevie out to guide a trip if there was any chance for inclement weather, but the report gives me an idea.

"I'm going to Asheville in a bit to pick up Hazel from the airport if you want to come," Mom says.

I shake my head. "I think I'm going to hike The Mountain today."

Mom stares at me. To be fair, it's a little ambitious. We're surrounded by mountains in Fontana Ridge, but there's one that the locals have creatively dubbed *The Mountain*. It's a 4.2-mile hike, all uphill, but there's a fire tower at the top, and the views are always worth it.

"Have you been hiking *at all* recently?"

"Nope," I answer. The hike will probably kill me, but the strenuous labor will hopefully be enough to keep my mind off Ellie all day. And if it's not, at least I can scream and wail in the mountains alone with nothing but the trees and bears to hear me.

"Are you sure that's a good idea?"

I point at the TV. "You heard her. The weather's great, so this might be my only chance. Who knows when a winter storm will blow in."

Mom's brow furrows, but I can tell she knows there will be no dissuading me. I wonder briefly if Dad mentioned our talk in the orchard last night to her, but I don't really care. If he did, I'd much rather be miles away on top of a mountain than here alone with her inquisitions.

"Fine, be safe," Mom tells me.

I WAS RIGHT AND wrong about my hike—yes, it's going to kill me, and no, it didn't take my mind off Ellie one bit. Actually, being all alone with my thoughts has only brought her to mind that much more.

I swear I can hear her laugh echoing on the breeze and see her smile every time I blink.

Maybe I'm just dehydrated.

I finally crest the last hill and see the fire tower up ahead. Sweat beads on my forehead and stings as it drips into my eyes. Pushing back the hair that won't stay out of my face, I pause and take a drink of my water. Although I'm flushed and sweating, the air is crisp and cold, especially at this elevation.

I look around me, taking in the view, and wish I had brought my camera. But after the sick feeling in the pit of my stomach last night when I tried to force myself to take photos, I decided to leave it back in my childhood bedroom. It feels weird being without it, like something is missing—a vital organ or a limb.

Me without my camera is like Ellie without her smiles, and my heart hurts knowing she's probably feeling as empty and bereft as I am right now.

Tucking away my water bottle and thoughts of Ellie, I make my way to the stairs. There are at least a hundred rickety ones leading above me. *It will be worth it*, I try to remind myself.

The stairs creak beneath my weight, and the wind whips a little harder, drying the sweat on my skin, but I finally make it to the top. Without fail, this view always takes my breath away. From here, you can see the whole town nestled in the trees far below on one side and miles and miles of uninterrupted forest on the other.

My heartbeat slows into a steady rhythm as I stare out into the distance, and I feel it again, that urge to snap a picture. This time, I'm not forcing myself to. This time, I'm driven by this want to capture a moment in time.

I pull out my phone, making do the best I can with what I have on hand. The pictures will never live up to the real thing or what I could have taken with my film camera or my DSLR, but they'll still be a reminder that I did the hard thing. They'll remind me that when everything was falling apart, I did something hard, and it was worth it.

My heartbeat finally slows as my eyes take in the view. My problems don't seem so bad up here, with the wind and the trees to keep me company. Closing my eyes, I breathe in and out, feeling some of the tension finally leave my shoulders.

Things aren't magically better—I still feel like there's an Ellie-sized hole in my chest, a spot reserved for tea and soup, daisies and stars, slow dancing and honeyed kisses—but it's helping.

Opening my eyes, I pull out my phone for one last photo. I want this picture to remember this moment of *letting go*. Leaning forward, I hold my phone out one of the shattered windows, angling it just right to catch the sun glittering on the river below.

I press the button and watch the shutter click.

And then I drop my phone.

CHAPTER THIRTY-FOUR

I'm not sure exactly how it happened, but one moment, it's in my hand, and then next, it's hurtling to the ground below.

A loud crack reverberates as it hits one of the metal beams before slamming into the rocky earth.

I definitely won't need that photo to remember this moment.

Thirty-Five

ELLIE

The event venue looms ahead of me, the bright lights at the entrance refracting off the raindrops covering my window. I can't bring myself to go inside. I'm the guest of honor, but I don't want to celebrate. Everything is such a jumbled mess. I feel like the ball of cords you end up throwing out because trying to untangle them and find the device they belong to would be too much effort.

My passenger door swinging open snaps me out of my reverie. I look over just in time to see Sadie sliding in. She shuts the door, trapping us inside this stifling silence.

"I don't like how we left things," Sadie says into the quiet.

I tuck my hands under my thighs to stop my fingers from tapping. "Me neither."

"I wasn't trying to agree with him."

Turning back to face out the window, I say the thing that's been haunting my every thought for days. "Maybe he *was* right."

I feel Sadie's stare on me, but don't look over. "Do you really think that?" she asks quietly.

I let out a long breath. "I don't know. I know what I told him was true—that they wouldn't let me keep my job if they knew."

Sadie is quiet for a moment. "But…?"

"But he also made some good points," I say, finally meeting her eyes.

"What did he say?"

"That while I love my job, working for them has made me kind of…miserable." I hesitate, unsure of how she will react.

I certainly don't expect her next words. "You could quit, you know."

I stare at her, unblinking. "You want me to quit?"

She gives me a small smile and reaches for my hand. "No, I don't want you to quit. I couldn't imagine anyone else on the other side of that window. You're my best friend, and I love working with you."

"I love working with you too," I say, fighting against the lump lodging in my throat.

"But," she says, "if working at The Flats, working for *your parents*, isn't making you happy, I want you to be happy more than I want you to be in the office next to mine."

I can't help the tear that drips down my cheek now, coming to splash against the black velvet dress I bought since I thought the sequin emerald one I'd originally purchased was no longer appropriate.

A knock on my window stops me from responding, although I'm not entirely sure what I would have said.

I look up to see Alex standing outside my car, the rain misting around him and causing his hair to curl up around the edges. Turning back to Sadie, I say, "We better head inside."

When I shut off the car and step into the rain, Alex wraps me in a hug.

"Hey, loser," he says, but his tone is soft. I texted him and Adam yesterday to give them an update in case Mom or Dad mentioned Cam to them. They were both heartbreakingly sympathetic, asking if I wanted them to come over or if I needed to talk, but I just wanted to be alone.

I sink into him, grateful for his familiarity when everything else feels so messed up.

"You okay?" he asks, and I'm horrified at my sniffle.

"Yeah, I'll be fine."

He pulls back, hands still wrapped around my arms, and searches my face. "You're a liar, but I'm going to leave it alone anyway because I don't want to get soaked."

Alex flashes Sadie a smile as we head toward the doors. "You both look great, by the way." He glances sideways at my dress. "Mom will love this."

"Gee, thanks."

He presses a hand to his chest, feigning offense. "Mother and her society members have excellent taste."

I bite back a smile, the first one I've had in days, and follow him into the building. With my brother and my best friend at my side, it feels a little less scary.

"Thanks for coming," I say when we walk through the doors. Crystal chandeliers line the entryway, casting a golden glow all around the ornate room.

Alex crooks a grin back at me. "Wouldn't miss it for the world. Adam and Kelsey are already here. They're trying to make up for being late to Thanksgiving."

We head through the double doors to the ballroom and locate our seats at the front table.

"Where are Gary and his wife?" I ask Sadie when we sit down, nodding to the empty seats reserved for them.

"I don't know. He sent me a text earlier saying they couldn't make it."

"Hey, Ellie," Adam says, dragging my gaze away from the empty chairs. He lowers his voice. "You doing okay?"

CHAPTER THIRTY-FIVE

Dad walks out on the stage then, saving me from answering, and I spin around to face forward. Silence descends on the room, and all eyes focus ahead.

"Welcome to the annual Bates Property Management Winter Gala," Dad says, a charming smile lighting his face. I got all of my charisma from Dad and none from Mom, who is sitting a few tables away, her face set in a firm line as she watches Dad on stage.

"We're so glad you're here," he continues. "Dinner will be brought out shortly, and then we will begin our awards ceremony. You've all accomplished great things this year, and we're thrilled to celebrate you. In the meantime," he says, spreading his hands out wide, "eat."

Noise slowly fills the room again, and I turn back around in my chair, fingers tapping on my thigh under the table. I don't want anyone to press the issue because I honestly don't know how to answer their questions. I'm so utterly relieved to still have my job, but the relief is usually overwhelmed by crippling despair and emptiness.

"I'll give ten bucks to the person who spots Mom smiling tonight," Alex says, reaching for one of the rolls sitting in the middle of the table.

"Spots Mom what?" Mom asks, coming up behind Alex.

The tips of his ears turn pink, and I almost feel bad for him, but then he turns around and flashes Mom one of his crooked grins. "You look lovely tonight, Mom. Has anyone told you that yet?"

She smooths her hands down the fabric of her black lace dress. "Thank you, Alexander. I actually came over to talk to your sister."

All eyes swivel to me, and I resist the urge to give into a shudder.

"Do you mind stepping out with me, Ellie?"

I swallow against the lump lodged in my throat and nod. Pushing to my feet, I follow her out. When we've made it far enough down the hall that the noise from the ballroom has quieted, she spins to face me.

I'm short, but my mom is shorter. I have no idea how she is able to be so commanding and confident in every situation, but it's one of the qualities I admire about her. It's something that, despite trying to emulate for years, I've never quite been able to manage.

She stares at me for a long moment, long enough that a bead of sweat forms between my shoulder blades.

"Your father has told me that I may have been too harsh with you lately," she says finally.

I clear my throat, searching for words, but she continues.

"I want you to know that, despite everything, I *am* proud of you. We've always been different, you and I. I like everything in my life to be in neat boxes, and you've never quite fit into one. You've been your own person from the very start. I guess I didn't think I'd have such a hard time letting you be *that* person." She smooths a hand down her stomach, and I wonder, for the first time, if my mother is nervous. It makes my heart soften just a little. "Having you follow in our footsteps has been a dream come true, but it also makes it difficult for me to separate my daughter from my employee."

I pause for a moment. "I understand." And I do.

It's just that, for the first time, I'm starting to see the problems with it.

She gives me a smile and gives my hand a squeeze—a rare gesture of affection from my reserved mother. "Good, I'll be glad to hand you that award tonight, Elizabeth."

CHAPTER THIRTY-FIVE

We return to the ballroom, but I can't bring myself to ask Alex for my ten dollars—I don't think I want it like that.

AN HOUR LATER, I'M pushing my slimy catered chicken around on my plate as we sit through the awards.

My hands are getting tired from clapping, and the smile I've had plastered on my face all night is making my jaw ache. All I want is to go home and drink a cup of too-sweet tea, even though I haven't been able to touch the honey since Cam left. If his goal was to get me hooked on how he made it, it worked. The herbal tea that once used to taste perfect to me before I met him is now bitter and tasteless.

"And now, on to Manager of the Year," Dad says, snapping my attention back to the stage. "As you know, every year, each one of our property managers is evaluated through an unbiased set of qualifications. Online reviews are taken into consideration, as well as revenue, closing ratios, and accomplishments. Once those top few are narrowed down, the managers with the best resident and employee recommendations are considered. Finally, the manager with the best overall score wins the title for the year. This year I could not be prouder to present the award to my daughter, Elizabeth Bates, manager of The Flats at Inglewood."

My heart stutters in my chest when all eyes fix on me. I stand on shaky legs and make my way to the podium. Mom and Dad are smiling at me, looking for all the world like they couldn't be more proud.

And while it should make me feel thrilled, I can't help but wonder what mistake will wipe that look off their faces—because there *will* be one.

I take the award from them and stare out at the table full of *my* people. There's one person notably missing, the one person I wanted to be here from the start.

Thirty-Six

ELLIE

"You sure you don't want to go out to celebrate with us?" Adam asks one more time as the cleaning crew starts to descend on the ballroom, tearing down the gala decor.

I give him a small smile. "No, I have something I need to do."

Sadie's hand finds mine under the table and squeezes. I don't know how, but she's figured out why I'm still sitting here at this table, waiting on my parents to finish telling everyone goodbye.

"Do you want me to stay?" she asks quietly.

I shake my head. "No, I need to do this alone."

Alex looks between us. "What are you doing?"

I let out a deep breath, gathering the courage to say the words aloud. It's scary, but it feels right. "I'm going to quit."

The table is silent for a long moment, and then it erupts. My brothers come around to give me hugs and Kelsey flashes me a grin.

"I'm proud of you," Alex says in my ear.

"This will be good," Adam says.

"What will be good?" We all freeze at our father's voice behind us. Adam and Alex each give me one last hug, then back up.

Alex winks. "Call me later." Turning to our parents, he gives them a mock bow. "Mom, Dad—delightful as always."

Mom is not to be deterred. "What will be good?"

Sadie, Kelsey, and my brothers file out, each giving me a reassuring pat on the shoulder as they walk by. I don't look away from my parents, for once not feeling intimidated or small.

This—the scary leap into the unknown—feels like the right path. I'm not sure how they're going to take it, but I think this is the first step on the road to recovering our relationship.

When we're finally alone, my heart a steady beat in my ears, I say, "We need to talk."

Mom's eyes me warily, and I can tell she's hoping I haven't messed up again.

"Okay," Dad says, gesturing to the table. "Let's talk."

A sudden urge to begin a nervous tap of my fingers strikes me, but I clasp my hands together behind my back. "I don't think it should be here."

Dad tilts his head quizzically. "Why?"

"Could we go back to your office?"

Mom and Dad exchange a silent conversation with their eyes before Mom finally nods. "We can meet you there."

I FOLLOW MY PARENTS' Cadillac to their office, the noise of my wipers hiccuping across the windshield the only sound for the entire drive. I'm too nervous for music, and the only person I want to call is the one person I can't. Not yet. I don't want to call Cam until I have good news.

CHAPTER THIRTY-SIX

The Bates Property Management headquarters are in an old factory turned office park near downtown. I've always loved it. As a kid, I would follow my dad around the office and make copies for him or brew tea for my mom and bring it to her in her favorite mug from the break room. She would take a few sips and then let me have the rest. She kept a bottle of honey in her desk drawer just for me.

I don't know how things got so messed up between us—if it was the job or my debilitating need to try and please them—but something was critically altered along the way. And I think quitting is the first step to fixing that.

Dad flips on the lights in his office, bathing the room in the glow from the fluorescent light. He motions to the chairs across from his desk, and Mom and I each take one. I expect him to sit behind the desk, but he drags his desk chair around so we're sitting in a circle.

It feels like the world's smallest start, but I grasp on to it for dear life.

"What did you want to talk about?" Dad asks.

His eyes are a warm, chocolate brown, just like mine. They're apprehensive, and I want to change that.

I turn away, no longer able to look at the suspicion there. My gaze fastens on a picture on the wall. It's of our family on some vacation years ago. Italy, I think. All of us kids had complained about spending the day seeing the sights when all we wanted to do was swim in our hotel pool. At the end of the day, tired of our whining, they'd stopped at a random gelato stand and let us pick whatever flavor we wanted. I'd ended up with blue all over my lips, Alex shoved his cone in Adam's face, and Adam had retaliated by pouring his cup of soda in Alex's lap.

We were a mess, and Dad snapped a picture. I remember seeing it on his wall the next time I came to work with him and wondering why that was the moment he wanted to remember. When I asked him, he said that sometimes the messiest moments in life are the ones we look back on most fondly.

I really hope he was right.

"I would like to resign from my position as property manager of The Flats at Inglewood," I say on an exhale.

Mom blinks, as if not understanding what I just said. "You what?"

I swallow and clasp my hands tightly together in my lap to keep them from shaking. "I think working together has put an unnecessary strain on our relationship."

"What do you mean?" Dad asks, his brow furrowing.

Chewing at my bottom lip, I try to figure out the best way to explain all the thoughts running through my mind. "I think I want so badly to please you that I've started to...sacrifice pieces of myself."

Mom massages her temples. "What is that even supposed to mean, Ellie?"

I gesture at my dress. "Look what I'm wearing, Mom. Does this look like your daughter?"

"You look great," she protests.

Knowing I'm getting nowhere with her, I turn to Dad. "Look at me. Do I look like your daughter—do I look like *me*?"

The crevices between his eyebrows deepen as he looks at me, no doubt taking in not only my outfit, but the purple circles beneath my eyes. "No," he says softly. "No, you don't."

Tears prick at the back of my eyes. "I just think things would be best this way."

CHAPTER THIRTY-SIX

"I'm still not understanding," Mom says, sounding exasperated.

I huff out a breath and turn to face her. "The boxes, Mom. It's the boxes." Hot tears make a slow path down my cheeks. "You said it yourself—I don't fit in one. You can't separate your daughter from your employee, and I don't think it's worth continuing to try. I'd rather just be...your daughter."

Mom pushes back a lock of her pale blonde hair, managing to muss it up. It's disconcerting to see her out of sorts when she's always so put together. "You can't quit. Imagine what people would say."

I turn to Dad. "*Please* tell me you understand where I'm coming from."

His gaze searches mine for a moment before his shoulders slump. "I understand."

"Daniel!" Mom flails her hands. "This is going to reflect so badly on us."

"Say you fired me."

She pins me with a hard stare. "That's not any better, and you know it."

Dad keeps his eyes locked on mine for another long minute. The corner of his mouth tips up in the barest of smiles, so small you wouldn't see it unless you were looking. But I've always been looking, waiting for that smile to return because of me. "It's not her job to figure it out. She doesn't work here anymore."

CAM ISN'T ANSWERING HIS phone. In fact, it's going straight to voice mail. For a split second, I think he might have blocked me, but this is *Cam*.

The sound of the ringing over and over again grates on my already frayed nerves, and by the time I arrive back at The Flats, I'm a ball of barely contained energy. I run through the rain, puddles splashing beneath my bare feet, and unlock the door to my apartment.

The light is on upstairs, and for one moment, my heart stops, imagining Cam returning and using his key. I can almost picture him sitting on my couch, a pot of soup simmering on the stove, waiting for me to return.

But then Sadie appears at the top of the stairs, no longer in her formal attire. Her pale hair is in a bun atop her head, and it bounces precariously as she slides to a stop. "How did it go?"

I climb the stairs two at a time. "It went okay. No, it was good—I think. Mom…" I trail off. "She's going to take some getting used to the idea, but it will be okay in the long run."

Sadie gives me a small smile. "So this is it, then?"

I nod, reaching for her hand. "Yeah, this is it. I have to be out in five days."

A crinkle forms between her eyes. "Where will you go?"

"Alex has a spare room," I say with a shrug.

Sadie laughs, and I realize how much I've missed it these past few months. It's *liberating* to have everything out in the open between us.

"I bet he's going to love that," Sadie says.

"Oh, definitely."

She pauses. Then, "What about Cam?"

I pull my phone from my pocket, checking for missed calls. "He's not picking up."

Sadie's face falls. "I'm sorry. I'm sure he just missed them and will call back soon."

I nod, trying to convince myself that she's right, and feel all the spark drain out of me. "Yeah, maybe."

She grabs my hand, tugging me into my living room. I finally notice there's a movie playing on my TV.

"Making yourself cozy, huh?" I ask.

She grins back at me. "I couldn't sit at my place and wait around for you to call, so I came here."

Her words are a lightning zap to my brain, lighting me up with an idea and charging me with energy once more. "Sadie, tell me I'm not crazy."

She spins around, staring at me. "What?"

"You're right—I can't sit around here and wait for a call."

She tips her head to one side. "That's...not at all what I said."

I charge past her and into my bedroom, already stripping the damp velvet dress from my body.

"What are you doing?" she asks, following after me.

I grab the first things from my drawer that I can find—a bright orange loungewear set. I tug it on haphazardly. I'm pretty sure the sweatshirt is backward. "I'm going to North Carolina."

"You're *what?*"

When I spin around, looking for my sneakers, Sadie's hands are propped on her hips.

"I'm going to see Cam." I stop, letting my breath out in a whoosh. "I can't sit around and wait for him to call, Sadie. I'll go crazy."

She stares at me for a long moment. "It's like that quote from *When Harry Met Sally.* 'When you realize you want to spend the rest of your life with somebody, you want the rest of your life to start—'"

"As soon as possible," I finish for her.

She looks around my room for a moment before disappearing into my closet. When she comes back out, she's holding my cherry-red leather pants. "Then you're going to want to take these."

Thirty-Seven

CAMDEN

Light filters through the trees and colors the world in burnt oranges and warm golds. I walk the fields, my camera a familiar weight at my side, the air heavy and damp and chilled with morning fog. I take a deep breath, filling my lungs, and exhale, watching the cold air puff out around me.

I reach for my phone to check the time, but remember it's still shattered at the bottom of a fire tower on top of The Mountain. For the most part, not having my phone has been a pain, but there's a small part of me that's glad for it. I don't have to keep staring at it, waiting for Ellie to call. I don't have to keep reading through our messages or sit with my finger hovering over her contact.

Now I'm just existing—in a world without Ellie. It feels dull and colorless.

So I thought I'd come out here with my camera this morning, when the sun and the clouds douse the stars and make their own color.

It still hangs at my side, wrapped in its leather case, and I keep walking. I don't know where I'm going until I round the corner and see the store up ahead, nestled in a copse of trees. All it would take is one twist of the spare key hidden under the mat, and I could be inside, where everything smells like Ellie.

My feet keep going of their own volition until my eyes snag on the lone car in the parking lot.

Ellie.

My heart beats erratically in my chest as I move closer. It can't be her. It *can't* be, but I feel that tug low in my stomach, the one I always feel when she's close. It's like there's a string tying us together, and she's given it a firm pull.

I come around the driver's side, and my breath hitches at the cascade of dark hair. Ellie's chest rises and falls in sleep. She's wearing an orange sweatshirt and matching pants, and the outfit is so *her*, so like the clothes she used to change into when we would lounge on her couch at night, that my heart melts just a little.

I don't know why she's here, can't imagine a single reason that makes sense, and a small piece of me doesn't want to wake her up to find out. If she's asleep, she can't give me bad news. If she's asleep, she can't tell me again that she can't be with me. If she's asleep, I can choose to believe she's here for a *good* reason.

Her eyelids flutter, and I know I should move away so I don't scare her, but I have to know how she reacts to seeing me. Ellie has a horrible poker face—she wears her heart like a badge of honor, and I have to know if there's hope.

Warm, sleepy brown eyes lock on mine, and she doesn't even look surprised—like she knew she'd wake up to find me right here. Like this is where she was *wishing* I'd be. I swallow against the lump rising in my throat as she reaches for the door handle.

The sound of the door squeaking open shocks me enough to remember to breathe. I don't think I have since I got here. If this is a dream, I don't want to wake up.

CHAPTER THIRTY-SEVEN

Ellie swings her legs out and stands in one fluid motion. And then she's *right there*, her head reaching just below my chin, her eyes sleepy, and her lip tucked between her teeth.

"Hi," she says.

As I look down at her matted hair and the crease on her cheek from where it was resting against her palm while she slept, I feel such an overwhelming surge of affection for her. "Hi."

A slow, small smile blooms on her face, and it threatens to take my breath away. "So, I'm in North Carolina."

"I hadn't noticed," I say, unable to keep my own lips from twitching up.

Ellie watches me, her eyes cataloging every inch of my face, like I am with her. It's only been a week, but it feels like a lifetime.

Finally, she tears her gaze away and fixes it on something behind me. "Want to show me around?"

I blink at the change in subject. "You've been here before."

"But not with you."

The words are so simple, but they burrow beneath my skin. I don't know why she's here, and I don't know if she will ever be back, but I want to show her my home, the place that now reminds me of her as much as it does of my childhood.

Leaves kick up in the breeze, waving their hello to us.

"Okay, Daisy, let me show you around."

The sun slowly crests the mountains as we walk. Ellie and I keep to ourselves, although every few steps, my arm brushes against the sleeve of that furry beige coat we bought at the thrift store. When she pulled it out of her back seat and tugged it on over her orange getup, I wanted to reach over and tug her hair free from the collar, finally feel her skin against mine again, but I held back.

Leaves crunch beneath our feet, a steady rhythm as we weave through the rows and rows of trees. "This isn't exactly the best time to visit the farm," I tell her.

She kicks her feet through the leaves, sending them spraying. "When is?"

I shrug, considering. "Early fall is nice because of the apples. There are apples everywhere—cider, donuts, muffins, you name it. Pumpkins too. Fall is nice."

Ellie peers at me sideways through her lashes. "But that's not your favorite."

It's not a question, and I wonder briefly when she came to know me so well. These past few months seem both like a blip in time and an eternity. "No," I say softly. "Spring is my favorite."

"Because of the flowers?" she asks after a long moment.

We break through the rows of trees and end up on the dirt road that circles the farm. "I like the daisies the best, but the peonies are pretty too."

She makes a humming sound in the back of her throat but doesn't say anything else.

I point to the base of a hill. "That's where the flowers grow in spring."

The breath huffs out of her. "It's beautiful."

And it is, even though everything has died off. With the mountains in the background, a thick layer of fog looking like smoke rising from the trees, it's magical. "You should see it in spring."

"I'd like to," Ellie says, her voice so quiet I can barely hear her.

My feet stop before my brain can tell them to keep going. Ellie spins around a couple of paces ahead of me, sending up a cloud of dust behind her.

When her brown eyes meet mine, I realize I can't pretend anymore. I can't hope to stay asleep in case I'm dreaming. "Ellie, what are you doing here?"

Ellie swallows, and out of the corner of my eye, I see her fingers drumming against her thigh. She's *nervous*. I want to grab her hand and squeeze, assure her that everything is going to be okay, but I hold myself back.

Already, I can feel my resolve crumbling like a sandcastle in a summer storm. If I close the distance between us, if I wrap my arms around her, I'll give in to whatever she asks.

"Last night was the gala," Ellie says.

"I know," I whisper, my voice a little strangled. I'd been at war with myself all night, wanting to figure out a way to contact her. I wanted her to know that even though I didn't love how things happened with us, I was still so proud of her.

Ellie meets my gaze once more. "Right, okay. So last night, I got my award, and I was standing out there looking at the table with my people." She moves forward a step, and although I tell myself to move back, my feet grow roots and anchor me to the ground. "I was looking at the table, and there was one person I wanted to be there."

I exhale as she takes another step. "Ethel?"

She shakes her head. Another foot closer. She's within arm's reach now, but she stops.

"Your brothers?"

"No, they were there. Any other guesses?" she asks.

I stare at her, my chest rising and falling on uneven breaths. I won't say what I'm thinking. I have to hear it from her. "No."

Ellie hesitates for one second, one blink of an eye, before stepping into my space. She's close enough now that she has to tilt her head all the way up to look at me. So close that I can see the faint dusting of freckles beneath the rosy tint of her wind-chapped cheeks. So close that I can see the exact moment the corner of her mouth curls.

"It was you," she breathes. "I wanted you to be there."

I clench my hands at my sides to keep from reaching for her, to hold myself back from giving in to the heady pull of her words. "I'm sorry I couldn't be, but your parents—"

"Are back to being *just* my parents."

Maybe it's the early morning, or maybe it's the proximity to Ellie, but it takes a minute for her words to register. When they do, my heart stops. "What do you mean?"

Ellie pauses, then reaches for my hand. Her fingers are cold as they wrap around mine and squeeze. "I quit."

"Daisy—"

"My parents aren't bad parents, Cam," Ellie says, cutting me off.

I blink at the change in direction of the conversation.

"Things between us…" She stares up at the sky, as if looking for the right words. "Things between us just got so messed up. I never should have worked for them. I thought it would make them proud, but, well, you saw what happened."

I did—and I still wanted to give Kristin Bates a piece of my mind.

Ellie must notice the fire behind my eyes because she grips my hand a little tighter. "It's okay, really. Things aren't fixed, but I think this is the first step."

I nod, knowing this isn't my battle to fight. This is Ellie's relationship with her parents, and if I want to fit into it somewhere, I have to follow her lead. And I do want to. I'll find my place if she'll let me.

"So where does that leave us?"

"On a dirt road in the middle of the mountains."

"Daisy…"

CHAPTER THIRTY-SEVEN

She tucks her bottom lip between her teeth and meets my gaze. "My life is a little up in the air right now."

My stomach swoops at the words, and I curse myself for getting my hopes up.

"But there's one thing I know I want for sure."

I swallow against the lump rising in my throat. "Tea with honey?"

"Okay, two things," she says, that smile I've missed so much returning to her face. It's a hit to my solar plexus.

"Homemade soup?"

"Three things. You're very bad at guessing today," she says, pushing up onto her toes.

Staring down at Ellie, into the warm brown eyes and bright smile that captured me from day one, I know exactly what *I* want.

"What do you want, Daisy?"

Her palms slide up my chest and come around my neck, fingers sifting through my hair, and my hands curve around the gentle slope of her hips. She leans forward until we're nose to nose, until it's like looking through a camera lens that hasn't focused.

"You, Camden Lane. I want you."

Epilogue

ELLIE

The kettle beeps, and I fill my mug, adding a heaping dollop of honey to the bottom. I wrap both hands around it, letting the heat seep through to warm my hands as I exit my cottage and cross the parking lot. The air is finally starting to lose the chill from winter, and peonies and daisies in every color imaginable are beginning to bloom in the little flower bed in front of the cottage.

I take a sip of my tea. It's pleasantly warm, and almost too sweet, just the way I like it.

"Morning, Ellie," one of my residents says as they pass me, their dog trailing ahead of them on a leash.

"Morning," I call back and veer to the left toward my office building.

Unlocking the front door, I flip on the light switch and take in my office. Early morning light filters in through the open blinds, illuminating the little dust motes in the air. The building is dusty and old, although well cared for. And, since I started working here, full of color.

My desk is pink, and the rug is yellow. The couch is a lovely shade of lilac. It's cozy and welcoming, which is why I have tenants stopping by to hang out with me every day. I hardly get anything done, but it's fine because there's not much to do at a property this size. There are only ten units, plus my cottage, and it's exactly the right size for me. Plus, the owners encouraged me to get to know the people living here, which is what made me accept the job just a little over a year ago.

My phone rings on the desk, and I pick it up.

"Hey, Ellie," Gary says.

"Morning, Gary," I say, settling down behind the desk. It's covered in papers and empty mugs that I have to shift around to make room for the one in my hand.

"I'm going to be a little late this morning. Delores has a doctor's appointment."

"No problem. How is she feeling today?"

"She's doing really well," he says. "They're running some scans to make sure everything is still looking good."

"Good, I'm glad to hear it. Give me a call when you're on your way here." Shortly after I left Bates Property Management, Gary resigned. It turned out that his wife had been sick for a few months, which is why he'd been calling out of work so often. I'd just gotten the job here and was trying to hire a maintenance manager. This is a perfect fit for him since the place requires much less maintenance than The Flats.

The front door swings open, and the other person I brought with me from The Flats walks in.

"Morning, Ethel," I say. Three months ago, I had a unit open up right around the time Ethel's lease was up, and the rest is history.

I grin as I notice the Tupperware in her hands. "New recipe?"

"You betcha," she says and shuffles over to sit in one of the chairs across from my desk. She peels the lid off the container and hands me a phallic-shaped pastry on a lacy napkin.

"I've told you I'm not entirely comfortable eating these, right?"

She waves a dismissive hand in my direction. "And I've told you the best way to start the morning is with a mouthful of—"

"Wow, this is really tasty!" I interrupt.

Her mouth splits in a wide smile. "I think that's the one. All those bachelorette groups are going to lose their mind over these. They'll finally have something for brunch."

I roll my eyes and set the pastry down next to my keyboard. "What are you up to today?"

"I've got a big order to deliver this evening, but nothing much other than that."

My brow crinkles. "Do you need help? Cam and I are supposed to go see Tyler's band play tonight, but we can move something around."

"Nonsense," she says with a shrug. "I can deliver it on my own."

"What time do you have to take it? You're not supposed to drive at night anymore."

"That was a suggestion."

"That was a warning," I correct. "From a police officer. After you backed into a light pole in a parking lot."

"I still say it wasn't there."

"The dent in the back of your car says otherwise. Sadie is out of town, but here, let me call Alex and see if he can drive you."

"It's really not necessary, Ellie," she says quickly.

The phone rings twice before Alex picks up. "Hey, loser."

"Hello, dear brother. I need a favor."

"As long as it doesn't involve you crashing in my guest room for a few months, I think I can make it happen."

"It was one time." After I moved out of The Flats, I moved into Alex's spare room for a bit. Needless to say, he was not thrilled to share his new bachelor pad with his baby sister, but those few months gave me time to sort myself out and to figure out how to move forward. I was right when I guessed that none of my parents' big competitors would want to hire me, but a lot of smaller, privately owned companies weren't concerned about my family name.

"One time was plenty," he says, but I hear the teasing in his voice. "What do you need?"

"Can you help Ethel deliver an order tonight?"

"Um, actually…I can't."

"What? Why?" I ask.

"I have to pick up someone from the airport."

"Who do you have to pick up from the airport?"

I startle when Ethel jumps up from her chair and snatches the phone from my hand faster than I thought someone of her age could move. She puts the phone up to her ear. "Thank ya, dearie. Don't you worry about it."

She slaps the phone back down on my desk, and I blink at her.

"I better get going," she says. "Need to finish my order for tonight."

"Are you sure you don't need help?"

Ethel waves me off. "I'm fine," she says before disappearing out the door.

THE REST OF THE afternoon passes by with few distractions, and while I usually have a stream of texts going with Cam, I don't hear from him all day.

Residents filter in and out, mostly coming in to chat. I love the relaxed atmosphere here, the easy way everyone is with each other. It's everything I ever wanted when I worked with my parents.

My phone buzzes on my desk as I'm finally closing up the office for the night, but it's still not Cam. It's a text from my therapist, reminding me of our appointment tomorrow.

During the months I lived with Alex, I realized I had a lot I needed to work through. Things Cam or my job couldn't fix. I started seeing a therapist once a week, and although I still have a long way to go, it's helped me navigate my life a little more easily—especially in my relationship with my parents. Things with them are still far from perfect, but we're learning how to patch up the holes we created.

I let myself into my cottage and flip on the lights. It's still very much my space, but there are little touches of Cam all around. It's tidier, and there are a lot more spices in my cabinet and far fewer microwave meals in my freezer. Most nights he comes over and cooks dinner, and we end up on my couch, my feet tucked under his thigh, the golden stars from the pendant light that used to hang in my room painting the walls around us.

I head into my room and rifle through the closet, looking for something to wear. When Tyler emailed me a flyer for his band playing a gig at the same place Cam and I met, I knew immediately that we had to go. I plan to spend the whole night wrapped in his arms, dancing slower than the beat.

Maybe making out against the wall outside.

Yeah, definitely some of that.

My gaze snags on a striped sweater tucked in the corner of my closet, and I get an idea.

I hear the front door open. "Ellie, you here?"

Just like it always does, my heart picks up its rhythm at the sound of Cam's voice. A year and a half later, and he still gives me butterflies.

"I'm changing in my closet!" I yell back. "I'll be right out."

I pull my hair out from the neck of the sweater and tug on my boots. When I exit the closet, Cam is there, leaning against my bedroom doorframe, his legs crossed at the ankles.

A slow smile tilts his lips as he takes in my outfit—striped sweater, black skirt, yellow tights, and white boots—the same thing I wore the night we met.

You're a striped sweater in a sea of black dresses, he told me once. It's something I repeat to myself often when I'm feeling lost or unsteady. I may not always know exactly who I am or who I want to be, but Cam does.

"You look beautiful," he says, inching forward. His hands slide against the curve of my hips, drawing me forward for a long, lingering kiss.

Kisses with Cam never fail to steal the air from my lungs—from the very beginning, he made me feel a little reckless.

He squeezes my side, his fingers burning through the fabric of my sweater, and leans back. His forehead is pressed to mine, and I'm pleased that he's a little breathless too. "You ready to go?"

I nod as he nudges his nose across my cheek and down the slope of my neck, inhaling right where I spray my perfume. I never did get that bottle back from him all those months ago.

He places a kiss there, and I'm tempted to pull him in for more, but I don't want to be late.

"Tyler's band is going on soon," I say as his hands tighten on my hips and his mouth trails across my neck.

"Who's Tyler?" he mumbles into the skin there.

I shove against his stomach, a laugh bubbling in my throat. "Come on."

A YEAR AND A half ago, the place was full, but there were still open tables. Tonight, it's standing room only, and the only place easy enough to move around is the dance floor, so that's where we end up. Tyler's band plays a mix of upbeat songs and slow ballads, but we don't change our pace, drifting to our own tempo.

My head is against Cam's chest, and I can hear his heart beating against my ear. It's a slow, steady rhythm I don't think I'll ever grow tired of.

I shiver against Cam as his hand slips under my hair. He tilts my head up so his mouth is right against my ear. "Want to get some fresh air? I promise not to murder you."

My laugh fans against the exposed skin at his collar, and he tugs me toward the door.

Although it's another season and the world is coming back to life instead of dying off, this night feels just like that first one. There's a chill to the air and the heavy feeling of incoming rain. The stars are barely visible beneath the glow of the city, but I can see a few of the brightest ones as Cam leads us down the sidewalk.

Just like last time, I can hear music in every direction, but for some reason, this little spot feels quiet—like it was waiting for us.

Cam moves until my back is against the cool brick wall, and his hands come to bracket my hips. I wait for his lips to find mine, but he doesn't move. His gaze is heavy as he takes in every line of my face, like he's committing it to memory. I wonder if he wishes he had his camera.

I think I feel a tremble in Cam's hands as he leans forward, nudging his nose against my cheek. "A year and a half ago," he whispers, his breath fanning my skin, "I never could have imagined this moment—being here with you like this again." His lips brush against the spot just below my ear. "I love you."

It's been over a year since he said it the first time, and it still makes a warm feeling spread through my chest.

"I love you too," I breathe.

He pulls back, and there's a faint blush staining his cheeks. As he pulls his hands away, I know I see the tremor in them now.

I want to ask him why, but my question is answered when he takes a step back and bends down to one knee.

Watching him, knelt before me with his hair ruffled from my hands, his face bright, and his midnight eyes glittering like stars, I think my heart might burst from my chest.

"Will you marry me, Daisy?"

THE END

Also By

JUST US SERIES

Just Go With It
Wes + Lo's Story

Acknowledgements

WRITING A BOOK IS never easy, but I'm lucky to have people out there who make it easier.

Josh, you make this passion of mine possible. Thank you for single-handedly taking care of our house and dog when I'm on deadline. And thank you for always filling up my water bottle. I would be severely dehydrated without you.

Kelsey, Amanda, and Juliana, I don't know how I wrote a book without you—it seems impossible now. Thank you for answering all the plot questions I send at 2AM. Thank you for encouraging me to write and telling me my stories don't suck when I want to give up. Thank you for forcing me out of my comfort zone. This book wouldn't be in the hands of nearly as many people without you guys telling me to do all the scary things. I love you guys so much, and I can't wait to write many more books with you by my side.

To my wonderful beta readers, thank you for reading my bad drafts of this book and making them better. I couldn't do it without all of you.

Mary Lee, this book was inspired by your job and all the crazy stories you tell me every day. I couldn't have done this without you. Also, thanks for being my best friend. You're a baddie queen.

Jamie, thank you for loving my books and my characters. Thank you for reading early drafts of this book and sending me texts in all caps of the things you loved. I know you thought it wasn't helpful, but it was. Your enthusiasm kept me wanting to write, even when I would have preferred to throw this book in the trash and start over.

Sam Palencia, you have made all my beige book dreams come true. I could write a whole page about how grateful I am to get to work with you, but I know that would make you uncomfortable, so I'll keep it short. Thank you for working with me and for being patient with the way I tell you everything is perfect and then send you fifteen emails throughout the night of teenie, tiny changes to make. I promise to be better next time. Also, Feyre is jealous of your skills.

To the entire bookstagram community, and to people who have found my books in other ways, THANK YOU. I'm still pinching myself that people are out there reading and connecting with my words and characters. I will never get over it, and I am so, so thankful for each and every one of you.

Above all, to God, who gave me this dream, and who keeps allowing it to come true.

About The Author

Madison is a romantic comedy author living her own happily ever after in Nashville, Tennessee. After falling in love with reading at a young age, she always dreamed of writing her own stories.

Madison spends most of her time with her head in a book—usually when she should be doing other things. When she's not reading, she's probably watching *The Office*, consuming excessive amounts of chocolate, or spending time with her husband and dog.

https://www.instagram.com/authormadisonwright/

Printed in Great Britain
by Amazon